M000222729

The Tunnel Mystery

J.C. Lenehan

First published: London, 1929

This edition published 2023 by

OREON

an imprint of

The Oleander Press
16 Orchard Street
Cambridge
CB1 1JT

www.oleanderpress.com

ISBN: 9781915475190

Sign up to our infrequent newsletter
to receive a free ePub of
Fatality in Fleet Street
by Christopher St John Sprigg and get
news of new titles, discounts and give-aways!

www.oleanderpress.com/golden-age-crime

A CIP catalogue record for the book
is available from the British Library.

Cover design, typesetting & ebook: neorelix

The language and views expressed herein are those of a
bygone era and, whilst probably obvious, it should still
be noted that they are not shared by this publisher.

Contents

Chapter 1

The Murder

A deafening crash of thunder heralded the arrival of the train at Boxfield Station.

Mr. David Hyde, Hatton Garden diamond merchant, moved over to the corner of his third-class compartment and mentally prayed that at last he might be able to travel alone, for his fellow-travellers from the Yorkshire town, where dwelt the shady knight with whom he had concluded such a satisfactory stroke of business, had been none too congenial.

"Twenty thousand!" he muttered with a complaisant smile. "And the necklace is easily worth twice that amount! Ah, well! Sir Joshua had to pay for the privilege of absolute secrecy. Didn't want Lady Jordan and their daughter to know he was selling it. That's why he chose today while they had gone to London on a shopping expedition. And, of course, his reason for insisting beforehand that I must pay in banknotes was the fear that the transaction might be traced through the bank if I paid by cheque. I don't think much of Sir Joshua's powers of description, though..." His face clouded. "If only Connie could be persuaded to—"

The thread of his reflections was broken, and his hopes of privacy were dashed to the ground by the opening of the door. But the intrusion was in some measure atoned for by the appearance of the intruder.

The girl who entered was young and undeniably pretty. Her eyes were as bright as the diamonds that reposed in Mr. Hyde's pocket, and he had seldom seen rubies to equal the beauty of the parted lips that revealed two rows of pearl-like teeth. Naturally, Mr. Hyde thought in terms of precious stones.

The girl seated herself opposite to Mr. Hyde, with her back to the engine, but not directly opposite. On the corner of the seat beside her she placed a rather long, but shallow, attaché case. For the moment, Mr. Hyde wondered whether she was reserving a seat for a friend of hers.

In one respect at least, the British travelling public resembles a flock of sheep. Passengers seeking a seat naturally drift towards a door that is already swinging open. And so it was now, although there were other compartments quite empty.

The pretty intruder was closely followed by a boy and a girl, their green caps and blazers proclaiming them to be pupils of some Secondary School. These lost no time in monopolising the remaining two corner seats near the door by which they had entered. Next came two women who sat on the same side as Mr. Hyde and balanced shopping baskets on their knees. A man who looked like a butcher in his Sunday suit pushed his way through the door and flopped down midway between the schoolboy and the girl with the attaché case.

A porter slammed the door shut, and the train creaked into slow motion. Before it had gained much momentum, however, the receding posters were partially blotted out by a tall, well-dressed, slouch-hatted man, who grasped the door handle and walked alongside the moving train, his deep-set eyes keenly scrutinising the occupants of the compartment. As though satisfied with what he saw, he pulled the door open, sprang inside, and banged the door to behind him. Then, although there were fewer people on the other seat, he pushed past the schoolgirl and the two shoppers and sat down beside the diamond merchant.

Had the coach been provided with a corridor, Mr. Hyde would, perhaps, have sought another compartment before the invasion was complete. Then again, perhaps he would not. The girl opposite was good to look upon, and Mr. Hyde had an appreciative eye for beauty. Anyhow, it was an old-fashioned coach, and he had no option but to retain his seat.

It was a habit of Mr. Hyde to travel third-class. In his journeyings he often carried valuables and large sums of money on his person, and he maintained that one never attracted undesirable attention in the cheaper part of the train. For the same reason, he invariably dressed in a sober suit of darkish grey.

"Gosh!" exclaimed the butcher-like individual, as a blinding flash of lightning danced and zigzagged across the windowpanes. "That wor' a whopper an' no mistake. Now listen for—"

An ear-splitting crash drowned not only the remainder of his speech but the roar and rattle of the now swiftly-moving train. Nobody answered the man's remark. The only persons who spoke were the schoolchildren engaged in an animated discussion as to the rival merits of rounders and stool-ball. And it was obvious that they were talking merely for the sake of demonstrating to themselves, as well as to the others, their utter indifference to the raging elements.

The train rushed on. Every minute or so there came a flash and a crash. The fat man made one or two more attempts to start a conversation. Soon, however, he shrugged his shoulders with a gesture of resignation and abandoned the attempt. Even the boy and the girl finally lapsed into silence.

From under the brim of his slouched hat, the tall man was furtively staring at the diamond merchant. But his scrutiny was so unobtrusive that it passed unobserved by the others.

The girl opposite to David Hyde opened her attaché case and withdrew a box of chocolates. Very slowly she removed the transparent paper with which the box was covered. But she made no attempt to remove the lid. Presently she glanced at the watch on her wrist, then, letting down the window a little at the top, she threw out the piece of paper.

A few drops of rain splashed on her face, and she banged up the window. Then, stepping backwards, she sat down again, seemingly unaware that she had moved closer to the portly man. With the utmost nonchalance, she opened the box and placed a chocolate between her lips.

"Good job you shut that theere winder, Miss," remarked her loquacious neighbour. "We'll be goin' through the tunnel in a minute, an' if the winder wor' open we'd be blessed well smothered wi' smoke."

John Lofthouse was a true prophet. There came a piercing shriek from the whistle, and the next moment they plunged into Highpen Tunnel and absolute darkness. No light came on. Even the usual flickering pencil-point of flame in the bowl at the ceiling was absent, for, in ordinary trains, it is not usual to have the light turned on for the passage through Highpen Tunnel.

"More lightnin'," grunted the talkative one out of the darkness, as a flash flickered across the windows for an instant. "Wot wi' the din the train's makin' in 'ere we'll not 'ear the thunder this time."

He was right. Only a super-crash could have been heard above the reverberating roar of the train as it tore its way through the inky blackness.

Soon a faint glimmer of light was visible, and a second later they were in broad daylight once more.

"Good Gawd!"

The fat man placed a hand on the seat on either side of him as though to heave himself up. But his will, or his muscles, refused to act. His body straining forward, he sat there in that peculiar attitude, staring, staring at Mr. Hyde in the corner by the window.

And both he and the others had good reason to stare. The diamond merchant sagged in his seat, his mouth wide open and his face contorted as though in agony. His eyes rolled in their sockets, and a choking gurgle rattled in his throat.

"Good Gawd!" repeated John Lofthouse, as the train lurched and Mr. Hyde fell forward, his face thudding against the edge of the opposite seat. "That's death or I'm a Dutchman!"

As though his words were an incantation that released all of them from a binding spell, both he and the others became suddenly active. The schoolgirl screamed; the two women grabbed their baskets and backed towards the door, away from the crumpled-up body; the cadaverous man and the fat man, assisted by the girl with the attaché case, struggled to lift the diamond merchant back to his seat. Of the three engaged in the gruesome task, the girl seemed, by far, the coolest.

But it was left to the schoolboy to do the one thing that was really helpful. He was not particularly anxious to help, but he was quick to see his opportunity to gratify the impish ambition of his short lifetime. He could pull the alarm signal and stop the train without being called upon subsequently to pay the penalty.

Again and again he pulled down and released the chain.

Amidst a grinding screech of brakes the train jerked to such a sudden standstill that the fat man sat down on the girl's attaché case to the accompaniment of the sound of a broken catch. The man grunted an apology, and the girl quickly retrieved her case. Pale and tight-lipped, she regarded the body of the diamond merchant, now lying on the seat before her.

The guard hurried forward from the rear of the train. Already a crowd was collecting around the door, but until the appearance of the guard no one attempted to enter.

"What's up?" asked the official in curt tones, for more than once a train in his charge had been stopped on some trivial pretext.

They all seemed too stupefied to reply.

The guard entered, saw the body on the seat.

"What's up?" he asked again. But this time he spoke in a different key.

"Guard, I'm a doctor. Is there anything I can do?"

The speaker was standing outside in the forefront of the crowd. Of medium height, and dressed in professional black, everything about him, from his large horn-rimmed glasses to the grey spats that encased his shining patent shoes, proclaimed him to be what he said he was—a healer of the sick.

"Come in, Doctor," said the guard in obvious relief. "You're the very man that's needed."

The doctor placed his little black bag on the seat where the girl's had lain. Then he felt the diamond merchant's pulse and gravely shook his head.

"All over, I fear," he said in quiet tones. "But let's make sure."

He opened his bag, thus exposing to view several instruments and an assortment of little bottles and stoppered glass tubes as well as bandages and other odds and ends usually found in a medical kit. He withdrew a stethoscope and applied it to his own ears and the prone man's heart.

Again he shook his head.

"Dead," he said with a note of calm finality.

"A fit?" asked the girl, speaking for the first time since she had entered the compartment. "Or was it the lightning?"

"I doubt it." The doctor replaced the stethoscope and snapped the bag shut. "Seems to me very much like foul play."

The thunder had practically ceased, but the rain was now pouring down in torrents. Nevertheless, the tense-eyed crowd round the open door made no attempt to return to shelter. Many of them had heard the doctor's suggestion of foul play, and their gaze travelled from one to another of the occupants of the compartment.

"Bet a bob as it's the fat un wot's done it!" came a raucous voice. But the weedy youth with the sodden cigarette between his pendulous lips found no takers.

His remark, however, focussed all eyes on the butcher-like individual. But John Lofthouse soon managed to outstare them.

"You'd better keep yer dam' mouth shut tight!" he then roared at the offending youth.

"It wasn't the fat one, but the thin one," piped the schoolboy, again making an interesting contribution to the proceedings. "He's just dropped a wallet on the floor and kicked it under the seat."

The slouch-hatted man made a wild dive for the door. But John Lofthouse was too quick for him. There ensued a determined struggle, in which some men from the crowd were quick to join. The tall man was speedily overpowered, and when he saw that escape was impossible he apparently resigned himself to the inevitable, except that his piercing eyes glared balefully and his rat-like teeth bit into his foam-flecked lips.

"Guard, you'd better let him ride as far as Blackton in your van," counselled the doctor. "No doubt you'll find plenty of volunteers to help you look after him till we get there."

The volunteers were forthcoming, and the prisoner was hustled back to the rear of the train.

Meanwhile the boy had retrieved the wallet, which he handed to the guard upon his return. Inside were a few Bank of England notes, some letters, and about half a dozen business cards on which were inscribed the dead man's name, profession, and business address.

"Seems a small amount of money for a man in his line of business to carry about with him," observed the doctor.

The guard fidgeted uneasily, for already his train was many minutes late.

"Afraid you will have to take the body on to Blackton," said the doctor, as though reading the guard's thoughts. "The police there will have to be informed, of course. And"—he glanced at the others in the compartment—"I think you had better find another carriage for these people. Keep them together, for the police are certain to want to question them. I noticed that there are three or four empty compartments towards the front of the train."

The guard, however, bundled them into the compartment immediately behind, and the doctor frowned, apparently because his suggestion had not been carried out to the letter. One window of this compartment was completely down, and the smoke which had entered it while the train was passing through the tunnel had not yet entirely cleared away.

The other passengers returned to their several compartments, while the guard locked in the potential witnesses and returned to the compartment in which the tragedy had occurred.

"I'll stay with the body till it's handed over," said the doctor.

"Foul play!" remarked the guard, recollecting the words used by the other man a short time before. "How was he killed?"

The doctor pointed to a blood-rimmed wound on the dead man's forehead.

"Shot," was his terse answer.

Chapter 2

Inspector Parker Takes Charge

T he train resumed its tragically-interrupted journey, and the doctor was left alone with the murdered man. The first thing he did was to draw on a pair of thin rubber gloves, and then he commenced a systematic examination of the body. He touched the back of the head many times, though he was careful to leave this part of the work until last. The gloves became blood-stained, and with a piece of boracic lint he wiped them clean. Then he replaced the lint and the gloves in his bag.

His task completed, he looked up and, for the first time, observed that the window near which the girl with the attaché case had been sitting contained a hole that looked as though some mischievous boy had hurled a marble through it. The doctor removed his hat and scratched the crown of his head with his left forefinger, while his little finger stuck up in the air almost vertically.

The moment the train stopped at Blackton—a town of fair dimensions served by two different railway systems —the guard raced across the metals, for the station buildings were on the west side of the line, and into the station-master's office. In as few words as possible he explained what had happened, and the station-master despatched a porter posthaste to inform the police.

Police Constable Brent, who had been discovered a short distance away, hurried on to the platform. Quick to grasp the essentials of the case, he immediately took charge.

"I've sent your man to headquarters," he said to the station-master, "for I should like the inspector to see the body before it's removed. In the meantime, I think we might get those witnesses off the train. Where can you accommodate them?"

The station-master suggested the first-class waiting-room, and they crossed the permanent way at the end of the platform. By the same way, after the guard had unlocked the carriage door, six of the seven persons who had accompanied Mr. Hyde on part of his tragic journey were marshalled towards the waiting-room.

The boy and the girl were frankly and unashamedly jubilant. A real murder had happened under their very eyes. At least it would have happened under their very eyes had not the compartment been so terribly dark.

They would be called as witnesses. Perhaps their photographs would appear in the newspapers. They would be envied by all their school-fellows, acclaimed as heroes. Even the girl, such is the modern feminine trend, thought in the masculine term.

The women, too, seemed glad of the promised notoriety, although one of them considered it necessary to register a protest.

"I 'ope," she said, carefully skirting a puddle, "as you're not goin' to keep me long. I've brought a nice piece of 'addock from Boxfield for me owd man's tea, an' 'e'll soon be 'ome from the pit."

But Constable Brent was paying no attention to her half-hearted remonstrance. He had eyes and ears only for the pretty girl with the attaché case.

"Why, Miss Lowe," he exclaimed, "surely you aren't one of those who saw it done?"

The girl laughed.

"Yes, and no," she said with complete self-possession. "I saw just as much as the others—no more, no less. And the fact is, none of us saw anything—till afterwards."

"You know the lady?" asked the station-master, who had yet to wait some months before he could celebrate his first anniversary at Blackton.

"Of course. I thought everyone knew Mr. Lowe, the potter—and his niece."

"Old Dick, the potter? Yes, I know him right enough. But his niece..." He glanced at her appreciatively. "Well, she can't be much of a traveller or I'd have noticed her before now."

The implied compliment seemed to please the girl, and again she laughed.

"I drive Uncle's old Tin Lizzie," she informed anyone who cared to hear. "That's why I rarely travel by train."

This brief interlude over, they were escorted inside the waiting-room, and it was noted by the observant guard that John Lofthouse seemed very worried and ill at ease.

The attitude of the tall man, when he was brought from the guard's van, came as a surprise to those who had witnessed his previous conduct. Gone from his face was the saturnine expression, and the eyes that had burned so fiercely now held a merry twinkle. The brim of his hat was now turned back, revealing well-cut features and a fresh complexion that many a girl might envy.

Freda Lowe regarded him keenly.

"Acting a part," was her unspoken comment. "He's anxious to create a good impression."

"Well, Constable, what are you arresting me for?" demanded the tall man in a jaunty, self-confident voice.

But Constable Brent was equal to the occasion.

"I'm not arresting you," he said. "You are merely being detained, along with the others, until the inspector comes along and takes charge."

Just then Inspector Parker bustled in. Behind him clumped a portly sergeant, obviously hot from his efforts to keep pace with his more active superior.

The inspector got down to business at once. He rapped out a few questions that quickly gave him a working knowledge of the case, and then demanded to be shown the body.

Leaving the sergeant and the young constable to guard the occupants of the waiting-room, he and the guard and the station-master hurried across to where the dead body lay, still in charge of the doctor. He threw a brief glance at the inert form, and then listened to what the doctor had to say.

"You have no doubt that death is the result of a gunshot wound?" he enquired.

"None whatever, Inspector. True, my examination has been very superficial; but it was sufficient to show the cause of death. He's been shot through the brain. See for yourself,"—and he pointed to the wound in the dead man's forehead.

"H'm," said the inspector. "That seems plain enough. Then, turning to the station-master, he went on: "Will you get a couple of your men to bring a trolley along? And don't forget a covering of some sort."

The body was covered with a piece of tarpaulin and lifted on to the trolley, the proceedings being watched by dozens of pairs of curious eyes.

As the inspector was about to leave the compartment, he observed the pocketbook lying on the seat.

"The dead man's," explained the doctor. "It was found lying on the floor and handed to the guard, who dropped it on the seat when he had finished inspecting it."

The inspector took a silk handkerchief from his pocket and threw it over the wallet. Then he carefully deposited both wallet and handkerchief in his pocket.

The rain had now ceased. The trolley, with its ghastly load, was wheeled across to the cloakroom, and the dead body, still covered, was lifted on to the counter.

"It can remain here for the present," said the inspector. "Mr. Brown,"—to the station-master—"will you please lock the door and don't let the key out of your possession until I ask for it."

The station-master obeyed, and they returned to the waiting-room.

Then the guard asked for permission to proceed.

"The train's already nearly half an hour late," he said, "and I can't see what good I can do by remaining here any longer."

Inspector Parker agreed.

"But first let's hear all you know about the affair," he said.

The guard, however, was unable to throw any real light on the affair. The alarm had been rung, he had applied the brakes and stopped the train, to learn of the tragedy that had occurred. That was all he knew.

"I see. Where are you taking this train?"

"To Midtown. I shall be free then if you should require me."

"Thanks. Well, I think you may proceed."

"Will you give me the same permission, Inspector?" put in the doctor. "Any local doctor will confirm what I have said as to the cause of death. And it's necessary that I should get to London without loss of time. There's an important conference which I must attend tonight. I expected to have half an hour's wait at Derwent Junction for the London Express, but now it's doubtful whether I shall be able to catch it at all. Here is my card," he laughed, "in case you should consider it necessary to arrest me at some future date. But remember," he added, still laughing, "that I was in a compartment further forward when the murder was committed."

The inspector glanced at the card, which showed that the doctor's name was Victor Peters and that he boasted a Wimpole Street address. Whilst reflecting that the doctor's joke was not in the best possible taste, he gave the required permission, and soon afterwards the train proceeded on its journey.

The compartment in which the diamond merchant had been murdered was locked by the guard, and Doctor Peters rode as far as Derwent Junction in the compartment immediately behind.

At the junction he alighted and watched the arrival and departure of the London Express. Soon afterwards, instead of travelling south, he caught a west-bound train that carried him as far as Hartby.

Meanwhile, back at Blackton, Inspector Parker interrogated the persons who had travelled in the ill-fated compartment. And he took the precaution of questioning them separately, except that he summoned the boy and the girl to his presence together.

These two were quickly disposed of. They were brother and sister, and their home was in Blackton. They attended the Secondary School there, but had taken the afternoon off to visit a very sick aunt at Boxfield.

The only part of their statement to which Parker paid particular attention was the boy's assertion that he had seen the tall man drop the wallet on the floor and then kick it under the seat. Not once, while he was making his statement, did the boy look the inspector straight in the face, and Parker concluded that the boy's nerves were not under proper control. The children gave their names and address, and then they were allowed to go.

The two women with the shopping baskets were also quickly dismissed, one at a time. Both lived in Blackton, and were the wives of colliers.

The next person summoned to the inspector's presence was Freda Lowe, the girl with the attaché case. The investigations were taking place in the station-master's office, and Constable Brent was assisting, for he had a good knowledge of shorthand.

The girl calmly supplied the particulars for which she was asked, and, while she was speaking, the inspector keenly scrutinised both her and the young constable, without seeming to do so.

Her name, she said, was Freda Lowe, and she lived with her uncle, Richard Lowe, in a little cottage just outside the town.

"Richard Lowe? That's Dick, the potter, isn't it?"

The girl nodded.

"I know him pretty well," said Parker, smiling. "And, now that I come to think of it, I recollect having seen you about the cottage once or twice when I happened to be passing that way. You drive a car, too, don't you?"

The girl's laugh was like the tinkle of a silver bell.

"Uncle calls it a car," she said. "But I call it—something else."

Parker joined in the laugh, and then, pretending to be serious, said:

"No need for you to worry any longer, Miss Lowe. I know old Dick, and the fact that he's your uncle clears from my mind all suspicion of your guilt."

"Thanks so much," retorted the girl, and the inspector fancied that there was a shade of mockery in the emphasis she placed on the middle word.

Like the others, Freda Lowe could throw no light on the mystery of the diamond merchant's death, and as she took her departure George Brent's gaze followed her to the door.

"Know her well?" rapped out the inspector.

"I've met her a few times, sir," answered his subordinate with obvious embarrassment.

"And hoping to meet her a few more, eh?"

A reply seemed unnecessary, so Constable Brent said nothing.

The worried expression on John Lofthouse's face seemed to have deepened, as he was ushered into the presence of Inspector Parker.

"Name and address?" was the inspector's curt request.

The fat man mopped his brow with a large red handkerchief.

"My name's Lofthouse," he said—"John Lofthouse. An' I'm proprietor o' the Red Reynard in Midtown. Seein' as 'ow I ought to be openin' in another 'alf-'our or so, you might—"

But the inspector was already scribbling on a piece of paper.

"Brent, take this to Sergeant Hopkins," he said, "and ask him to attend to it immediately. You take his place until he's at liberty again."

The constable took the slip of paper and then left the room.

"Tell me everything you can about what took place in the train," requested the inspector. "Everything, remember."

The fat man rambled on for several minutes, but all his information added nothing to what the others had already said in fewer words.

At last the constable returned, bearing in his hand another slip of paper which he handed to his superior.

Parker studied the paper for a minute or two, and then looked John Lofthouse straight between the eyes.

"Mr. Lofthouse," he said, with slow deliberation, "you have recently been in trouble with the Midtown police. You have allowed your premises to be used for betting purposes, and the Red Reynard is the regular meeting-place of the most notorious of the Midland racing-gangs. Isn't that so?"

John Lofthouse gasped.

"Good Gawd!" he cried. "Who's bin a-tellin' you that? But it's all a lie. I'm not denyin' as I've bin convicted, but—"

"You may go now," interrupted the inspector. "I don't need you any further—for the present."

At the door John Lofthouse hesitated, looked back. Then he shrugged his shoulders and lurched on to the platform.

"Reggie Robinson," said the tall man jauntily, when asked for his name. But he refused to disclose his address or his occupation.

"Most of my people are toffs," he explained, winking at the constable, "and I don't want to disgrace them by having it known that I was mixed up with the police."

"Right!" snapped the inspector. "Then I shall detain you on suspicion."

The following morning a young woman of about twenty-five was ushered into Inspector Parker's office. Her face bore evidence of acute distress, and she nervously clasped and unclasped her hands.

Refusing the chair which the inspector offered her, she cried out in a voice of extreme agitation:

"I am Miss Hyde—Constance Hyde. I got the telegram you sent to—to father's business address last night. It was too late to come then, but I hurried here first thing this morning. May I—may I—see him?"

"Yes," he answered. "But not just yet. When you've rested a little you'll be better able to... Do sit down Miss Hyde."

The inspector had risen to his feet, and this time the girl obeyed. And it was as well she did, for she seemed incapable of standing upright much longer.

"Thanks," she said. "Oh, it's awful, awful! I think I could have borne the horror of it better if only we had parted differently yesterday morning. But the things he said!... the things we both said!"

Inspector Parker was a keen officer of the law. But he was also a humane man—a husband, and the father of two girls.

"Compose yourself, Miss Hyde," he said gently. "And don't say anything more just now. Later, when you are more yourself..."

But the girl was too distracted to heed his warning.

"He threatened to cut me out of his will," she went on in a semi-hysterical voice. "Threatened to make a new one this very day with the proviso that I'd lose everything if I married Jack. And now—" She covered her face with her hands, and her shoulders shook. "The night before last he dismissed Jack, dismissed him at a moment's notice."

The inspector was only human after all.

"I presume Jack is the man you had meant to marry," he said. "Does Jack know all this—about the row yesterday morning, and your father's threat to make a new will?"

"Yes. I ran round and told him as soon as father had left home."

"Ah! And where is the young man now?"

"I don't know."

"You don't know, Miss Hyde?"

"I don't know with any certainty, I mean. When I had told him all about Dad and the will, he took out his motorcycle and said he was off to visit some friends—somewhere in the Peak District."

"The Peak District!" exclaimed Inspector Parker. Then his mouth shut with a snap. The murder was committed at Highpen Tunnel, and Highpen was on the fringe of the Peak District.

Chapter 3

Dick, the Potter

E arly on that same Tuesday morning, Police Constable Brent was walking slowly along the Hartby road, just outside Blackton, his thoughts enmeshed in the tangle of mystery that surrounded the murder of the diamond merchant the previous afternoon. Rather, his thoughts were busy with one of the persons indirectly and unwittingly connected with the crime—Freda Lowe.

And in a few minutes' time he would be passing the cottage in which Freda and her uncle lived. Would he be able to catch a glimpse of her as he passed?

George Brent was very much in love with Freda Lowe. But Freda? Well, whenever they happened to meet she seemed frankly pleased with his company. George, however, had an uneasy feeling that her friendliness was merely the result of her spontaneous good nature. Probably, she treated all young men of her acquaintance in a similar manner.

As he passed the wide gate that gave access to the cottage, he saw both Freda and her uncle inside the open doorway of a lean-to wooden structure that was half garage, half potter's shed. Freda beckoned, whereupon he opened the gate and walked up the gravel-covered drive.

The girl was enveloped in a flowered overall, whose cut displayed to advantage the alluring contours of her perfect figure. How homely and business-like she looked, yet, withal, how beautiful! George Brent's heart lost one beat and gained several. Freda had always been friendly, but never before had she called him to her side.

Freda's uncle sat in front of an improvised potter's wheel, that was mainly a discarded sewing-machine with an added spindle to which was affixed a circular piece of wood in a horizontal position. When the treadle was worked the spindle and the wooden disc rotated.

When old Dick Lowe first came to the place some three years before, his hobby had excited the curiosity and the admiration of many of the townspeople. Pottery-making was an unknown art in Blackton, and they loved to stop and watch the shapeless mass of clay quickly form into a beautiful vase, or bowl, or other vessel under the magic of Dick's skilful fingers.

Dick was undoubtedly an expert. But he took no undue credit for that. For years, he said, he had been manager of the most important pottery works in a famous Staffordshire town, and the work was now second nature to him. He had always loved the work, and had been unable to give it up completely when age had compelled him to retire. That was why he had taken up pottery as a hobby when he left the Pottery district and came to Blackton.

And he never denied that he endeavoured to make his hobby a paying proposition. He was able to do his own burning and painting and glazing, and he had a friend in London who managed to dispose of the best of his work at a handsome profit. Some of the copies of Greek and Chinese and Egyptian art old Dick turned out were so perfect that only an expert could have distinguished them from the real thing. Dick, however, never pretended that his wares were anything but copies. Had he been less honest, he might have reaped a rich harvest from gullible amateur collectors.

There were those who said that the old potter's love of clay was so great that he hated to wash it off his hands and face. And their statement was not altogether without foundation. His hands were usually coated with clay, and his face was generally a crazy pattern of lines and smears, obviously the result of rubbing his unwashed hands across it.

"What does it matter?" he was wont to say with a whimsical smile. "We've all got to eat a peck of dirt before we die; and, anyhow, clay is clean dirt."

Old Dick threw a lump of clay on the centre of the revolving wheel and, with a few deft touches, shaped it into a perfect dome. Then he removed his foot from the treadle and looked up at the young constable.

"Good morning, George," he said cheerily. "Out hunting for the murderer, eh? But tell me all about it, will you? Freda's account was as clear as mud, and I'm inquisitive enough to want to know how it all happened. When I saw you at the gate I asked Freda to call you for I saw my opportunity to get first-hand information."

Brent would have preferred to hear that Freda had called him on her own account, but he endeavoured to conceal his disappointment.

"Afraid I can't give you the information you want," he said. "The thing's a complete mystery."

"But there's no doubt that he was shot?"

"No. He was shot through the forehead—so the doctor said, and the wound's there plain enough."

Old Dick opened wide his clear, sparkling eyes and rose to his feet.

"Gee!" he said. "Shot through the forehead, was he? The murderer, whoever he was, must have meant business."

George nodded, and watched Freda, who was now at the back of the shed wiping down a ramshackle old car with a piece of rag. The car was wet, and water trickled along the joints in the flagged floor. From the nozzle of a flexible hose-pipe, hanging from a nail in the wall, water was still dripping.

"And there's nothing to show which of the two men did it?"

Brent's gaze came back to the other man's face.

"There's nothing," he said, "to prove that either of them did it."

But it must have been one of them," insisted the potter. "Rule out these two and whom have we left?—a boy and a girl, mere children; two women with shopping baskets; and... Freda." He turned and called to his niece: "Freda, my girl, are you quite sure you didn't shoot the diamond merchant?"

Freda's musical laugh rang out.

"Quite sure," she cried, evidently enjoying the joke.

"Anyhow," said the policeman, anxious to justify his argument, "the person who fired the shot couldn't possibly have been the man who calls himself Reggie Robinson."

"What grounds have you for saying that?" asked old Dick.

The young constable smiled the smile that denotes superior knowledge.

"I should have thought that was sufficiently clear," he replied. "Reggie and the murdered man were sitting side by side, Reggie on the left. Unless he were a contortionist, Reggie couldn't have done it, for the wound is towards the right side of the forehead."

"A left-handed man could easily have done it," retorted Dick, after he had, apparently, studied the matter for some moments.

George Brent started.

"Jove!" he exclaimed. "I hadn't thought of that."

Old Dick laughed.

"No," he retorted dryly. "You wouldn't think of anything so simple. Yet you policemen deny that you run in grooves. Just because you and I and most people use the right hand, you never even considered the possibility of that shot having been fired by a left-handed person."

"I plead guilty. Now if we can only prove that Reggie uses the left—"

"There you go again!" interrupted the other. "Another groove! What was to prevent his using the left hand merely as a blind? No, George, even if you should discover that the man is right-handed, you mustn't jump to the conclusion that he's innocent. Remember, he'd got the pocketbook... Of course, the man opposite may have been the guilty party. He was really in a better position to do the shooting. Nevertheless, I believe Reggie's the man you've got to hang."

But Brent still felt dubious.

"There's something in your argument," he conceded. "But you are ignoring the weapon that fired the shot. No weapon has been found on Reggie Robinson."

"Has a weapon been found on anyone else?"

"No. But—"

"Then you may be sure that Reggie managed to dispose of it somehow."

"It would have been extremely difficult. All our information goes to show that he was under observation every moment of the time after the train emerged from the tunnel until he was searched by the inspector."

Old Dick half-closed his eyes and gazed at some unfinished pottery that stood drying on one of the shelves which ran round the shed.

"Then he got rid of it in the tunnel," he said at length. "Sure he didn't hurl it through the window?"

George Brent almost cried out, so great was his excitement. For hours he had vainly striven to resurrect something that had buried itself in his subconscious brain, and now, by a process of mental cerebration, that Something had come to light when he least expected it. Last night it had occurred to him that, some hours before, his brain had received a vague impression of something wrong, something unusual, about the appearance of the carriage from which the dead body was being removed. He had endeavoured to recall the impression, but without success. Now, however, it had come back in a flash. Without being fully conscious of it, he had noticed that one of the windows was broken.

"Good heavens!" he exclaimed. "You've hit upon the very thing! A window in that compartment was broken. Why, it was the very window beside which Miss Lowe had been sitting. Wonder whether she happened to hear the crash?"

"Freda," called the potter, "come here a minute." Freda moved over to them, and then old Dick went on: "George tells me that the window beside you in that carriage was broken. Did you happen to hear the sound of breaking glass?"

Freda shook her head.

"No. But the train and the thunder were making such a deafening din that it would have been impossible to hear anything else."

"Didn't you notice afterwards that it was broken?"

"No, Uncle." Freda shuddered with a pretty grace. "Such dreadful things were happening that I had no eyes for anything so trivial as a broken window."

The girl went back and resumed her polishing of the car.

"You say that the tall man was searched," enquired old Dick. "Was anything incriminating found on him?"

"Nothing whatever. Just a packet of cigarettes, matches, some loose money—oh, all the usual things that are to be found in any man's pockets."

"What account did he give of the affair?"

"He denied all knowledge of how the murder took place. Of himself, he refused to say anything. He didn't even trouble to conceal the fact that the name he was giving was false."

The potter pondered for several moments. Not for the first time did it strike George Brent that the old man's face bore an extremely intellectual look. And George had always found him a clever, almost a brilliant, conversationalist. Had he not been aware of the responsible position the old man had held in the past, he would have considered it incongruous that such logic and such educated speech should be found in one whose outward appearance suggested thoughts of a builder's labourer.

George's own education was far above that of the ordinary constable. Before he became a policeman he had been studying for the law, until an unexpected financial crash had flung his father on the brink of bankruptcy.

He enjoyed his occasional talks with the old potter; though, needless to say, he would have enjoyed them even more with the potter's niece. Old Dick had told him more than once that his favourite books were about crimes and criminals, and that the man he envied above all others was the detective. He would cheerfully give all he possessed, he said, to be given the tangled skein of a complicated murder mystery with a free hand to unravel it. It now occasioned the young policeman no surprise to find the old potter taking such a keen interest in the tunnel mystery.

"The dead body was also searched, I suppose?" was Dick's next question.

"Yes. His wallet contained less than ten pounds in notes and some ordinary business cards. As for the pockets, there was nothing—a pipe, matches, and so on."

Again there was a long pause.

"George," said the old man, "I would give my eyes to have the opportunity your inspector has now. I shouldn't sleep day or night until I'd run in the murderer."

Brent laughed.

"That's easier said than done," he retorted. "We've practically nothing to work upon. And the other fellow's job, you know, is always a pleasant one until you've had a shot at it yourself. Now, supposing you were in charge of the case, what would be your first move?"

George's motive in asking the question was not merely a good-natured attempt to catch the old man napping. The potter was undeniably clever, and he might drop a hint that would prove helpful. George Brent was ambitious; and if he could manage to make himself useful to the inspector, promotion would hardly be delayed very long.

"Can't say off-hand what I'd do," said the potter, scratching his head in the effort of concentrating on the problem. "I might—yes, bearing in mind the broken window, I most certainly should examine the tunnel to see whether anything was to be found there. But I daresay that's what Inspector Parker means to do?"

George shook his head.

"I can't say. He hasn't told me. But I fear I must be off. I ought to have met Constable Wilkins at the Four Lane Ends ten minutes ago. Good morning, sir. Good morning—Miss Lowe."

Freda, however, escorted him to the gate.

"You must call again soon," she said, as they parted outside on the road.

George vowed that nothing in life could give him greater pleasure.

"Finished the car?" asked old Dick, as Freda returned.

"I've done all I can with her, Uncle. But it would take more than water and a piece of rag to make her look respectable."

"Never mind, my girl. Looks aren't everything. The old rattler suits our purpose, and, remember, she's never broken down yet. After all, nobody expects an old potter to drive a Rolls-Royce."

"Lizzie certainly rolls," was Freda's flippant rejoinder.

When Constable Brent returned to the station, he was informed that the inspector wished to see him. Going into the office, he found his superior using the telephone, and he was not a little surprised at the excitement in the other's voice.

"What!" Parker was shouting into the instrument. "Impossible! ... Sure?... Oh, all right!... Simplifies matters? Wish it did. Seems as though it makes them even more complicated... Yes... Goodbye, sir."

The inspector banged down the receiver on its stand.

"Brent," he said, his excitement still evident, "there was something I wanted you to do, but it will have to wait now. I've just been speaking to the Chief Constable of Donmoor. He saw an account of the murder in this morning's papers, and, knowing that the body is here, he rang me up."

"The Chief Constable of Donmoor!" repeated Brent. "Does he enter into this affair?"

"Very much so, Brent, if I'm not mistaken. He tells me that a man named Sir Joshua Jordan was found tied to a chair in his own house last evening. When he was released, he was almost apoplectic with rage, but he was able to say that he had been attacked hours before, drugged, tied to the chair, and robbed almost under his very nose; robbed of a diamond necklace worth £40,000."

"And is Sir Joshua's assailant known, sir?"

"Yes. His alleged assailant is here."

"Reggie Robinson?

"No, Brent. Mr. David Hyde, the Hatton Garden diamond merchant."

Chapter 4

An Important Find

When Jack Davis came downstairs to the flagged kitchen of the farmhouse in which he was staying, his dark-rimmed eyes told of a sleepless night. To his friend's good-natured chaff about the pangs of a guilty conscience, he responded with ill-assumed gaiety.

Upon his arrival the previous day, he had given Fred Bates a brief account of the quarrel with Connie Hyde's father, hence Fred's flippant remark.

Jack made a pretence of eating the generous breakfast which his friend's wife placed before him, and then, in moody silence, he left the house and wandered over the hills.

"That row seems to have cut up Jack pretty badly," remarked the young farmer to his wife. "He must have changed a lot. Jack was never the kind to let anything worry him."

"That's because he was never in love until now," replied the wife with confident sententiousness.

Jack returned two hours later. His host met him at the door with a newspaper in his hand.

"Better read this, Jack," he said, holding out the paper.

As Jack read the brief account of David Hyde's murder, his face paled and his lips set in a grim, straight line. For long after he had finished reading, he stood in silence, crumpling up the paper in his hand, whilst his friend regarded him keenly.

"I shall have to leave you, Fred," said Jack at last, as he put the paper aside.

"You're not... not..."

"I'm going to Blackton."

"I... see." But Fred Bates did not see at all.

Later, Jack stood beside his motorcycle outside the farmhouse gate.

"I may return tonight, Fred," he said. "I may not. If I don't, you will understand."

Fred said nothing. Understanding was very far from him just then.

Jack's motorcycle tore along the road, and ate up the miles with greedy enjoyment. Tight-lipped, Jack sat on the seat staring straight before him. But his eyes saw more than the white stretch of road that rushed back to meet him.

The road gradually converged towards the railway lines, and, at last, he saw a crossroads in front. Jack knew that if he turned to the left here he would soon reach Highpen Tunnel. He turned, and his machine roared up the steep incline.

The road crossed the tunnel at the end nearer Blackton. Jack stopped the engine, dismounted, and leaned the cycle against the high limestone parapet that bordered the road. Across the top of the parapet he saw the glistening railway lines running south between high banks. And he knew that if he placed his hands on the top of the parapet and levered himself up he would be able to see the mouth of the tunnel itself.

But not until he had walked along, almost to the end of the parapet, did he raise himself. Then he looked down a full fifty feet. In a moment he released his grip. Standing at the mouth of the tunnel, clear of the lines, was a policeman looking up at the spot where Jack had left his cycle. No doubt the constable had been attracted by the stopping of the engine, and had Jack mounted the parapet at that point he could not possibly have escaped the watcher's notice.

Jack tiptoed back to his machine, and pushed it all the way back to the crossroads before he mounted it again and started the engine.

Inspector Parker, alone in his office, was puzzling over the startling information he had received from the Chief Constable of Donmoor, when a sergeant knocked and entered.

"Gentleman called Mr. Davis wishes to see you, sir," he said.

The inspector sat up with a start.

"Show him in," he ordered, endeavouring to mask his surprise.

Jack Davis stepped briskly in.

"Yes?" was the inspector's unhelpful greeting.

The young man moistened his lips with his tongue, and for some moments he stood there in silence.

"I saw an account of the murder in the paper," he began at last. "I considered it my duty to come here at once. I know the dead man."

"Yes. And I know that he gave you the sack a day or two ago."

The curt statement, so bluntly rapped out, took Davis completely by surprise. For several moments he was in the grip of stupefied amazement, and then he gasped:

"You... know... that?"

"Yes, that and a few things more. Better tell me all about it. But, remember, you are not compelled to say anything."

The inspector's manner, more than his actual words, fired Jack's blood.

"Am I to regard that as the usual caution?" he demanded.

"If you like."

Inspector Parker had the feeling that his shot had missed its target. He had hoped that his abrupt reference to the younger man's dismissal would have startled him into some unwilling admission. But nothing had come of it. True, the other had seemed almost astounded at first. But his start of surprise might have been equally the result of a guilty mind or—just natural surprise at the inspector's knowledge.

"Tell me about your relations with the dead man," went on Parker. He was careful not to ask a leading question. After she had regained her composure, the murdered man's daughter had told him all that she was able to tell, and he was now keenly anxious to see whether there should be a discrepancy in Jack Davis's story.

Afterwards, however, the inspector had to admit to himself that he could detect no discrepancy. And Jack told his story with apparent frankness, except that he hesitated now and then when referring to his feelings for the dead man's daughter.

The diamond merchant, he said, was hard and unyielding; unscrupulous even, when carrying out a business transaction. But, apart from business, he was a just man—rigidly just, too just, the kind that would consider it a weakness to temper justice with mercy.

Jack Davis had been Mr. Hyde's assistant for several years, and, although he had never been able to experience any warmth of feeling towards his employer, he had been compelled to admire his business acumen.

"Despite his hardness," continued Jack, "we got on fairly well together until"—and here came one of the young man's pauses—"until he discovered that I loved his daughter. For a considerable time, Miss Hyde and I had managed to conceal our love from him, for we both knew that his ambition was to marry her into what is called Society. In the end, however, he found out. That was the day before yesterday. There was a terrific row. He ordered me to give up his daughter. I refused. Then he used some forcible words to describe what he termed my presumption, whereupon I, too, lost my temper and said things that in calmer moments I would have left unsaid. The upshot of it was that he gave me the sack, threw a month's salary at me and almost kicked me out."

"And threatened to disinherit the girl?"

"Your knowledge of the affair," said Jack after a long pause, "seems equal to mine. Well, he did make such a threat. Not to me, though. Evidently that plan occurred to him during the night. Next morning—yesterday morning—he had a row with Connie and told her that he was making a new will, containing the proviso that, should she marry me, all his wealth would go to an institution upon his death."

"You think he would have done it?"

"I am sure he would."

"How fortunate that he—died when he did."

In an instant, the younger man flared into a terrible passion. Striding over to the inspector, he stood before him with clenched fists and flashing eyes.

"That's a damned insult!" he cried hotly. "And if you weren't a police officer you'd take it back jolly quickly. But, of course, you'd never have dared to make the rotten suggestion if you hadn't your position to back you up. One can afford to take risks when one has a uniform to shield—" Suddenly he broke off. Until now he had seen only the fringe of the cutting innuendo. But now, now he saw, or fancied he saw, the very centre of the hideous allusion.

"Good heavens, man!" he cried, aghast, "surely you don't mean to insinuate that—that I—killed...?"

"An innocent man, or a very clever actor?" the inspector asked himself. Aloud he said: "Calm yourself, Mr. Davis. I mean to insinuate nothing. But I think we'd better not discuss that part of the business further... Do you happen to know why Mr. Hyde travelled north yesterday so soon after the unpleasantness with his daughter?"

Jack swallowed hard, and for several moments he did not answer. His outburst had left him shaking, and he was trying hard to regain a semblance of composure.

"Yes," he replied at last. "I know why he went. But his going had nothing to do with—with the row. The journey had been under discussion for over a week, or, rather, it had been the subject of correspondence. Mr. Hyde went to Donmoor to inspect, probably purchase, a diamond necklace belonging to Sir Joshua Jordan."

"Sir Joshua Jordan! The man who was robbed?"

Jack stared.

"You have the advantage of me there," he said. "I didn't know that Sir Joshua had been robbed."

"I didn't, until quite recently." The inspector rose and began to pace up and down the room. He was considering the advisability of making an important disclosure to the man before him. Finally he decided that the revelation could do no harm. "Half an hour ago," he said, "the Chief Constable of Donmoor rang me up and told me that Sir Joshua had been assaulted and robbed in his own house, assaulted and robbed by—Mr. David Hyde."

"Are you telling me the truth?" asked Jack, after a silence that had lasted a full minute.

"I don't usually tell lies, Mr. Davis."

"Perhaps not. But that's a hellish lie, anyhow. I don't mean to say that you are telling a deliberate untruth, but your information is grossly inaccurate. Although I have no reason to love the dead man, in justice I must say that I am convinced he would never have done that. He may have been unscrupulous, may have been guilty of sharp practices now and then. I have known him to provide a jewel with a history it didn't possess; but he would never have acted like a common house-breaker or purse-snatcher."

For several minutes they discussed the matter further, but no new facts were brought to light.

"There is a young lady in this town in whom you are interested," said the inspector at last, wishing to terminate the interview. "Miss Hyde arrived this morning."

"What!" cried Jack. "Connie here?"

"Yes. And one of my men has found rooms for her." He scribbled a few words on a piece of paper. "Here is the young lady's address. I presume that you, too, will wish to remain in Blackton for a day or two. As soon as you've found temporary accommodation, will you let me know? Thanks. And now I shall have to say good morning, Mr. Davis. Glad you called."

"Innocent?... Or very, very clever?" the inspector again asked himself when Jack had gone.

After deep deliberation, Police Constable Brent had arrived at what he considered the safest method of drawing his superior's attention to the broken window. He would have done so the moment he had returned to the police-station had he not remembered the inspector's ironic smile on the previous day. George Brent was too deeply in love not to resent being chaffed about the object of his affections. Then again, the inspector would probably have disapproved of his discussing the murder with the old potter and his niece.

"But why mention them at all?" was the question he finally asked himself: "Why not say that I suddenly remembered the broken window whilst on my way to meet Constable Wilkins at the Four Lane Ends? It will be the truth, although, perhaps, not the whole truth."

His mind made up, George Brent entered the presence of his superior. Apart from necessary disciplinary routine, Inspector Parker treated the young constable almost like an equal. He knew that Brent's intellect was at least equal to his own, and he was sufficiently large-minded to be glad that he had such a capable officer working under him. More than once he had asked for the young policeman's advice on some legal technicality and the advice, when received, was invariably followed. Parker now listened with interest to what the other had to say.

"I was a blind fool not to have observed it myself," he frankly admitted, when George had finished. "And, apart altogether from the broken window, I ought to have inspected that compartment yesterday. It might have contained some valuable clue. But there were so many other things to claim my attention just then—the removal of the body, interrogation of witnesses, and so on. And the guard was in such a hurry to take on the train to Midtown. But perhaps it is not yet too late. I shall ring up the traffic manager and see whether he can do anything to help."

He picked up the telephone and was soon in communication with the traffic-manager's office. For several minutes he talked and listened, and when, finally, he put down the telephone there was a satisfied smile on his lips.

"Better luck than I deserve, Brent," he announced. "The window has not yet been repaired, and the traffic manager was decent enough to offer to place the whole coach at my disposal. He has promised to send it back here to the Blackton sidings."

"And now to explore the tunnel," said the inspector. "Of course, Brent, I shall want you to come with me."

Police Constable Brent smiled quietly to himself. Matters were working out splendidly, after all. No need now for him to mention that this was the very thing suggested by old Dick, the potter.

Armed with nothing more deadly than a powerful electric torch, they set out to explore the sinister tunnel.

The inspector had decided not to make enquiries about the times trains might be expected to pass through. The fewer who knew what he was about, the better. There was a constable on duty at either end of the tunnel, and these could be trusted to prevent any untoward happening.

Almost in silence they covered the mile and a half that stretched between Blackton and Highpen Tunnel. Arrived there, Parker gave strict orders to the constable on guard to keep eyes and ears alert for trains coming north. The moment he became aware of an approaching train, he was to blow his whistle for all he was worth. This would give the explorers plenty of time to cross to the other side of the tunnel.

Inspector Parker was fully aware that he was not taking every possible precaution. But, rather than waste time, he decided not to warn the constable at the other end. Moreover, there would be no danger from a train running south. His investigations, he reasoned, would have to be carried out along the west side of the tunnel, for anything thrown through the broken window would have dropped on this side.

The inspector leading, they followed the beam of light that stabbed through the inky blackness. Progress was very slow. Keeping close to the left wall of the tunnel, Parker switched his light from left to right, and both carefully scrutinised the floor as they moved forward. The ground, they observed, was, for the most part, covered with gravel, now weathered to the consistency of coarse sand; whilst here and there, particularly near the side, were bare patches of sticky clay.

"Hark!" cried the constable when they had been in the tunnel for what seemed an hour, but was in reality only a few minutes. "I believe a train's coming." They heard the shriek of a whistle, shrill and prolonged.

The inspector sprang towards the other side of the tunnel. But Brent grabbed him by the arm and held him fast.

"Back, sir!" he yelled. "That wasn't a police whistle. It was an engine entering the tunnel at the other end."

The inspector stood there undecided, and Brent saw that he would have to act promptly.

"Let's lie down close to the wall," he shouted, to make himself heard above the thunder of the approaching train. "Whichever way it's coming we ought to be safe there."

Parker obeyed, and in another moment a south-bound train roared past, the illuminated smoke that belched from its chimney making it seem like a monstrous fiery dragon.

For several moments neither spoke. Then Inspector Parker laughed a quavering laugh.

"Thanks, Brent," he said, and the hand he placed on his subordinate's shoulder was violently shaking. "I lost my head completely. Funny the tricks one's brain will play. I had told myself that when I heard a whistle I was to run to the other side. Well, I heard a whistle, and... Brent, I shan't forget this."

But Brent hardly heard him. From his prone position he reached over and picked up a pistol that he had seen lying half-buried in a patch of sand. He had a fleeting glimpse of a tiny furrow that had obviously been ploughed by the weapon before it came to rest after striking the ground.

Chapter 5

The Missing Tobacco Pouch

"The case against Reggie Robinson seems to be getting clearer," said the inspector as they walked back towards Blackton. "This weapon ought to prove his guilt."

"I suppose, sir, you are thinking of fingerprints?"

"Yes." The inspector had now regained his composure. "As soon as we get back I shall apply the usual test to the pistol."

Constable Brent reflected.

"But even if you do find fingerprints, sir," he asked, "how are you to know that they are Reggie's? You don't possess his."

"No, Brent. But there are ways and means."

Brent nodded. He knew what his superior meant.

They walked along in silence for a considerable distance, the young policeman busily revolving in his mind many problems that puzzled him.

"Your face is like an open book, Brent," said Parker with a smile, observing the other's abstraction. "But the language is foreign. What is it?"

"Reggie, as we must still call him, gave a false name, sir. Why, having given it, did he not also give a false address?"

The inspector still smiled.

"The false name, Brent, was simply a polite way of giving no name at all. And Reggie, you may have observed, can be polite when he likes. A false address, however, is in a very different category. Unlike the name, we could easily prove it to be false. But, to my mind, his refusal makes one point clear: he is crooked. He didn't give a false address, for the reason I've already mentioned. And he daren't give the true one, because we should then be able to learn something to his disadvantage."

They kept close to the shelving bank while an engine and a long string of laden coal-trucks rumbled past.

"Brent," said the inspector, his gaze apparently fixed on the lamp at the back of the receding guard's van, "you use a camera, don't you?"

"Yes, sir. But I'm not an expert."

"An expert isn't needed. All I shall want you to do is to take a few snaps of Reggie, from different angles if possible. I shall see that you get the opportunity, without his knowing what you are about. I have decided to get in touch with Scotland Yard. Our own Chief Constable, as you know, has his hands filled with the Hellifield murder, and he has given me what amounts to a free hand here. But he has been in consultation with the Yard, and has received the assurance of someone in authority that the Criminal Investigation Department will be pleased to give me any help I may need. And it has been arranged that I may apply direct instead of through the Chief Constable. Well, Reggie may be on the Crime Index, and if I have a few snaps to send along with his fingerprints the Department's job ought to be easy."

Brent nodded.

"I believe I've heard of the Index, sir," he observed. "Doesn't it contain particulars of all known criminals, both British and foreign?"

"Correct, Brent."

They discussed the best methods of obtaining the photographs, and then the constable brought forward some of the arguments that had been used in his conversation with the potter, without, however, mentioning the old potter's name.

But Inspector Parker did not attach much importance to the left-handed theory.

"Reggie could easily have done it with the right hand," he asserted. "If a train in which one is travelling plunges into a tunnel, and no artificial light comes on, what is one's first instinctive action? Why, to turn one's eyes to the spot from which the light ought to come. There can be little doubt that the diamond merchant did what nine persons out of ten would have done. He glanced towards the ceiling, which meant that he was practically facing Reggie. No, Brent, I cannot agree that Reggie would have found it difficult to shoot Mr. Hyde through the forehead."

Constable Brent kicked a pebble out of his way.

"I must admit, sir, that that solution hadn't occurred to me," he confessed. "Having in mind the position of the wound and the seats occupied by the various occupants of the compartment, I was inclined to think that John Lofthouse must have been the guilty party."

There was an amused twinkle in the inspector's eyes.

"Seems funny," he remarked dryly, "that your reasoning should have ignored Miss Lowe. Her position was the most favourable of the lot, you know."

The constable said nothing. His expression, however, said much.

"Anyhow," went on the inspector, "I am not forgetting the possibility of John Lofthouse's guilt. I have asked the Midtown police to keep an eye on him, and any suspicious move on the publican's part will be reported to me immediately. Should his conduct seem to justify such a step, he will be arrested forthwith."

Very little more was said until they were back in a room at the police-station and making arrangements for the forthcoming interview with Reggie Robinson.

"Reggie will be coming across the yard in a few minutes," exclaimed Parker. "Get your camera ready at one of the windows, and keep out of sight if you can until the snaps have been taken."

George Brent pulled open the folding camera and approached one of the two large windows that looked on to the yard. Raising the lower sash a short distance, he swung the camera from left to right, thus bringing every part of the yard within focus in turn. At a certain angle there came a slight flash as the sun caught the lens.

"Ready?"

There was no answer for several moments, and Inspector Parker was about to repeat his query when Brent left the window and moved over to the table where his superior sat.

"We've been forgetting the flash, sir," was his somewhat cryptic remark.

The inspector stared.

"The flash?" he echoed. "What do you mean, Brent?"

"The compartment was in complete darkness. When the pistol was discharged everyone must have seen the flash. Yet not one of them has mentioned it. That seems peculiar, sir. The noise of the train would drown the report, I suppose. But the flash...? I can't understand it, sir."

The inspector still stared. After a long silence he picked up a pen and commenced to draw imaginary figures on a sheet of blotting-paper.

"That's certainly a poser, Brent," he finally admitted. "But there's probably a simple explanation. No one mentioned the flash because no one was asked. Or, which is more likely, they saw the flash, but thought it was lightning."

"But they couldn't have seen lightning when they were well inside the tunnel, sir."

"I know. But there was nothing to prevent their thinking it was lightning. They wouldn't have paused to reflect on the matter... Let's waste no more time, though. Get ready at the window, Brent."

He struck the bell on the table, a signal to the sergeant outside the door that Reggie Robinson was to be conducted to the inspector.

A few minutes later, the camera clicked three times during the progress of Reggie and his escort across the yard.

Reggie, who had been allowed full facilities for a shave, was looking spruce and debonair. And his attitude was still one of jaunty defiance.

"Well?" he asked, boldly confronting the inspector. "What's the trouble?"

"There's not going to be any trouble, I hope," was Parker's smiling reply. "I just thought I'd give you an opportunity to amend your statement, if you cared to do so."

"Amend my statement, Inspector? Did I really make a statement?"

The inspector leaned back in his seat. His left elbow rested on the table, and the fingers of his right hand drummed on the arm of his chair.

"Take a seat, Reggie." With a nod he indicated a chair. "I think you'll find that chair quite comfortable."

For a moment the mocking smile was wiped clean from Reggie's face. But it soon returned. In that brief moment, however, Parker had learned much. He had a friend at Scotland Yard who had taught him some of the ropes, and now he had deliberately used the formula by which certain of the Yard's officials begin to interrogate a suspect. Reggie's start of surprise had proved conclusively that he was familiar with the formula.

Reggie sat down.

"That's better. Well... are you going to talk?"

"Sorry to disappoint you, Inspector; but I've said all I mean to say."

The inspector crossed his knees. "Just as you like, Reggie," he said in a friendly tone. "By the way, have you any objection to my taking an impression of your fingers and thumb?—just as a matter of routine, you know."

"Just as a matter of routine, you know," mimicked Reggie, "I have the strongest possible objection." His mocking smile became intensified. "And you daren't do it without my consent."

Parker politely inclined his head.

"You're right, Reggie. In the circumstances, I daren't... You still maintain, I suppose, that you never had possession of the murdered man's wallet?"

"Of course I do. You don't think I'm going to admit it just to please you—and that nosy young school-kid?" A little of the urbanity seemed to be oozing away from Reggie Robinson.

"You'd be a fool to admit it for that reason," agreed the inspector. "So you refuse to say anything? Rather a pity. No use wasting any more time, then. Time we were having our lunch, I think. Perhaps you wouldn't mind telling me which is your favourite lunchtime beverage? Water-Bright, I expect?"

"Champagne's said to be more palatable," said Reggie, slowly rising to his feet.

"Constable Brent," rapped out the inspector, "will you see that Mr. Reggie Robinson has a glass of beer with his lunch."

Again he struck the bell. The sergeant entered and conducted the grinning Reggie out of the room.

Inspector Parker gave some concise instructions to Brent, who then departed to provide Reggie Robinson with the promised glass of beer.

Left alone, the inspector unlocked the drawer and withdrew the dead man's wallet and the pistol found in the tunnel. With a powerful magnifying-glass he examined the pistol for fingerprints; but, except for a few smudges near the tip of the barrel, he could detect none. And he strongly suspected that these smudges had been made by

Brent when he picked up the weapon in the tunnel. Not yet satisfied, however, he moved over to a cupboard and returned with a little box of French chalk. But when he had dusted the weapon with the fine powder, and blown off the surplus chalk, he was forced to the conclusion that the pistol contained not the slightest trace of a fingerprint.

"Funny!" he mused. "There ought to be fingerprints. Looks as though they had been deliberately rubbed off. But the pistol was half-buried in the sand. Perhaps that's how the prints disappeared."

The pocketbook, however, was not so barren of results. The inspector possessed other appliances for the reproduction of fingerprints, and he had obtained several more or less perfect prints by the time Constable Brent returned. Not all of them were alike, for several people had handled the wallet.

"Well?" he asked, as Brent entered and placed a glass tumbler on the table. "Did Reggie enjoy his beer?"

George chuckled.

"He complained that he'd ordered champagne, sir," was the laughing answer. "But he drank the beer all the same—and seemed to enjoy it, too."

"Good. I feared that his suspicion might have been aroused. And now to examine the fingerprints he left on the tumbler."

Five minutes later, Inspector Parker would have been prepared to swear in any court of law that the man who called himself Reggie Robinson had handled the murdered man's pocketbook. And no one with any knowledge of the infallibility of the fingerprint system would have dared to contradict him, for his proofs were incontrovertible.

"Good!" he said again. "Now I have something worth sending to Scotland Yard. Brent, I think you had better remove that film from your camera, and I'll send it along just as it is. The Yard experts will be able to deal with it more expeditiously than you or I could. Nevertheless it will take some time for the packet to reach London. Wish we could wireless the things. Anyhow, I can put through a call and let them know what I am sending on."

The conversation that took place between Inspector Parker and the Assistant Commissioner, New Scotland Yard, was long and interesting, and, when it was finished, the inspector put down the telephone with a sigh of satisfaction.

"I gave him all the particulars I could about the crime," he told the constable, "and a detailed description of Reggie. But, of course, you heard all I said. Pending the arrival of the fingerprints and photographs, he is having the Index looked up, and, judging by the way our unwilling guest gave himself away, I have little doubt that it will contain some particulars of Reggie."

Parker passed Brent his cigarette-case, lighted his own pipe, and then resumed:

"The Assistant Commissioner suggests that we get in touch with Sir Joshua Jordan through the Donmoor police. And, from a hint he dropped, I have formed the opinion that he'd like to send a man along to help us. But we can manage very well without a Yard man. There's no mystery about the affair, after all. Reggie robbed and murdered the diamond merchant, and nothing remains but to prove his guilt."

Police Constable Brent thoughtfully inhaled some smoke and expelled it through his nostrils.

"Sounds easy, sir," he agreed. "And yet—what facts have we to go upon? The diamond merchant was murdered. But did Reggie murder him? Did he commit the robbery even? True, he had the wallet in his possession for a moment or two. But what about the necklace? Mr. Davis says that his employer went to Donmoor to purchase a diamond necklace from Sir Joshua Jordan. Sir Joshua, on the other hand, has declared that Mr. Hyde took the necklace from him by force. Whichever story is the true one, the necklace ought to have been in Mr. Hyde's possession—or in Reggie's if he robbed Mr. Hyde. But, although both Reggie and the dead body have been thoroughly searched, no trace of the diamonds has been found. I wonder, sir, whether the case is really so simple as it seems."

The inspector had listened with respectful attention to the arguments raised by the young constable. He now took several turns up and down the room, his gaze apparently concentrated on the floor. Finally, he came to a halt.

"I wonder, Brent," he echoed, as though the other had spoken only the moment before. "You've shown me a few nasty snags that had escaped my notice. And—and—Brent," he cried suddenly, "bring me the list of things found on the dead body."

Wondering, George Brent obeyed.

"Now, Brent, I want you to read through the list. Never mind the contents of the wallet. Just what was found in the pockets—slowly, Brent."

Brent slowly read through the list—watch and chain, fountain pen, coins, keys, return half of a railway ticket, handkerchief, matches, pipe.

"And that's all, sir," he wound up.

"I've got it!" exclaimed the inspector. "I knew that there was something funny about the contents of Mr. Hyde's pockets, but I didn't tumble to it until now. Brent, can you tell me what's missing from that list?"

"Nothing, sir," came the unhesitating answer. "I wrote down the name of every item."

Parker smiled.

"I know you did, Brent. But that's not what I mean. Now what other article ought to have been in one of the pockets, but wasn't? I'll tell you though, for we cannot afford to waste time asking riddles. A pipe and matches are useless without tobacco. There ought to have been a tobacco pouch in one of Mr. Hyde's pockets. But there wasn't. Why? Well, Brent, unless I'm very much mistaken, Mr. Hyde had a pouch when he left Donmoor. And the pouch contained not only tobacco, but—the necklace. Quite a clever hiding-place, too. Nevertheless, it wasn't clever enough to deceive Reggie Robinson."

"And where's the tobacco pouch now, sir?" asked Brent after a long pause.

"Wish I knew, Brent. But wait a minute! Why, it must be in the tunnel. Reggie threw it out after the pistol. We ought to have made a more thorough search there."

In imagination, Constable Brent was again lying in the tunnel as the train thundered past. By the light of the torch, he saw the pistol lying in the sand, saw the little trench it had made before it came to rest. And, strangely enough, although the weapon lay motionless, it set him thinking about certain of the Laws of Motion.

"The pistol," he declared with a startled exclamation, "was never thrown through the window of that moving train."

Chapter 6

Brent Explains His Theory

"I believe that confounded inspector thinks I've had a hand in it, Connie."

"Well, what else can you expect?" answered Connie Hyde. "Had you stayed in London instead of flying down here you would have had a—an—"

"Alibi," suggested Jack Davis.

"Thanks. That's the word I wanted."

They were together in Connie's sitting-room. As soon as he had got her address from Inspector Parker, Jack Davis had rushed off to the girl he loved. The meeting had been painful at first; but, gradually, the girl had become her old vivacious self, and she was now quite different from the distraught young woman who had called on Inspector Parker. Sensibly, she had come to realise that tears were more a hindrance than a help; and she was honest enough to admit to herself that Jack's unexpected presence had done much to restore the usual buoyancy of her spirits.

"But, Connie, how was I to know that this would happen?" protested Jack. "Months ago, I promised Fred Bates to pay him a visit at the first opportunity. My chance seemed to have come yesterday. I was out of a job… Moreover, I couldn't forget some of the hard things your father had said. On a sudden impulse I decided to—"

He paused abruptly, and the girl's suspicions were instantly aroused.

"Yes," she said. "You decided to… what?"

"Oh—just think things over," he answered evasively.

There followed a long silence, which was finally broken by the girl.

"Jack," she said, and there was a funny little catch in her voice, "you are keeping something back. Won't you tell me what it is?"

Jack bit his lip, and swallowed hard.

"Don't ask me now," he begged. "Later you will have to know all; but—don't ask me now, Connie."

Another long silence followed. Suddenly the girl roused herself, as recollection flashed upon her.

"Jack," she said, "let us not be selfish. There's this dreadful business of my father to be thought of. We mustn't let our own little troubles intrude."

"You are right, darling. That mystery must be cleared up at all costs." He laughed rather mirthlessly. "Until the guilty person has been discovered, I shall live every moment with the fear of arrest upon me. That is why I must stay here and play my part in solving the mystery. Already I think I can see one or two lines of investigation that might lead somewhere."

Soon afterwards the landlady was summoned. She recommended rooms in another street, and then Jack took his departure, his immediate object being to provide temporary accommodation for himself.

But in Connie's heart the seed of suspicion steadily grew.

Old Dick, the potter, stuck his thumb in the whirling mass of clay, and quickly fashioned the inside of a bowl. Then, stopping the wheel, he inclined his head to one side, and scrutinised his handiwork.

"Freda, my girl," he said, looking up at his niece, who was standing by, "I hear that the murdered man's daughter arrived in Blackton this morning. Poor girl! This must be a dreadful experience for her! The awful shock of it all! And then to be alone in a strange town! I want you to befriend her, Freda."

Freda's steady gaze met the kindly gleam in the old man's eyes.

"I understand, Uncle," she said simply. "You want me to…"

"I want you to do what you can, what you think is best."

"Right, Uncle. I'll get my hat and coat, and go at once."

At the gate, Freda turned and looked back. Her uncle sat in front of the wheel, his gaze concentrated on the unfinished bowl.

The girl set off with a brisk step, and was soon in sight of the house that provided Connie Hyde with a temporary home. When she was less than a dozen yards from the house, the door opened, and a tall, well-set-up young man stepped out. Glancing neither to left nor right, he crossed the road and went down a side street.

Freda advanced and watched him out of sight. She had a trustworthy memory for faces and figures, and she felt sure that the young man was a stranger to Blackton.

A few minutes later, Freda stepped briskly into Connie's room, whilst the landlady held the door open.

"Thought you might be feeling lonely," she cried gaily; "so I just breezed in to cheer you up."

Without waiting for an invitation, she took a seat, introduced herself, and explained more fully the object of her visit.

"But I expect you're admiring my cheek," she wound up.

Connie, however, had taken an instant liking to Freda.

"It was awfully good of you to call in like this," she said with genuine gratitude. "I have been feeling dreadfully lonely all the morning."

"Then the young man I saw leaving hadn't been visiting you?" was the other's innocent query.

Connie, banishing her worry, laughed. Then, impulsively, she told her newly-made friend many delicious secrets.

"That mustn't stand in the way of our being friends, though," she declared. "Jack will be busy most of the time he's here."

"Hunting for clues, eh?"

"Yes, hunting for clues."

"How delightfully thrilling! I shall be frightfully interested to know what progress he's making. He has his suspicions, of course?"

But Connie couldn't say. If Jack suspected any particular person he hadn't told her.

"How mean of him!" exclaimed Freda with a pretty little sniff of disdain. "Now, if I had a young man I'd make him tell me everything, every single thing. And I suppose that police inspector was just as secretive?"

"Quite," agreed Connie. "He told me nothing. As far as—"

"Let's talk about something more pleasant, old thing," interrupted Freda. "You play tennis, of course? Well, you must promise to come with me to my club. I belong to the Elite and can bring a friend any time I like."

"I should be delighted to come if I could," answered Connie truthfully. "But, in the circumstances..."

"I'm so sorry," said Freda. "For the moment I had forgotten."

Thereafter, they discussed various topics.

"What the devil do you mean, Brent?" was Inspector Parker's blunt demand. "The pistol not thrown from the train! Sure you haven't been sampling Reggie's beer?"

But Police Constable Brent remained quite unperturbed.

"It's quite true, sir," he insisted. "Perhaps you didn't notice the little furrow in the sand."

"The furrow in the sand!" repeated the inspector, staring. Was Brent taking the liberty of indulging in an ill-timed jest? But, no. Brent's expression was too serious for that. "What do you mean, man?"

"The furrow," explained George, "was in the wrong place. I shall try to make the thing clear. The pistol, had it been thrown through the window of the moving train, would, naturally, have had an outward motion. But it would have had a forward motion as well. At the instant it left Reggie's hand it would have been moving forward at the same rate as the train. And it would have wanted to continue that movement. You know what happens when you alight from a moving bus or tram-car: you want to continue moving forward even after you have stepped on to the ground. Something similar happens if you throw a ball into the air whilst you are running along. The ball returns to your hands several yards in advance of the point from which you threw it. The ball has moved forward as well as upward, because it was moving forward at the instant it was thrown. Is that clear enough, sir?"

The inspector nodded. "Go on, Brent," was all he said. But his face still bore a perplexed expression.

George Brent continued:

"To go back to the pistol: the weapon would, of course, have had a third motion—a downward motion. Now, assuming for the moment that it was really thrown from the train, it must have done one of two things: either it stopped dead the moment it struck the ground, or it slid forward for a short distance. You still follow, sir?"

"Ye-es. I think so. But wait a minute. What about that outward motion you've mentioned. Couldn't the pistol have continued to move in that direction after it had struck the ground?"

Brent gazed thoughtfully at a fly on the ceiling.

"It might, sir," he conceded at last. "Depends, I should say, on the force with which it was thrown. Anyhow, that doesn't affect the point of my argument. The pistol I picked up in the tunnel seemed to have done an impossible thing. The position of the little channel in the sand shows beyond doubt that the weapon moved neither forward nor outward, but—backward."

"What!" The inspector's excitement was patently apparent. "You mean—?"

"I mean what I said at first, sir. The pistol wasn't hurled through the window at all."

Parker's pipe had gone out. He carefully selected a cigarette, and several minutes later he was speaking out of a dense cloud of smoke:

"And what's your theory now, Brent? You've got one, I suppose?"

"I don't believe the murder took place in the train, sir." The young constable's voice was full of quiet confidence.

"But, damn it, man!" was the other's unceremonious retort, "that's ridiculous! We all saw the dead body in the carriage. Don't tell me that our eyes—"

"I'm afraid I haven't made my meaning clear, sir," Brent interrupted with a smile. "I meant the murderer wasn't on the train."

The inspector smoked thoughtfully for several minutes.

"Then you believe he fired from the tunnel as the train passed?" he finally asked.

"Yes. It's my belief that he was standing somewhere near the Blackton end of the tunnel. And when he had fired the shot he threw away the pistol, threw it further into the tunnel. That would clearly account for the position of the furrow in the sand. You may remember that we found the pistol less than a stone's throw from the mouth of the tunnel."

Inspector Parker rose to his feet, and, hands behind his back, stood gazing into vacancy. He was picturing the darkness of the tunnel, the murderer standing there with upraised pistol, the string of carriages rushing past...

"Brent," he said, raising his gaze to the other's face, "your theory may be the right one. I don't know. It may be that the feat you have suggested is too difficult to be practicable. But it's well past your lunchtime now. Clear off and have something to eat. When you get back we'll pay another visit to Highpen Tunnel. I fancy we shall be better able to discuss your theory on the spot. There's the tobacco pouch, too, to search for. And, Brent, until this case is finished, you are to perform no more ordinary duties. I can't afford to have you wasting your time directing traffic. You are too good a man for that. Except when I require you in connection with the murder, you may pursue whatever line of investigation you think fit. I hardly think it's necessary for me to warn you against doing anything—unusual without first consulting me."

"Thank you, sir," said Police Constable Brent.

It seemed a fortunate coincidence that when the young constable was returning from his belated lunch Freda Lowe happened to be on her way home after paying her kindly visit to Connie Hyde.

They stopped and talked. Brent was feeling happy with all the world. His superior had shown him a signal mark of his favour, and now here was the girl he loved, obviously pleased to see him.

The man was young and very human. Like most men, he possessed a strong vein of vanity, unknown to himself. He was anxious to impress, and Freda was a sympathetic listener; consequently he did most of the talking.

"Why, George," she cried at last, lowering her eyes, "how clever you are! Fancy learning all that from a little mark in the sand! You'll be promoted in no time. I—I am proud of you, George. And, George, now that you've been given a free hand, we—I—we shall be able to see a lot more of each other...."

As he strode back to the police-station, George Brent realised, for the first time in his life, what poets and lovers mean when they sing about the "Seventh Heaven."

Meanwhile, Freda reached home. Knowing how interested was her uncle in the tunnel mystery—in all mysteries—she told him what she had learned from the young constable.

"So the murderer wasn't on the train, after all?" he exclaimed, his smeared old face wrinkling into a smile. "And that young man worked it out all by himself. He'll make a name for himself yet, I'm thinking. Freda, my girl, I believe you couldn't do better than..."

He left the sentence unfinished. But Freda seemed to understand.

A disinterested listener, had one been present, would immediately have classed the potter as a well-meaning old match-maker.

The darkness fled before the light of their electric torch as the inspector and the young constable made their way into the tunnel. This time they had made enquiries and learned that no north-bound train would be passing through for another hour at least.

They searched long and carefully, but their most painstaking efforts were barren of result. There was no trace of the tobacco pouch or of anything else that might throw a light on the mystery.

The inspector glanced at the watch on his wrist.

"A train will soon be coming south," he said. "Let us go back a bit. You say the murderer must have been standing near the mouth of the tunnel, don't you?"

"Yes, sir. The train was without lights, remember. Except the person who fired the shot stood where the daylight could reach, he would have been little better than a blind man."

"True. Well, let's put ourselves in his place."

They took up their stand about twenty feet from the tunnel's mouth, and even there the light was dim when the torch had been switched off.

"He couldn't have been standing any nearer to the open," remarked Parker. "The Midtown publican noticed what had happened the moment they got into the light."

For several minutes they waited in silence. Then at last they heard the warning screech of the whistle as the train plunged into the tunnel at the other end. Soon they heard the resounding roar of the approaching train. A moment later, they saw the fire and smoke belching from the engine, and then the procession of coaches thundered past.

The gaze of both policemen had been steadily fixed on the windows that dashed by. But all they had been able to distinguish was a quick succession of ghost-like blurs.

The inspector shook his head.

"Your theory will have to go by the board, Brent," he said with decision. "Had we been murderers, or would-be murderers, we couldn't
possibly have killed a man on that train. I mean we couldn't have killed
a particular man. We could have done nothing but let our pistols go
bang, and trust to luck. If Mr. Hyde was killed by a man standing here,
then the killer was a madman who fired blindly."

Constable Brent was quite despondent. He had felt so sure his
theory must be the right one, but he was compelled to admit the logic
of his superior's remark.

"But the murderer wasn't a madman," he said, after a thoughtful
silence. "The whole thing was too deliberate—the missing necklace,
the absence of fingerprints on the pistol, the—" Suddenly, he broke
off. "Footprints!" he exclaimed, pointing to a clayey patch, wet from
the water that dripped from above. "Rubber soles! Neither of us has
rubber soles. Someone has been in here lately, sir."

"You're right, Brent," agreed Parker, after he had examined the
impressions made by rubber-soled shoes. "Wonder who it can have
been? What a fool I was to take away the men on duty here, after we'd
found the pistol!"

Out in the open, some plate-layers were working on the line.

"Perhaps it was one of them," observed the inspector. "Let's enquire."

None of the plate-layers, however, had entered the tunnel. But the
foreman was able to shed light on the mystery.

"Not ten minutes afore you kem along, sir," he said, "I see'd a bloke
slip out o' the tunnel an' climb up the bank. I didn't see 'im go in,
though, for we'd only just started on this section."

"Can you describe him, my good man?"

The foreman could, and did. And, though his description was
somewhat long-winded, it was none the less lucid.

"H'm," reflected the inspector, his brow wrinkled in a puzzled
frown. "Wonder what Mr. Jack Davis was trying to find—or hide—in
there?"

Chapter 7

Light-Fingered Freddie Talks

The moment he got back to the police-station, Inspector Parker was informed that a call had come through from Scotland Yard. Hastening to the telephone, he was soon listening to the voice of Brigadier-General Norman, the Assistant Commissioner.

"One of our men has been looking up the Index," said the voice, "and I think we can let you have the information you want. Your description suits a man who has been through our hands more than once. The name by which we know him is Frederick Wilson, though he's commonly called Light-Fingered Freddie."

"Light-Fingered Freddie!" repeated the inspector. "That sounds like a pickpocket, sir."

"It does," agreed the other. "And that's what Freddie is. Quite an artist in his profession, too. He's so clever that, although we've been confident of his guilt in dozens of cases, we've never been able to lay him by the heels more than twice. He's a superb actor, and he lies so convincingly that when he has sworn black is white you begin to think that black really is white. Freddie, however, has never been guilty of robbery with violence. And criminals are usually consistent in their methods. Of course, in the present case, he may have been in a tight corner—"

"I don't think he was, sir. In fact, the murder seems to have been quite unnecessary; madness even, with so many others in the compartment."

"Of course," said the voice at the other end, "your man may not be Freddie. When the fingerprints reach us, however, we shall know with certainty, for Freddie's prints are here. By the way, the necklace hasn't been recovered, I suppose?"

"No, sir. Its whereabouts is a complete mystery."

"Ah! Do you know, Parker, the necklace makes me doubtful about Freddie. Purses and pocketbooks are his particular line of business. He has never been known to touch a precious stone. Seldom, indeed, has he troubled about even a watch. I wonder now?" went on the voice reflectively. "For the past year or two we have been uncomfortably aware of the existence of a gang of jewel thieves, but we have never been able to discover any definite facts to work upon. Parker, if the gang is responsible for Mr. Hyde's death, you really must let me send a man to Blackton."

Parker promised that if the murder were proved to be the work of a gang he would apply forthwith for the help of Scotland Yard, and the conversation then terminated.

"Another interview with Reggie might not be out of place," mused the inspector as he put down the telephone and rang for a constable.

Reggie's jauntiness, as he entered, seemed less spontaneous than it had been earlier in the day. That he was considerably worried was obvious, and his efforts to appear carefree did not escape the keen eyes of the police officer.

Parker motioned him to a seat. Reggie swaggered over and sat down facing the officer. He knew that the chairs had been arranged before his entrance, but he was too clever to object to the light striking full on his face.

The inspector was aware of the advantage of a prolonged silence as a prelude to the interrogation of a suspected wrongdoer. For several moments he sat there staring at the man before him. His fingers played piano scales on the arm of his chair, but he spoke not a word. Under the steely glare of the inspector's eyes, Reggie's nerves seemed to become jumpy. He shuffled uneasily in his chair, and, although he endeavoured to out-stare the other, his gaze dropped more than once.

"What the hell do you want now?" he demanded at last, unable to endure the inspector's scrutiny any longer. His voice was harsh, and on his lip was an upward curl that resembled a snarl.

The other's smile was inscrutable. His fingers continued to tap-tap on the arm of his chair.

"What have you done with the necklace... Freddie?" he asked in silken tones.

The tall man flinched as though from a threatened blow. One of his hands flew suddenly to his throat and tugged at his collar. His shifty gaze swept alternately from the inspector to the door by which he had entered. But the constable who had escorted him was standing just inside the room.

"What the hell—" he began again, then stopped abruptly.

"Light-Fingered Freddie," rapped out the inspector in merciless, incisive tones, "the game's up. What about it?"

But Reggie, or Freddie, did not give in without a struggle.

"Well, what about it?" he echoed harshly. The first shock of discovery over, he was getting a grip on his emotions, and his nervousness gave place to truculence.

"Listen—Freddie. That kind of talk is wasting my time and your breath. You needn't attempt to deny that you are Light-Fingered Freddie. I know you are he."

Parker did know it as surely as if he had received confirmation of the fingerprints and photographs from Scotland Yard. Freddie had given himself away the moment his name was mentioned.

"Well, supposing I am? What then?"

"I'm not supposing. I am stating a fact." Withdrawing his gaze from the other's face, he picked a pen off the tray and carefully regarded its broad-pointed nib. "You're a common pickpocket, Freddie. You robbed the diamond merchant."

"It's a lie! I—"

"Don't talk about lying, Freddie. It's you who lie. You'd got the pocketbook. But when you saw that discovery was imminent you dropped it and kicked it under the seat. The boy saw it all."

"Oh, I've heard all that already, Mr. Clever Inspector." Freddie's mirthless laugh matched the calculating glance of his eyes. "I've denied it. Want me to deny it again? It's just that school-kid's word against mine, you know."

"It's more than that, Freddie. In your profession you ought to wear gloves. You left your fingerprints on the wallet."

Freddie sat bolt upright. He opened his mouth as though to hurl out a vigorous denial, but closed it again without speaking.

"That's right, Freddie." Parker's smile was blandly disarming. "Think well before you speak. And at this point I should like to give you the usual caution. Remember, you are not bound to say anything. But if you do talk—be careful!"

Freddie's tongue shot out between his lips like the fangs of a poisonous snake.

"Thanks," he said, and whether or not he meant it, it would have been difficult to say. Then he went on slowly, carefully choosing each word, as one picks one's steps crossing a treacherous bog: "You say you found fingerprints on the wallet. Perhaps you did. But what's that got to do with me? Why do you say they are mine? It's all bluff. You cannot possibly know what my fingerprints are like."

"Can't I, Freddie? Remember that glass of beer you had with your lunch?"

Freddie was no fool. At once he saw the trap into which he had fallen. His mouth opened wide and his jaw dropped.

"You blasted snake!" he snarled. "I can have you for that. You have no right to take a man's fingerprints against his will."

"I didn't take them, Freddie. But if you think fit to leave your fingerprints lying about on tumblers—well, that's your look out, isn't it? But we're wasting time. Now I should think you will no longer trouble to deny that you robbed the diamond merchant, robbed him of a valuable diamond necklace, and then"—the inspector paused—"and then... murdered him. Or did you murder him first?"

Freddie's eyes goggled. His nostrils dilated with the intense emotion that gripped him.

"I didn't do it!" he cried in panic. "Honest to God, I didn't!" There seemed no fight left in Freddie now: he was simply a terrified, broken-down outcast. He had had previous experience of the firm hand of the law, and had taken his punishment more or less philosophically. But this? This was entirely different. This was a hanging matter. And he knew, or thought he knew, that the law would never cease its efforts until it had brought the crime home to him. Nevertheless, he went on in desperate, high-pitched vehemence:

"I know nothing about it, I tell you. I never even knew that there was a necklace. And I didn't know the man. I got into that carriage because he seemed a likely one to have money on him. Oh, yes, I admit I am Freddie Wilson. I admit that I tried to pick Mr. Hyde's pocket. What the boy said was true. I'd got the pocketbook, but dropped it again when I saw—"

He broke off with startling abruptness, horror in his eyes.

"You must believe me!" he continued with a panting rush when he had partially regained his breath. "You've got to believe me! I know no more about the—the shooting than any of the others. But it must have happened just at the moment I was taking the wallet from his pocket. While my hand was at his breast, I felt him sort of crumple up and sag forward. That's all I know. It's God's honest truth..."

Freddie's voice trailed off into silence. Parker raised his finger and beckoned. The constable advanced, and, a moment later, Light-Fingered Freddie lurched out of the room with downbent head and drooping shoulders.

The inspector watched his departure.

"A superb actor," he said to himself, remembering the words of Brigadier-General Norman.

Left to himself, Inspector Parker reviewed in detail the very puzzling facts in his possession.

Mr. David Hyde, a Hatton Garden diamond merchant, had been shot in a train as it sped through Highpen Tunnel. And there seemed little doubt that he had been robbed also. Jack Davis and Sir Joshua Jordan had told conflicting stories about the manner in which Mr. Hyde had gained possession of the necklace, but, whatever the means by which he had acquired it, there seemed little doubt that he had it in his possession when he left Donmoor.

Where was the necklace now? In the dead man's tobacco pouch? Judging by the amount of caked carbon inside the bowl of his pipe, Mr. Hyde had been a heavy smoker, and it seemed inconceivable that he should have travelled all the way to Donmoor without the wherewithal to indulge in a smoke. True, he might have forgotten his pouch when leaving home. But, if that were so, he would almost certainly have purchased a packet of tobacco on the way to Donmoor, or in Donmoor itself. No tobacco, however, had been found on his person; therefore it was safe to assume that he had not left home without his pouch. There was only one conclusion to draw: the pouch had been stolen with the necklace inside it.

But how and whither had the pouch vanished with its valuable contents? Light-Fingered Freddie had been searched, and the search had availed nothing. The pouch must have been thrown through the window, yet diligent search had failed to reveal it in the tunnel.

Then a sudden new thought struck the inspector. Had he searched the wrong person, the wrong place? Of course, with one exception, the others were above suspicion. But the exception? Might not the Midtown publican be the guilty one? John Lofthouse was a shady customer, who was known to associate with all kinds of undesirables. There was nothing fantastic in assuming that it was possibly he who had committed the robbery. He and Light-Fingered Freddie might even be partners in crime.

The inspector's thoughts jumped on to the other and greater crime. Who had shot Mr. Hyde? Light-Fingered Freddie, came the answer. Naturally, Freddie had denied all knowledge of either the necklace or the murder. But, according to Scotland Yard, Freddie was a superb actor and a convincing liar.

It was peculiar, though, that Freddie's fingerprints had not been found on the pistol. The man could hardly have had time to obliterate them before throwing away the weapon. And he hadn't been wearing gloves. No gloves had come to light during the search. Of course, as he had already surmised, the sand might have destroyed the fingerprints, but he doubted whether it could have done so without leaving even a trace.

Was Lofthouse, then, the murderer? Parker frowned in perplexity, for the same difficulty again confronted him: why were not Lofthouse's fingerprints on the pistol? Of course, Lofthouse might have had gloves...

Again, why had none of those present mentioned the flash of the explosion, the smell of the burning powder? Was it because of the natural excitement consequent on the discovery of the murder? But the flash had taken place before the discovery, had taken place a fraction of a second before the murder even. Perhaps, as he had already argued, they had seen the flash and thought it was lightning. Perhaps the murderer had been clever enough to conceal the flash by screening the pistol with a coat or some kind of material. And the smoke from the engine had probably mingled with the smoke of the gunpowder.

Brent's theory next flashed across the mind of Inspector Parker. But, in the light of his own observations, he discarded that theory. Had the train been standing still it would have been a different matter. But even a Bisley prize-winner could hardly have performed the feat while the train rushed past at well over twenty miles an hour.

And the broken window made Brent's theory more fantastic than ever. Though he had not yet seen it, Parker knew that it was not the window near which the murdered man had been sitting. To shoot Mr. Hyde, in the circumstances, the murderer would have been compelled to discharge the pistol long before the compartment had got in line with him. Apart from the question of marksmanship, the line of fire did not seem at all practicable. Had the bullet crashed at an angle through the window beside Freda Lowe, it would have been far more likely to kill Freddie or one of the women with the shopping baskets.

Suddenly the inspector's thoughts switched back to the missing to-bacco pouch. And in that same instant he thought of Jack Davis. What had Davis been searching for in the tunnel? Did he know that the pouch had been, or was to have been, thrown through the window? Had he had prior knowledge that the murder was to be committed? Davis had had a very strong reason for wishing the diamond merchant dead before the will could be altered. What had he been doing in that part of the country, anyhow? Had he actually fired the fatal shot? Or had he had a confederate on the train whose business it was to do the shooting. Davis's part of the business might have been the comparatively easy task of removing the pistol and the pouch from the tunnel.

The inspector hesitated. If such were the case, why had Davis waited so long before attempting to carry out his part of the work? A possible explanation occurred to Inspector Parker. He rang the bell, gave an order to the man who answered, and a few minutes later the constable who had been on guard at the Blackton end of the tunnel stood before him.

"No one entered the tunnel while I was on duty there, sir," said the constable, in answer to his superior's query. "But I believe an attempt was about to be made. A motorcycle stopped on the road above. I didn't see the cyclist, however. He must have seen me before I could catch sight of him. Anyhow, he cleared off. And he did it quietly, too, sir, for I didn't hear the motor again until it had reached the crossroads."

The inspector's lips tightened into a grim smile. He knew beyond the shadow of a doubt that Jack Davis was the motorcyclist. And he felt sure that Davis would have entered the tunnel then had it not been for the presence of the constable on guard.

Chapter 8

The Reckless Motorist

T hat evening Inspector Parker was notified that the coach in which the murder had been committed was now in Blackton sidings close to the railway station.

Both he and Constable Brent were soon at the sidings. Only one compartment held any particular interest for them, and this they subjected to the keenest scrutiny. But, from the inside, they learned nothing beyond what they already knew. The outside, however, though barren of clues, enabled them to put Brent's theory to some sort of practical test.

Almost half the glass was missing from the broken window. Inspector Parker moved about with careful deliberation. Now and then he stopped and fired an imaginary pistol at an imaginary target. The target was stationary, but the inspector took up a different position each time he went through the pantomime of firing.

"Brent," he said at last, "I've tried various distances and various angles, and I am now firmly convinced that the diamond merchant could not have been shot through this window. Unless the train were at a standstill, and the murderer held the pistol almost flat against the windowpane, Mr. Hyde couldn't possibly have been killed where he sat. But we know that the train was rushing along at a pretty fast speed.

Constable Brent, who had been an interested observer of his superior's actions, stood close to the broken window and attentively regarded the seat on which Mr. Hyde had met his death.

"Seems difficult, sir," he admitted. "Nevertheless, I'm still certain that the pistol wasn't thrown through this window." He paused for a moment, then went on: "Assuming that the pistol was fired from the outside, sir, where would the broken glass be most likely to fall? Inside the carriage, or outside on the line?"

The inspector gave the problem his serious consideration.

"Can't say for certain," was his final pronouncement. "As a matter of fact, I believe there would be little or no glass to fall anywhere. The pistol we found fires a small, high-velocity bullet, and it's my opinion that the bullet would have gone clean through the glass, leaving a neat, round hole. Instead of that, we find the window so badly shattered that little more than half the glass is left. No, Brent, I shall have to disagree with you. I still stick to the belief that the pistol was fired inside the compartment and was afterwards hurled through the window. Can't understand, though, how that girl, Miss Lowe, failed to hear the smashing of the glass."

"And," said Constable Brent, "I can't see why Freddie, if he fired the shot, should have thrown the pistol through this particular window. The other, on his own side, would have been much more convenient."

The inspector abruptly turned his back on the coach, and a frown ridged his face.

"Come on, Brent," he said, a trifle impatiently. "There are many things in connection with this confounded case which neither of us is able to understand at present. By the way," he went on, as they crossed towards the platform, "why did you ask whether the broken glass would have fallen inside or outside?"

"I had no particular reason for asking, sir. Just noticed that there was no glass inside the compartment, that's all."

"Crikey! Who's been making a jolly bigger mess of the window?"

It was the schoolboy, William Ernest Pardoe, who spoke, and the question was fired at himself rather than at the police officers as they stepped on to the platform.

At Blackton railway station the laws against trespassers are far from stringent, consequently William Ernest had no difficulty in attempting to gratify his morbid curiosity. As soon as his homework had been successfully scamped, he had hurried off to the station. What he had expected to find there, he could not have said. But the station was part of the railway system, and the murder was a railway murder. To William Ernest, that was sufficient inducement to steal away from accusative cases and problems that refused to be solved to a problem which, if it could not be solved, would at least provide plenty of interest.

The inspector was feeling irritable, because of his failure to probe the mystery.

"Now, my lad," he said to William Ernest in curt tones, "you know you've no business here. Off you go!"

William Ernest possessed a generous share of the exaggerated dignity that is peculiar to pupils of County Secondary Schools. And his dignity was now severely hurt. What right had this inspector of police to address him in such tones? Surely the man wasn't blind! The green cap and blazer were obvious enough. Yet he, William Ernest, couldn't have received more rotten treatment had he been wearing the nondescript cap and jacket of a common elementary-school pupil.

Conscious that he had not been detected in any form of wrong-doing, William Ernest felt no fear. Squaring his undeveloped shoulders, he tossed his head and bit his lower lip.

"Oh, all right!" he said, turning on his heel and strutting away.

"Stuck-up little devil!" snapped the inspector, when the boy had stalked off out of sight. "Oh, for the good old days and a good young birch!"

Inspector Parker had yet to learn that he made a big mistake in treating William Ernest in such a cavalier fashion.

Before ceasing work for the day, Parker paid a visit to the address which Jack Davis had sent him. He was not satisfied with Davis's behaviour, and there were some vital questions which he was anxious to ask the young man. To say the least of it, Jack's surreptitious visit to the tunnel was extremely puzzling.

But Jack was not in when the inspector called. He had gone out on his motorcycle, explained the landlady, without hinting where he was going, or when he was likely to return.

In the hope that Miss Hyde might know his whereabouts, the inspector called on her, but Connie was unable to give him any useful information. Jack had told her nothing of his intended movements, except that it was his intention to find rooms in Blackton for himself. She did not consider it necessary to inform him that Jack had also expressed the determination to solve the mystery of her father's murder, if it were within his power.

"Miss Hyde," said the inspector as he was about to take his departure, "perhaps you'll be good enough to do me a favour. Can you let me have a photograph of your father?"

"Certainly," Connie readily assured him. "I'm sorry I haven't one here, but I shall write to one of the servants and ask her to send one on immediately. Or would you prefer me to send a wire?"

"I wish you would wire, Miss Hyde. You will? Oh, thanks."

The inspector's face bore a thoughtful expression as he walked back to his office. He liked Connie Hyde, and—he was thinking of Jack Davis.

Meanwhile, Jack Davis, after searching the tunnel, had claimed his cycle from the garage where he had left it, and rushed off to Donmoor. He possessed knowledge of which the police were ignorant, and he had decided to make what use he could of that knowledge.

He reached Donmoor without mishap, and at once enquired for the private residence of the manager of the British Bank. It was past the usual closing hour or he would have gone to the bank itself.

"Yes," said the manager, when the two men were seated on opposite sides of a cheerful fire with cigars alight, "Mr. Hyde withdrew £30,000 as arranged. You are aware, no doubt, that I was warned by London headquarters to have the money in readiness, and when Mr. Hyde presented a cheque, after he had filled it in in my presence, he received the money—sixty banknotes of £500 each."

"You are sure it was Mr. Hyde himself, of course?"

"Of course. Not only did I know his signature, but I knew him personally. I often met him when I was cashier at London headquarters. But why do you ask?"

Jack Davis shrugged.

"This is such a funny business that I thought I would make sure."

"Yes," repeated the manager, "I paid out £30,000 to Mr. Hyde, your late chief."

Jack had refrained from mentioning his dismissal, therefore the manager was unaware that the 'late' applied in a double sense. "Afterwards he returned and paid £10,000 of it in again."

"But why?" demanded Jack, surprised at the news. "Didn't he make use of the thirty thousand, after all?"

The manager smiled.

"No need," he said, "for me to tell you that Mr. Hyde was a business man. Sooner than come away without the necklace, he was prepared to disgorge the full thirty thousand, but he managed to secure it for an even two-thirds of that amount. You ought to have seen his face when he came back with the ten thousand. It delighted him to have bested Sir Joshua.

"Sir Joshua," said Jack gravely, "declares that Mr. Hyde robbed him."

The manager's smile blossomed into a chuckle.

"And he isn't far wrong, Mr. Davis. I believe, and Mr. Hyde believed, that the necklace was worth £40,000. No one, however, can blame him for getting it as cheaply as he could, even though the seller may consider he was outwitted."

Jack Davis shook his head.

"I don't mean that. I am referring to actual robbery. Mr. Hyde is said to have overpowered Sir Joshua and taken the necklace from him by force."

"Preposterous!" exclaimed the manager, his first start of surprise over. "Surely you don't believe that rubbish?"

"I don't believe Mr. Hyde did anything of the kind. But I do believe that Sir Joshua has accused him. The Chief Constable of Donmoor informed Inspector Parker at Blackton, so it must be true."

The manager carefully studied the white cylinder of ash on the end of his cigar.

"Queer," he observed. "Very queer. In fact, the whole business seems peculiar. I suppose you are aware that Sir Joshua refused beforehand to accept Mr. Hyde's cheque. Nothing but banknotes would satisfy him. Why? Perhaps Mr. Hyde knew the reason, but, if he did know it, he didn't tell me. Furthermore, I may tell you in confidence that Sir Joshua is nothing better than a rascally company promoter. His head is screwed on in the right way, though. Yet he was willing to accept £20,000 for a necklace worth twice that amount—you will observe that I am accepting your chief's story as the true one. Then again, Mr. Hyde's own conduct was somewhat peculiar. No doubt you are well aware that he often carried large sums of money about with him? But in this case he wouldn't take the risk. He wouldn't even take back the £10,000 to London with him. Had he had a suspicion that everything wasn't quite as it ought to be? Had he had some foreboding of what was about to happen?"

Jack's brow corrugated.

"Wish I knew," he said, throwing his extinguished cigar on the ash-tray. "And I wish I knew what he did with the necklace. He didn't leave it with you, I suppose?"

"No. He took it with him. Seeing that he wouldn't risk carrying the money on his person, I asked him to leave the necklace in our strong-room, but he laughingly refused. He could carry it about, he said, concealed with such clever simplicity that a thief might search all his pockets and pass it over unnoticed."

"Yes," agreed Jack. "I have heard him make a similar boast myself. And this despite the fact that he believed in the existence of a clever gang of jewel thieves. Of course, the necklace might be easier to hide than the banknotes, but—" He abruptly broke off, and then demanded with a strong note of eagerness: "Do you know the numbers of the notes which Mr. Hyde is supposed to have paid over to Sir Joshua?"

"Naturally we have a record of the numbers. Of course, I couldn't let you have them without first referring to our books. But I can let you have them as soon as we open in the morning. Or we can go to the bank now if the matter's very urgent. May I ask what's the idea, though?"

Jack's excitement was obvious.

"Why, can't you see, sir!" he exclaimed. "With the numbers we ought to be able to prove that Sir Joshua is lying. Of course, you and I know that Mr. Hyde never committed the robbery. Had he done so he would not have parted with any of the £30,000. That being so, he would have handed back the whole amount to you—or none at all."

The manager scratched his chin and remained silent for some moments.

"I'm afraid that doesn't follow," he said at last. "Had Mr. Hyde been guilty, it would have been a clever move on his part to tell me a trumped-up story about the hard bargain he had driven, and then return £10,000 as proof of his assertion. I am confident, of course, that Sir Joshua's charge is absurd, but I'm trying to show you how the affair might strike an outsider—a police officer, for example."

Jack Davis nodded his agreement.

"Yes, I can now see the weakness of my argument. But if the banknotes can be traced we shall have all the proof that's needed. You said, I believe, that Mr. Hyde used the same taxi all the time he was in Donmoor?"

"Yes. He drove from the station to the bank, and from there to Hopeview House, Sir Joshua's residence. He returned to the station in the same taxi, calling at the bank en route."

"Well, if we find that he made no other call on the way. It's certain that he couldn't have changed any of those forty banknotes which he didn't return to you. That's why I am asking if you will be good enough to have them traced. If we can discover that even one of these notes has been changed, then it at once becomes clear that the £20,000 was paid over to Sir Joshua Jordan."

The manager nodded.

"To Sir Joshua or to someone else," he agreed. "Well, Mr. Davis, I shall place the matter in the hands of the Chief Constable without delay. If you will give me your present address I shall let you know immediately I learn anything of importance."

Jack Davis thanked him, enquired for the best way to get to Hopeview House, and then took his departure. However, he might have spared himself the trouble of calling on Sir Joshua. When he had rung the bell for the third time, the door was opened by a burly manservant with a surly cast of countenance.

"What d'you want?" was the servant's truculent demand.

"I should like to speak to your master for a moment or two. Will you please ask him if he'll be good enough to see me?" It cost Jack an effort to ignore the other's ungracious reception.

"Sir Joshua's not fit to see no one," growled the servant, and then the door was slammed shut.

For several moments, Jack stood on the doorstep, pondering. Why had he been refused admittance? Was it that the servant and the master had something to conceal?—something to fear? There had certainly been suspicion in the shifty eyes of the servant.

The puzzled young man walked thoughtfully from the door to the gate, mounted his cycle, and rode off. A few miles outside the city he narrowly escaped what might have been a serious accident. As he approached a sharp bend in the road he heard the engine of a car approaching in the opposite direction. He swerved sharply to the left, and the car whizzed past on the wrong side of the road, missing him by inches.

He caught a fleeting glimpse of the driver, whose turned-up collar almost met the brim of the hat that was pulled well down over the goggled eyes. Hardly a square inch of the man's face was visible.

"The damned fool deserves to break his neck," muttered Jack angrily as he continued his journey. "Only a madman would take that bend at such a reckless speed."

Jack Davis had not yet seen the last of that car.

Chapter 9

A Momentous Discovery

Inspector Parker had decided overnight not to bring forward any evidence at the inquest beyond what was absolutely essential to warrant the issue of a burial certificate. He did not wish to disclose the line his investigations were taking; and, it may be, he was reluctant to admit how little he had really learned.

The body was identified by the murdered man's daughter, and a local doctor gave medical testimony as to the cause of death. Stripped of its technical phraseology, what Dr. Green told the coroner and jury was that Mr. Hyde's death was directly due to a bullet wound in the brain.

At this point Inspector Parker made a not unusual request. He would like the inquest to be adjourned for a week so as to give him an opportunity to pursue his investigations.

The coroner, a busy lawyer, glanced round the court at the motley crowd assembled there. Particularly did he gaze at the occupants of the bench set aside for witnesses. His roving glance travelled from the Midtown publican to the two colliers' wives decked out in their Sunday finery, and thence on to Freda Lowe and Jack Davis and Connie Hyde. His gaze lingered on Light-Fingered Freddie sitting right at one end of the bench under the shadow of a stolid guardian police officer.

These witnesses were summoned in case the coroner saw fit to insist on hearing the evidence of those who had been in the compartment at the moment the murder had been committed.

William Ernest Pardoe and his sister were absent, Inspector Parker having considered it unnecessary to interrupt their school studies.

As proof of his interest in crime and criminals, Dick, the potter, sat immediately behind his niece, an intent expression on his wrinkled old countenance.

The coroner's gaze returned to the inspector's face. "These your witnesses, Inspector?" he asked, nodding towards the crowd he had just been surveying.

"Yes, sir. But, unless you insist, it is not my intention to call any of them now. Their evidence, I may say, will throw no light on the person responsible for the man's death."

"I see. So you wish for an adjournment, Inspector?"

"I should like the case to be adjourned for the usual week, sir."

The coroner tapped on his thumbnail with a dry-nibbed pen.

"Personally," he said, "I fail to see the need for an adjournment. It is really no part of my business to discover the murderer—if a murder has been committed. My duties, and the duties of the jury are, or ought to be, simply to determine the cause of death. And I think there's no room for doubt on that score." He turned to Dr. Green. "You are sure, Doctor, that death is due to a gunshot wound?"

"Quite sure, sir. The bullet penetrated the brain; and passed clean through the skull, I ought to add."

"And you say that it entered by way of the forehead?"

"Pardon me, sir, I said nothing of the kind. Mr. Hyde was shot from behind."

Though the coroner was accustomed to surprises, he allowed his face to express the bewilderment he felt.

"Shot from behind!" he repeated. "You gave me to understand, Inspector, when you were opening the case, that the wound was in the forehead."

Inspector Parker was patently perturbed, and it was the doctor who answered for him.

"There is a wound in the forehead, sir. But that's where the bullet came out. It entered by the back of the head, and there, because of the hair, the wound, naturally, is not so evident.

"Excuse me, sir," interpolated the foreman of the jury. "I should like to back up the doctor's opinion with my own observation. Years ago I was an officer in the infantry, and I have had considerable experience of bullet wounds. A few minutes ago when I viewed the body I saw by the broken skin round the wound in the forehead that that was the point at which the bullet had emerged.

The coroner again addressed the inspector, who had regained much of his normal equanimity.

"But, Inspector," he insisted, "you stated that he was shot through the forehead. What grounds had you for making such a statement?"

"I took the word of the doctor who saw the body immediately after death. Doctor Peters informed me that the dead man had been shot through the forehead. Or, if he didn't actually state it, he inferred it. I saw a wound there, and, naturally, I didn't consider it necessary to make a further examination myself."

The coroner made some rapid notes.

"Is this Doctor Peters present in court?" he asked.

The inspector shook his head.

"No, sir," he answered. "Doctor Peters is a busy London practitioner and I didn't consider it necessary to summon him."

"Rather a pity, Inspector. Apart altogether from the position of the wound, he might have been able to give some useful evidence. He was the man on the spot, you know. Well, gentlemen,"—turning to the jury—"I shall not ask you to return a verdict today. I consider it better to accede to the wishes of the police, and adjourn for a week." His next remark he addressed to Inspector Parker. "I would suggest that, in the meantime, you get in touch with Doctor Peters. It might be interesting to hear what he has to say."

The inspector promised, then the court rose, and, amidst an animated buzz of conversation, the people drifted out, singly or in small groups. At the door, Police Constable Brent found himself beside Freda Lowe and her uncle.

"Well, George," grinned old Dick, "that Doctor Green seems to have set up a new complication. Who d'you think's done it now?"

Brent felt in no mood for discussing the deepening mystery. He would much sooner be talking confidentially to Freda, with the old potter a thousand miles away.

"I'm hanged if I know," he answered shortly. "And I'm hanged if I care. All I want is to be allowed to forget the whole cursed affair." The constable's petulance was not entirely due to the presence of the unwanted third. In his own mind, he had reverted to his theory that the pistol had been fired from outside the carriage, and on that hypothesis he had been building up what he thought to be a fairly substantial structure. But the doctor's assertion had effectually disposed of both the structure and the theory upon which it had been so painstakingly built.

The old potter, however, was not be so easily turned aside.

"Can't you see," he said, "that the affair is now more simple than ever? Until a few minutes ago it was doubtful whether the publican or the other chap was guilty. But there is no longer any doubt. Only the man who sat beside Mr. Hyde could have shot him from behind." They were walking along together, the constable in the middle of the little group. Despite the girl's disturbing presence, the old potter's words had fired anew the policeman's enthusiasm.

"You may be right," he conceded. "If— But, no. I'm afraid that theory won't work. How could Freddie have shot him from behind?"

"He could easily have inserted his hand between his victim's head and the back of the seat."

"Perhaps. But why should he? It would have been much simpler to shoot him through the left temple. Moreover, it's Inspector Parker's belief that Mr. Hyde was looking towards the ceiling, and partly facing Freddie, as the train passed through the tunnel. In the circumstances, it would have been manifestly impossible to shoot him through the back of the head—just as impossible as to shoot him from behind through the broken window."

Old Dick walked along in silence for several moments.

"Yes," he said at last. "I agree that Mr. Hyde probably would have looked towards the ceiling. That is usually one's first inclination. But after that one tries to stare through the window for the first hint of daylight. Depend upon it, Mr. Hyde was looking through the window beside him, or trying to look through it, when Freddie fired the shot. There cannot possibly be any other explanation."

Police Constable Brent made no reply. He was too busy revolving this new theory in his mind.

For long after he had returned to his office, Inspector Parker sat lost in thought. The fact that the diamond merchant had been shot from behind introduced a new complication with which he felt unable to cope. Had he heard the old potter's theory that Mr. Hyde had been facing the window at the moment the shot was fired, he would probably have come to the conclusion that Dr. Green's emphatic statement made very little real difference to the problem in hand.

At last, after anxious thought, he rang up Scotland Yard. It was a simple action; nevertheless, it caused him real regret. He had hoped to be able to solve the mystery himself, but now he felt quite unequal to the task. The feeling rankled. But he was fair enough to admit that where his brains had failed another's might succeed.

"Ah!" said the Assistant Commissioner, when he had listened for a few moments. "I knew I should get this call sooner or later... So you've found it to be the work of the jewel gang?"

Inspector Parker shook his head. His mind was so filled with thoughts of the opportunity he had been unable to utilise that, for the moment, he had forgotten that he could not be seen by the man at the other end.

"I don't know whose work it is, sir," he confessed. "But I do know that the job needs cleverer brains than mine. Will you send a man along, sir?"

"First tell me what's made you change your mind, Inspector."

Parker related the new facts in his possession, and then the voice at the other end said:

"All right, Inspector. I shall send a man to investigate the affair on the spot. And I've already decided on the man. You may expect Detective Inspector Kilby to reach Blackton some time during the course of the day. Goodbye— Oh, by the way, I suppose Superintendent Smedley rang you up this morning and informed you that the photographs and fingerprints which you forwarded us were undoubtedly those of Light-Fingered Freddie?"

"Yes, sir. But, as it happened, I had already proved that to my own satisfaction." To himself he added, somewhat bitterly: "It was childishly simple, or I suppose I should have come a cropper over that, too."

He placed the receiver on its stand, and his lips shaped themselves into a grim smile.

Light-Fingered Freddie himself was the inspector's next worry. The magistrates' court would be sitting that afternoon, and some sort of charge would have to be brought against Freddie. The man could not be detained indefinitely without a trial; already he had been detained too long.

But the inspector could not charge Freddie with the murder. He lacked the evidence necessary to have the pickpocket committed for trial at the forthcoming Assizes.

Pickpocket! All at once the word suggested a way out of the difficulty. There was incontrovertible proof that Freddie had attempted to pick Mr. Hyde's pocket. He would charge him with that, and leave the other, and the greater, crime in abeyance for the present. Perhaps he had definitely finished with the other crime. When the Scotland Yard man came... Anyhow, Detective Inspector Kilby wouldn't find himself hampered at the outset by having to devise ways and means of placing Freddie under temporary legal restraint.

Inspector Parker found his task far easier than he had anticipated. Light-Fingered Freddie, obviously pleased at being charged with only the minor offence, was pathetically eager to plead guilty. This confession, coupled with the evidence of the fingerprints, was all that was needed to convince the Bench of his guilt. No other witnesses were called. The magistrates held a short consultation, and then the chairman informed Light-Fingered Freddie that he would be placed out of temptation's reach for the next fourteen days.

Meanwhile, the manager of the Donmoor branch of the British Bank had fulfilled his promise to Jack Davis. He had asked the Chief Constable to assist him in tracing the notes, whose numbers he supplied. The Chief Constable, Major Walters, had taken immediate steps to broadcast the numbers all over the country, and by early afternoon on the day of the inquest replies began to come in.

The first reply was from Hull. There it was learned that on the previous day a man had called at an Exchange Bureau and changed notes worth £2,000 into French currency. Later, somewhat similar reports were received from Liverpool, Glasgow, Leith, London, Southampton, and other towns, mainly ports; the only difference being in the amounts changed and the particular currency demanded. In Liverpool, for example, a £5,000 deal in dollars had been made. By four o'clock in the afternoon, practically the whole of the £20,000 had been accounted for.

When Jack Davis received the news he felt highly elated. He had known all along that Mr. Hyde had purchased the necklace honestly, and now he could prove it. Now the lie direct could be given to that rascally company-promoter, Sir Joshua Jordan. For Connie's sake, he was immensely pleased.

Gradually, however, his elation waned. Mr. Hyde's character had been cleared of a foul slur. But to what purpose? Valuable time had been wasted in vindicating the good name of one who needed no vindication. What of Jack, himself, though? He was sure that Inspector Parker suspected him of having murdered his late employer. Yet he had taken no steps to divert that suspicion. Reflecting on the strong motives he could be assumed to have had for wishing the diamond merchant's death, Jack Davis shuddered.

Rousing himself, he went round to see Connie Hyde. The first few minutes were exclusively devoted to each other; and when they spoke, which was seldom, they spoke only of themselves and their own personal affairs. Connie's suspicions of Jack's reason for rushing off to the Peak District had not yet been dispelled, but she managed to keep them in the background.

At length they moved slightly apart, whereupon the conversation became less spasmodic, but also less pleasing. Jack told the girl what he had learned from the bank-manager, and then they discussed the tragedy from every conceivable angle.

"Doctor Green," said Jack, "dropped the proverbial bomb-shell this morning when he stated that the shot had been fired from behind. Fancy no one discovering it earlier?"

Connie's gaze seemed to be concentrated on something that was not in the room.

"I suppose there's really nothing peculiar in that," she replied. "Nobody else took the trouble to make a careful examination. They were satisfied to rely on the word of Doctor Peters. He shouldn't have made such a stupid blunder, though... Jack, you often visit a friend in Wimpole Street, don't you? I wonder whether you've ever chanced to meet this Doctor Peters?"

"Not to my knowledge, dear. You don't happen to know his correct address, I suppose?"

The girl withdrew a little card from a bag lying on the settee.

"Here it is," he said. "The inspector gave it to me when I called on him yesterday morning. He thought that I might wish to consult the doctor who was present at—at the moment of father's death, or immediately afterwards."

Jack glanced at the card which Doctor Peters had handed to Inspector Parker.

"99A, Wimpole Street," he read. Then a peculiar exclamation escaped him. "Something dashed funny in this business!" he cried. "There's no 99A in Wimpole Street."

Connie gazed at him in wide-eyed surprise.

"I'm quite sure," declared Jack in answer to her unspoken query. "I know Wimpole Street pretty well, and I am positive that there's no 99A in it."

"Perhaps there's some mistake in the number," said Connie, finding her voice at last. "A misprint, perhaps."

"I don't believe it, darling. No doctor would carry, or present, a card bearing a wrong address. But there's no mistake about the street, anyhow. I noticed a pretty decent-looking library near the Square, Connie. It's almost certain to have a London Directory, Come along, darling, and we'll probe this mystery to the bottom."

When Jack put down the Directory some ten minutes later, his face was flushed and a light of excitement sparkled in his eyes.

"We've certainly discovered another mystery, Connie, old girl!" he cried, as soon as they had got outside the library. "That Doctor Peters is a complete fraud. The Directory is quite up to date, and you saw for yourself that there isn't a Doctor Peters in the whole of Wimpole Street.

Chapter 10

Brent Scores a Point

"I'm afraid, Brent," said Inspector Parker, "I shall have to deprive you of your roving commission. Now that New Scotland Yard is taking charge of the case, I expect we shall be reduced to the status of mere onlookers. Nevertheless, I shall let Detective Inspector Kilby know what a reliable chap you are, and it may happen that he will be glad of your assistance. Until tomorrow morning you may consider your time your own. Off you go now, Brent, and make the most of your freedom."

The constable thanked his superior and withdrew. The young police officer felt in a despondent mood and he knew not which way to turn. He was further away than ever from a solution of the mystery, and the realisation rankled deeply.

Nevertheless, he still clung doggedly to one theory, though he had been compelled to abandon others. Nothing would convince him that the pistol had been thrown through the carriage window. True, the window was broken; but against that, there was the little channel in the sand beside where the pistol had lain. And that channel provided more conclusive proof than did the shattered glass. So many things might have broken the window, but only the pistol could have made the furrows in the sand.

Of course there was the remote possibility that the pistol had been flung from the carriage, then picked up by someone and thrown further into the tunnel. But that theory struck him as too fantastic to entertain.

There must be plenty of other theories relating to the crime, plenty of clues, if he could only pick them up. He determined to do his utmost to discover them. The detective, when he came, might refuse his help; but not the whole of Scotland Yard could prevent him from using every spark of his intellect in an attempt to solve the tantalising puzzle.

His wandering footsteps had been carrying him towards the L.M .S. station, and suddenly he came to an abrupt stop. On the opposite pavement was William Ernest Pardoe, an impish grin on his freckled face. The boy was laughing at him. For what reason?

The constable remembered his last meeting with William Ernest, remembered how the boy had stalked off the platform in all the majesty of his outraged dignity. And across Brent's brain there flashed the recollection of the words the boy had used before being snubbed by the inspector.

He beckoned, and William Ernest crossed the road, nonchalantly swinging a tennis-racket to which a pair of white shoes was attached. His lips were pursed as though he were whistling, but no sound came from between them.

Brent was too wise to rush matters.

"Just getting back from school?" was his amiable greeting.

"Yes." William Ernest made a model swing-boat of the laden racket. He'd show this bobbie that he was perfectly at his ease.

"That's right," smiled the constable. "Oh, I just called you over to tell you that I'm sorry about last night. No one meant to hurt your feelings. The inspector was a bit off colour, though, and perhaps he spoke rather hastily. You didn't mind, of course?"

The racket came to an abrupt halt.

"I didn't mind him," was William Ernest's magnanimous reply. "Why should I? Tell me, though: did he send you to apologise?"

"Well, not exactly. You see—"

"It's the least he might have done after the beastly way he spoke." The racket began to swing more fiercely than before. "But what else might a fellow expect. I call it rotten, though."

A few discreet remarks induced in William Ernest a more reasonable frame of mind, and then the constable asked:

"What did you mean when you remarked that someone had made a bigger mess of the carriage window?"

The boy, elated at his superior knowledge, smiled knowingly. How he wished that it was the inspector who had asked the question. He'd soon pay him out for his high and mighty manner. Nobody could force a fellow to speak if he didn't want to, especially when no one could prove that the fellow had anything to speak about. The constable, however, was a decent sort of stick, and William Ernest decided not to have him on a piece of string.

"Because someone did make a bigger mess of it," he replied. "There was only a tiny hole in it when the train stopped after we'd found that the diamond chap was a goner. But you've seen what it's like now."

Police Constable Brent shifted his weight from one foot to the other while he watched old Dick, the potter, rattle past in his ancient car. The potter, however, was looking straight in front and did not seem to have observed the constable and the boy. But his passing served to divert Brent's thoughts for the moment. The inspector had told him to make what use of his time he liked until tomorrow morning. And Freda Lowe had expressed a wish to see him more often. These two apparently isolated facts wove themselves, in George's mind, into an harmonious whole. He was free, and Freda was willing. It would be the height of folly to let such a splendid opportunity pass.

Nevertheless, despite the strength of his inclination to be gone forthwith, he decided that his first duty was to sidetrack the boy Pardoe, or the young imp would go around saying all sorts of fantastic things about the broken window.

Had Brent been asked whether his sense of duty or his feelings for the old potter's niece were the stronger, he could have answered with perfect truth that he did not know. He might have added that the one bore no relation to the other, and, therefore, could not be compared. But his decision to waste some valuable minutes in hoodwinking the boy answered the question far more faithfully than the young policeman could have answered it in words.

"I'm afraid there's nothing in that," he said. "The coach had been at Midtown some time before it was sent back here. A cleaner or a glazier had probably started to remove the glass, but hadn't had time to finish it."

William Ernest's pursed lips made a jerky movement towards his nose.

"Pooh!" was his inelegant rejoinder. "Think I'm blind? You're not going to kid me with that stunt. I noticed the window again while they were putting the carcass on the trolley, and it was just the same as it is now. I'd forgotten that, though, until I saw it again last night."

"Then," countered Brent after a long pause, "the glass fell out between the tunnel and Blackton. It was badly cracked, and the jolting of the train shook it out."

"Oh that's all my eye! The glass wasn't cracked. I know because—" The boy bit off the remainder of what he had been about to say. What was the use of going on? This constable was just as bad as the inspector. Both seemed to consider that he, William Ernest Pardoe, possessed the brains of a gnat. They treated him just like a common elementary-school kid that required to be kept in his place. Well, let them find out things for themselves, then. He'd not help them. His hand dived into one of his pockets and closed on something round and hard. But a moment later he withdrew his hand, empty.

"Let them find out things for themselves," he repeated to himself, as he walked off.

The constable retraced his steps, strangely dissatisfied with the result of the encounter. He felt convinced that the boy could have said more, and he blamed himself for having mismanaged the situation.

But as he passed the North Eastern railway station and approached the potter's cottage, he threw his worry from him like a cast-off glove. The mystery could now go to the deuce, for all he cared. In a few minutes he would be seeing Freda and, thank goodness! There was no mystery about her.

George was really very much in love, and had a high opinion of his own perspicacity.

He found Freda cutting flowers in front of the cottage. At once she hurried to meet him, holding out her hand; and George was absurdly thrilled to find that she returned the pressure of his handclasp.

As they walked side by side to the door of the cottage, Freda stooped down and snipped off a little blue flower, which she added to the bunch she had already cut.

While the girl arranged the flowers in the cosy little sitting-room, George sat and watched her. He felt that he could desire no greater pleasure than to sit and watch her for the rest of his life.

Presently, Freda joined him on the settee. She did not sit sufficiently close for their shoulders or arms to come in contact, but she was near enough to set George's faculties in a bewildering tumult.

Like the Walrus and the Carpenter, they talked of many things. But for a time their conversation was mainly about books and tennis. The girl was an enthusiastic tennis-player, and, once or twice, when she was giving a graphic description of some game she had played in or witnessed she was so far carried away by excitement that she gripped George by the arm. In return, George told her of his ambitions and hopes and doubts and disappointments. But of his feelings for the girl beside him he did not speak. Perhaps he knew that there was no need.

A clock on the mantelpiece struck six. George was unpleasantly reminded of the passage of time. Perhaps even now Detective Inspector Kilby was in Blackton bent on solving the mystery which he, himself, had hoped to solve.

His thoughts were reflected in his face, and Freda was quick to note the change in his expression.

"You're worrying," she said in a voice that was soft and soothing. "What's the trouble?"

Brent laughed a somewhat mirthless laugh as he rose to his feet.

"Nothing, really," he replied. "I was just reminded how silly it is to buoy oneself up with false hopes that are even less dependable than toy balloons. A detective from Scotland Yard is taking charge of the case and he may have already arrived."

"Poor boy!" said Freda, when she had sufficiently digested this piece of information. "It's a shame not to have given you a better chance. I'm sure you'd have solved the thing before long without the help of any detective."

George was not so sure, but her sympathy was none the less delicious. However, he refused to take credit when he felt it to be undeserved.

"I don't think I could ever have solved it," he answered, a shade of bitterness creeping into his tone. "It was bad enough to start with, but now a new complication has cropped up. You've heard your uncle and me mention the broken carriage window. Well, it now appears that the breakage was only very slight at first. By the time the train had arrived at Blackton, however, nearly half the window was gone."

Freda studied the new problem.

"I shouldn't think there's much of a mystery in that," she observed at last. "The glass fell out, that's all."

But George shook his head.

"I'd thought of that," he said. "But I don't believe it's the true explanation. Someone broke it deliberately the second time."

"Good gracious! What a ridiculous thing to do! And who could have done anything so silly, even if he'd wanted to?"

There's only one person who could have done it, but I'm afraid it's absurd even to suggest that it was he."

"And who's that one person?" Freda asked the question as though to prevent the conversation from flagging, rather than because of any interest she felt.

"Of course, I know it is absurd," repeated George. "But, as far as I can see, the only person who could have done it was the doctor who travelled with the dead body."

Freda's amused laugh would have been a joyous thing to hear, only it gave George the uncomfortable feeling that she was laughing at him.

"And how," asked Freda, "did you manage to discover that the window had been broken twice?"

George told her of the part which young Pardoe had played in the affair, and he gave the account with much detail.

"I see," she remarked when he had finished. "So the coach is back again in Blackton? But let's forget the horrid thing altogether." She laughed and moved over to the vase of flowers which she had placed on the table a short time before. "Come here," she invited. "Let me put this in your button-hole—George."

It was the first time she had called him by his Christian name in such a tone, and George moved over to her side, his heart aflame... Her deft fingers became busy with the lapel of his coat.

George saw the little spray of blue forget-me-nots. Then he grasped Freda's hands. A moment later she was in his arms, her moist lips yielding to the hot pressure of his.

They heard a cough, and the next moment they were aware that old Dick, the potter, was standing in the open doorway.

The potter tactfully greeted them as though he had observed nothing unusual, and after a few moments' conversation Brent took his departure, feeling as embarrassed as a small boy that had been caught in the act of stealing jam.

When he had got beyond view of the cottage, he removed the spray of forget-me-nots from his button-hole and thrust it in his pocket. He was sufficiently the lover to press Love's token between the leaves of a book. His ardour might even have induced him to wear it in secret next his heart. But he fell short of the heroism needed to flaunt it on the breast of his plain-clothes jacket through the streets of Blackton.

"Very entertaining, Freda," grinned the old potter, when George had gone.

"Yes, Uncle," agreed Freda, smiling an enigmatic smile, and speaking as though she had misunderstood the old man's reference. "George's conversation was very entertaining, indeed. But why did you come in so quietly? I never heard the car."

The old potter chuckled.

"Lucky for me you didn't, my girl, or I should have been deprived of a delightful reminder of the days when I, too, was young. I left the car outside on the road, for I expected to find George here. And there was just the barest possibility that I might be called upon to use it in a hurry." Again he chuckled. "George might have carried you off, you know, and, naturally, I should have had to take up the chase without a moment's loss of time."

"Don't be absurd, Uncle. What made you expect to find him here, though?"

"A deep knowledge of lovers' ways, my dear. Perhaps, too, the fact that I saw him deep in conversation with the boy Pardoe may have helped my instinct, or my intuition, or whatever you like to call it. When I saw George leave the boy and head in this direction, I made use of my knowledge of psychology."

"Then you ought to be able to put it to better use. Constable Brent, I am sure, would much sooner you stopped using your gifts on him and used them on his quarry instead."

The potter removed his battered felt hat and threw it on the settee.

"Ah!" he observed, moving over and sitting down beside his discarded head-gear. "I told you that young man would find things out yet. So he's on the trail of another quarry, Freda? Or is it the same old one?"

"Another," was the girl's brief answer.

"And who's he after this time, my girl?"

Freda rearranged the flowers in the vase. Then she faced her uncle and answered quietly:

"He would like to find the person who broke the carriage window after the murder had been discovered."

"After? Gee! So the window was broken twice? And I expect George knows who did it, too?"

"He believes it to have been broken the second time by Doctor Peters."

Old Dick scratched his head.

"Doctor Peters," he slowly repeated, as though giving a sluggish memory time to function. "Doctor Peters?—Oh, I've placed him now. He's the man who attended to the diamond merchant, isn't he?"

Freda nodded.

"The man who attended to the diamond merchant," she assented.

"They'll never catch him, my dear. They haven't the brains. Moreover, how can they possibly connect him with the crime? It's a problem I should love to tackle, though. I'd back myself against all the police in England to succeed in running this Doctor Peters to earth. I must really ask George to let me help him. I'm sure he'd find my old brains at least as active as his."

Freda shook her head.

"You are too late now," she said. "Scotland Yard is taking up the case."

Chapter 11

Scotland Yard in Control

Detective Inspector Kilby, a tall military-looking man with a clipped moustache, arrived at Blackton early that evening.

"I am already acquainted with the main facts of the case," he said after he had conversed with Inspector Parker for some minutes, and viewed the dead body. "But I should like you to recapitulate the whole case, without omitting even a seemingly trifling detail."

For a long time after that Inspector Parker spoke without a break, except when the other interjected a pertinent question.

"Ah!" remarked Kilby when the narrative had come to an end. "The case certainly gives us something to bite upon. Suspicion seems to point to Light-Fingered Freddie."

"That's what I've thought all along." Inspector Parker was gratified to find the Great One agreeing with him.

"Yes, he seems to be guilty. But—the wrong window was broken." Parker stared.

"I'm afraid I don't quite follow you," he said.

"Several reasons occur to me, Parker. Why should Freddie throw the weapon through the window farther from him? The nearer one would have been much more convenient. Moreover, there was a young woman sitting close to the window that was broken. Freddie would surely have had enough common sense to know that she would be almost certain to hear the breaking of the glass."

"But the fact remains, she didn't hear it," countered Parker.

"Admitted. And it's rather surprising that she didn't. But to go on. There's a strong probability that the window was broken not by the pistol itself, but by the bullet. Now, Mr. Hyde was shot from behind. The bullet entered at the back of the head, slightly towards the left, and came out through the forehead, a little to the right. Freddie would have had considerable difficulty in making the bullet take that course. Remember, I'm assuming that the bullet, after crashing through the man's skull, broke the window opposite. Had Mr. Hyde been leaning forward, it might have been possible for Freddie to manage it. I very much doubt it, though. Now, Freddie's job would have been much simpler had the diamond merchant's face been turned towards the window on his right. But in that case— Well, you can see why I say that the wrong window was broken?"

"You haven't seen the state that window is in," protested the local inspector. "If you had, you'd hardly have come to the conclusion that it was broken by anything so small as a bullet."

"True, I haven't. But where is the bullet now if it didn't go out through the window? You searched for it, of course?"

"Yes. And I'm sure it's nowhere in the compartment."

"There you are, then. How did it leave the compartment if not by the window? Did you search for it in the tunnel?"

Parker shook his head.

"Not exactly," he confessed. "But, in addition to the pistol and the wallet, Brent and I had our eyes open for anything else there was to be found. We saw no sign of a bullet."

"It wouldn't be an easy thing to find in there, Parker. But we mustn't waste any more time in vague speculations. The day is yet young enough for me to interrogate some of the eyewitnesses of the tragedy—if, indeed, one can call them eyewitnesses. I know that you have already done all that, but it's just possible that when I get them talking some chance remark may suggest a particular line for me to follow."

It was Inspector Parker who accompanied him to the homes of the two marketing women and to the old potter's cottage. This task would probably have been given to Constable Brent, had not the young policeman been off duty for the remainder of the day.

Only Freda Lowe and the two women were visited that evening. Light-Fingered and John Lofthouse were not so easily accessible, and Kilby considered it inadvisable to disturb young Pardoe and his sister at a time when they were probably busy with their homework.

Inspector Parker had been of the opinion that he had induced Freda and the other two women to relate everything that they could possibly tell about the murder. But he was surprised to find that Kilby's questioning elicited many new facts. True, the new facts were apparently trivial; but, for all that, Parker had not heard them before.

From one or another of these three persons, the detective gleaned a detailed account, as far as they knew it, of everything that had happened from Freda Lowe's entering the compartment at Boxfield Station until the moment that the murder was discovered.

Kilby's powers of mental imagery were highly developed. As though he beheld it with his physical eyes, he saw Mr. Hyde sitting in the corner away from the door, visioned Freda Lowe enter and seat herself nearly opposite, with the attaché case between herself and the end of the seat. And he saw all the others follow and dispose themselves in their various positions.

He was able to form a clear picture of the peculiar behaviour of Light-Fingered Freddie both before and after he had entered the compartment and seated himself beside the diamond merchant.

So skilful was his questioning that Kilby received an account of practically every word that had been spoken. He learned of John Lofthouse's vain attempts to start a conversation; his remark when he saw a flash of lightning; what he said to Freda Lowe after she had opened the window and thrown out the piece of paper; his profane remark when he discovered that murder had been done.

"Well," enquired Inspector Parker, as they walked back together towards the police-station, "has any chance remark helped you to form a theory?"

"Can't say it has, Parker. The only actual conclusion I arrived at is that Lofthouse knows this part of the line pretty well."

"But no one told you that."

"Not directly. But you may remember that when Miss Lowe had closed the window after throwing out the piece of paper he observed that they were approaching a tunnel. He couldn't have known that, if he didn't know the line."

Inspector Parker remained silent for some moments.

"That may be so," he conceded at length. "But he travelled that way on the outward journey, you know. Anyway, it's quite likely that he does know his way about here. Midtown's not very many miles away."

Kilby seemed not to have heard. After a time he laughed and said:

"Another brainwave has just come my way. Miss Lowe is not in the habit of picnicking."

"What in the world do you mean?" demanded Parker, slightly amazed.

"If she were accustomed to picnics she would have known that it is the correct thing not to throw litter about without any regard for the feelings or the convenience of others. But you will have observed that she took the trouble to open the window and throw out her piece of screwed-up paper."

Inspector Parker wondered whether the other was a crank or a "leg-puller."

At the station they had a whisky-and-soda each, and then they strolled through some quiet streets to the private residence of Inspector Parker, where Kilby was being provided with sleeping accommodation.

After supper Kilby went to his room, where he spent upwards of an hour in a diligent effort to discover a workable clue.

"No doubt Parker's been very busy," he reflected. "But he ought to have got in touch with Sir Joshua Jordan before now. Perhaps, though, it's best as it is. Sir Joshua will now have got the idea that he is to be left alone. I shall pay a flying visit to Donmoor myself in the morning."

He unlocked an attaché case and withdrew some papers which he studied as carefully as if he were seeing them for the first time. Nevertheless, he had seen and read them all before.

Kilby had begun to work on the case long before Inspector Parker had made up his mind to ask for the assistance of Scotland Yard.

"As usual, they will wait as long as they possibly can," the Assistant Commissioner had said to him. "But when they find themselves sinking right up to the neck, they'll yell for help. Oh, yes, Kilby, they'll sink right enough. And they, as well as the public, will expect us to drag them out, just as they are going under. Let's be getting ready for the call. You might make a start by looking up the records of Sir Joshua Jordan. I've a vague idea that I've heard of him before."

Kilby had looked up the records, and the papers he was now studying would have given Sir Joshua much pain had he been privileged to read them.

Very many years before, when the Great War was at its worst, Joshua Jordan had had the honour of knighthood conferred upon him in return for the valuable services which he had rendered to his beloved country in the hour of her need. His enemies—and the great are never without them—had declared that the value of his services was measured by the extent to which his money had swelled the coffers of a certain Party. Furthermore these same enemies had the audacity to say that Joshua had amassed the money, in the first instance, by the skill—from his own point of view—with which he had executed certain fat contracts not unconnected with supplies of the men at the Front.

The Party, the Government Department concerned, and Joshua himself had all most strenuously denied those foul insinuations. The troops at the Front had never been asked for their opinions; so Joshua Jordan, while he was yet but in his early forties, had had his name emblazoned in the Honours List for all to see.

Many among his detractors had wondered why he coveted the honour. But the more astute among them had been heard to say that the title at the head of a prospectus would repay Sir Joshua a thousandfold for the initial outlay.

These conjectures may not have been altogether without foundation. At any rate, Sir Joshua had floated many new companies, each of which had eventually been engulfed in the quicksands. The promoter, however, was a man who admired the wisdom of rats in deserting sinking ships, and he was always careful to follow their example when the need arose.

Sir Joshua Jordan was now approaching his sixtieth birthday, and the defunct companies with which he had been associated could hardly be enumerated on the fingers of both hands. In each case, however, thanks to Sir Joshua's knowledge of high finance, the new company had at first appeared so seaworthy, and the subsequent grounding had seemed so natural and unavoidable, that its creator could not be held directly responsible for its untimely end.

All this, and much more, Kilby read, before finally putting away the papers.

"Sir Joshua's certainly a wily customer," he muttered; "and it would be extremely foolish not to hear what he has to say before proceeding further with the case. Wonder what's his motive in saying that Mr. Hyde robbed him of the necklace?"

But he was unable to answer the question to his satisfaction, so he went to bed, and was up betimes in the morning.

After an early breakfast, he and Inspector Parker motored to Hartby to interrogate Light-Fingered Freddie at the county gaol, but they had to return without having learned anything that promised to be useful.

When they had arrived back at Blackton, they consulted a timetable, and then walked to the railway station, which they reached a quarter of an hour before the Donmoor train was timed to depart.

"I can see," laughed Kilby, "that you are wondering why I allowed myself so much time to catch my train. But I thought I might as well have a look at the sinister coach before setting off for Donmoor. Is that it over there?"

Parker nodded, and they crossed to the sidings.

Kilby spent several minutes in keenly scrutinising the compartment with the broken window, but failed to discover any kind of new clue. He locked the door with the key which the station-master had given him, and was turning away, with the intention of regaining the platform, when a startled exclamation escaped him. Moving along a few paces, he carefully inspected the movable centre window of the compartment immediately behind that in which the murder had taken place.

"This seems dashed funny, Parker," was his excited comment. "Notice how the glass is smeared? Looks as though someone had been using some plastic material like putty, and afterwards tried to rub away the smudge it had made."

Parker looked, and frowned in perplexity.

"But what does it mean?" he asked.

"Someone's opened the window from the outside, and afterwards closed it again with the help of the putty. With a little care and patience, anyone can open this type of window from the outside. All that's necessary is to get it off the ledge on which it rests, and it drops itself. But it's a much more tricky matter to get it on to the ledge again, and that's why the putty was used. When the window had been banged right up, the person, whoever he was, had nothing to grip, and he used the putty to pull the window towards him on to the ledge. Naturally a smudge was left on the glass, and an attempt was made to clean it. But the attempt was not successful. The point we have to consider, though, is why should anyone want to enter this compartment in such a surreptitious fashion?"

"You are sure someone did enter?"

"Of course. The person must have done the job at night when no one could see him. Well, not even a lunatic would steal on to these sidings at night just for the sake of trying his skill in opening and closing a carriage window. No, Parker; he must have had a strong reason for entering this compartment. And here's the proof that he did enter."

As he spoke, he pointed to several tiny scratches on the woodwork. Then he took out the magnifying-glass, without which he never ventured abroad, and examined them more carefully.

"Yes," he observed. "I have no doubt that these scratches were made last night. Wish I could find some fingerprints; but there doesn't seem to be any."

He ceased talking, then picked a few greyish crumbs off the ledge and placed them in an envelope.

Next he unlocked the door, and both men entered the compartment. But, although, they subjected it to a fairly exhaustive search, they had to confess themselves baffled.

"It's a mystery," observed Kilby, with a shake of his head. "A complete mystery. It couldn't have happened at Midtown, for the glaziers had not commenced work on the other window, therefore it's perfectly clear that someone entered this compartment last night. And he's left no clue as to what he was after. But what was he after? That's the puzzle."

It was a puzzle. But, all at once, Inspector Parker fancied that he saw its solution.

"I'm afraid we are seeing a mountain where there is only an insignificant molehill," he said. "You haven't had the pleasure of meeting William Ernest Pardoe yet, so you cannot fully appreciate the vagaries of his enquiring mind."

Kilby looked hard at the speaker.

"William Ernest Pardoe!" he repeated. "Isn't that the boy who was present when the murder was committed?"

"The same. He made himself rather famous by using the alarm signal, you may remember. Well, I saw him prowling around on the platform here on Tuesday evening. He was looking hard at the coach, and he made some remark about the broken window. I chased him off, so there can be little doubt that he returned last night to nose around at his leisure."

"Wonder where he got the putty, if it was he?"

"You're sure it was putty?"

Kilby withdrew the envelope in which he had placed the few greyish crumbs, and examined them through his magnifying-glass.

"No," he said. "I am not sure."

A bell rang and, after re-locking the compartment, they crossed over to the platform.

Just as the train was steaming in, Inspector Parker handed a photograph to Kilby.

"Perhaps you'd better take this with you," he said. "It's the dead man's, and you might find it useful for identification purposes."

Kilby thanked him and watched the train grind to a standstill. Then, after entering the carriage, he leaned out and said with a smile:

"It's rather a pity that the mystery of the putty was solved so quickly. For the moment I fancied that I had discovered a first-class problem."

"And William Ernest Pardoe has solved it," retorted Parker with a smile that matched the other's.

This was the second mistake Inspector Parker made in his estimate of the schoolboy. William Ernest had not solved the problem of the putty. But he could have solved it, although in a manner totally different from that suspected by the worthy inspector.

Chapter 12

A Charge is Withdrawn

Detective Inspector Kilby hired a taxi outside Donmoor railway station and asked to be driven to the offices of the Chief Constable of the city.

Major Walters greeted him affably, and in a very few minutes cigar smoke was floating round the room in which they sat.

"I've called, sir," explained Kilby, "to hear what you can tell me about Sir Joshua Jordan. I am about to pay him a visit, and I think it advisable to learn all I can about him beforehand."

The Chief Constable leaned back in his chair and apparently studied the glowing end of his cigar.

"I can tell you very little about the man," he replied. "And, paradoxically, I can tell you quite a lot. Sir Joshua is a bit of an enigma. What kind of bird he was before he came to Donmoor I can't say, of course. I never troubled to enquire. But he came to this place a few years ago and took up his residence in a large, rambling old house on the outskirts of the city. He's lived there ever since, all alone, save for a couple of male servants. I've been given to understand that he won't allow a woman anywhere near the house."

"But what about his wife and daughter?" put in Kilby.

"His wife and daughter! echoed the other. "My dear man, they don't exist."

"That's peculiar," remarked Kilby after a thoughtful pause. "Mr. Davis told Inspector Parker that a wife and daughter were mentioned in the correspondence that took place between Sir Joshua and the diamond merchant."

"Really? And who is Mr. Davis?"

"The murdered man's assistant. Rather, he was his assistant, but he got the sack the previous night—the night before the day of the murder, I mean."

Major Walters pushed back his chair with such suddenness that its legs grated along the parquet floor.

"Got the sack the night before the murder!" he repeated. "What a significant fact!"

"Very significant, indeed. And you may be sure I shan't lose sight of it. But to return to Sir Joshua. May I ask, sir, what are your grounds for saying that he is a bit of an enigma?"

"That's a difficult question to answer offhand, Kilby. To begin with, no one seems to know why he came to Donmoor, or what he does for a living. Of course, he may have retired in the ordinary way and be living on the fruits of wise investments. Then, again, why will he have no women about the house? Is he a woman-hater? Or is it that he fears that women's tongues are not so discreet as men's? He is not a recluse, for, although he seldom goes outside his own gates, he frequently has visitors. Constables on duty have reported from time to time that it is not unusual for as many as half a dozen men to visit Sir Joshua in the course of an evening. Occasionally some of the visitors stay there the whole night."

A theory began to form itself in Kilby's mind. But he strove to suppress it until the time when he should be at liberty to give it more careful consideration.

"Please tell me about Sir Joshua's charge against Mr. Hyde," he said.

"There's not much to tell. Rather late on Monday evening one of Sir Joshua's servants rang up the King Street police-station and begged the sergeant on duty to send a man to Hopeview House immediately. The man was sent, and this is what he learned from Sir Joshua:

"That afternoon Sir Joshua himself had admitted Mr. Hyde, both the servants having been out. Mr. Hyde was conducted to the study, when, seizing a favourable opportunity, he attacked and drugged Sir Joshua, and, after tying the helpless man to a chair, decamped with a valuable necklace. Hours later one of the servants returned and released his master, who was just regaining consciousness. Then the servant was ordered to ring up King Street. That's really all there is to tell, except that Sir Joshua was in a dreadful rage when the constable answered the summons to Hopeview House."

"Ah! You interviewed Sir Joshua yourself, I suppose?"

"No. I was about to do so first thing in the morning, when my newspaper informed me of the murder in the tunnel. Though the facts were scanty they enabled me to put two and two together. At once I communicated with Inspector Parker at Blackton. Of course, I was now more determined than ever to investigate Sir Joshua's statement. But when I arrived at Hopeview House a burly servant refused to admit me. His master, to use the man's own words, was 'all of a shake from the shocking treatment what he'd got, and wasn't fit to talk to no one.' I had to leave without seeing Sir Joshua. Later in the day I called again, and was given a similar reception. Sir Joshua was still very 'groggy.' Moreover, he had heard of the diamond merchant's terrible fate, and, being of a forgiving disposition, he refused to blacken the name of a dead man by bringing such a dreadful accusation against him."

"But didn't you insist on seeing him, sir?"

The Chief Constable laughed a little grimly.

"My dear Kilby," he said, "you are forgetting that Sir Joshua is a gentleman of title. I don't fancy Home Office Inquiries and Royal Commissions at my age."

About fifteen minutes later Kilby's taxi pulled up outside the gates of Hopeview House, Sir Joshua Jordan's sombre home. Without waiting for the driver to leave his seat, Kilby opened the door and sprang out. "Wait here till I come back," he ordered.

He endeavoured to push open the heavy, door-like gates, set between massive moss-covered pillars. But the gates groaned in protest and refused to budge. Evidently they were barred, perhaps locked, on the inside. He stood there for some moments, his gaze wandering alternately from right to left along the high, forbidding walls that enclosed the house and grounds. A short distance on the left he saw a wicket door in the wall. This was only latched, and, pushing it open, he stepped through the doorway. He caught a glimpse of a straggling, grass-grown drive and untended trees and shrubs. But of the house itself there was no sign.

He stepped out along the winding drive. After many sharp twists, he reached the front of a grey stone-built house, down which ran many brownish streaks, obviously the result of defective eaves and broken spouts.

"Hopeview House!" he muttered. "Was ever a name so badly misplaced!"

He glanced about him for a second or two, then pulled an old-fashioned, rust-eaten handle that presumably set a bell in motion somewhere within the house.

After a long wait, and just as he was about to ring a second time, the door creaked open, and Kilby found himself confronted by a man who had ex-pugilist written all over his flat-nosed, scowling face.

"What d'ye want?" demanded this unprepossessing individual.

Kilby held out his card.

"Please take this to your master," he said; "and ask him if he'll be good enough to spare me a few minutes of his time.

"'Tain't no use, 'E won't see no one. 'E can't. So you'd better be—"

"Will you please do as you're told!"

The servant's knotted hand gripped the iron-studded door. Glancing down, he saw a substantial foot firmly planted on the step.

"Don't slam it," cautioned Kilby. "If you do you may crush my foot, and—well, I am quite sure you would be sorry for it afterwards."

The underlying threat did not escape Sam Grundy's ears. Growling something unintelligible, he took the card and, without troubling to glance at it, moved away into the dimness of the flagged hall.

Presently he returned, carrying Kilby's card on a tarnished salver. Obviously, the salver was for effect.

"I'm sorry as 'e won't see you, sir," said Sam in a new, and more respectful, tone. Kilby smiled, for he knew that Sam had read the name on the card. "Sir Joshua told me to tell you as 'e ain't in no fit state to see no one."

Kilby picked up his card and scribbled a few words on it.

"Take this back to your master," he said. "Perhaps he'll consent to see me then."

Though his speech had grown more deferential, the expression of Sam's face had become decidedly vindictive. He would have loved to slam the door in the other's face, or against the intruding foot. But all his life Sam had been in the habit of obeying the voice of authority, and he obeyed it now.

Presently, he slouched back. "'E'll see you, sir," he muttered, turning to lead the way.

Kilby followed Sam across the hall and along a gloomy passage. Outside a certain door, the leader stopped.

"'E's in there—Mr. Detective," growled the guide, and moved off down the passage.

Kilby knocked and entered, glad of the knowledge that a loaded automatic reposed in one of his pockets.

The room in which Kilby found himself was large and sparsely furnished, and, like all the rest of the house he had seen, depressingly gloomy. The man that rose from the chair by the fireless grate was even taller than Kilby himself, although not so strongly built. It was not the man's height, however, that attracted Kilby's attention, but the sallow face, with its deep-set, piercing eyes beneath black, beetling brows.

Kilby was prepared for a harsh reception, therefore Sir Joshua's greeting surprised him not a little.

"Come right in and sit down, Mr. Kilby," said Sir Joshua, with what was obviously intended for a genial smile. "I'm glad to see you. Sorry if that stupid servant of mine misunderstood me and kept you waiting at the door."

Kilby was quick to see that the chair he was expected to take was facing the window. The advantage of position would be with Sir Joshua. Smiling at this little bit of stage-managing, he sat down.

"Oh, that's all right, Sir Joshua," he replied. "The ideal servant is difficult to find."

"Glad you look at it like that, Mr. Kilby." Sir Joshua sat down and glanced at the scribbled message on the card in his hand. "By the way, did you really consider it necessary to remind me of this—er—this little past indiscretion of mine?"

"Some people might consider the first adjective inadequate, Sir Joshua. But what would you? Your servant said that you refused to see me. Of course, as you say, it was due to a misunderstanding, and there seems no need to pursue the painful matter further."

"None whatever, Mr. Kilby."

There was silence for some moments. Each was endeavouring to estimate his antagonist's strength, and both knew it. A casual observer, however, had one been present, would never have regarded them as anything but very good friends.

"You've come about the necklace, I suppose?" asked Sir Joshua at last, evidently deciding to force the other's hand.

"Yes, Sir Joshua. You've made a very serious charge against Mr. Hyde. It's only fair that the charge should be investigated."

Sir Joshua nodded.

"Perhaps you are right, Mr. Kilby," he assented. "But... I doubt it. Why not let sleeping dogs lie? Unfortunately, the poor man is now dead. Well, such being the case, wouldn't it be more charitable to let his—regrettable lapse, or the remembrance of it, die with him?"

"In certain circumstances it would. But I am not so sure that he was guilty of a regrettable lapse."

"Surely, Mr. Kilby, you don't think that I—?"

"Of course not. But you, yourself, have shown me how easy it is for a misunderstanding to arise. Moreover, his murder has to be investigated, and a complete knowledge of all the facts may be of vital importance. Sir Joshua, I want you to tell me all you can about Mr. Hyde's visit here on Monday afternoon."

"Mr. Kilby, I shall really have to refuse." There seemed genuine regret in the speaker's voice.

"And, Sir Joshua, I shall have to insist."

For the fraction of a second there appeared a steely glint in Sir Joshua's sunken eyes. But whether it was the officer's insistence or recollection of the treatment he had received at Mr. Hyde's hands that had called forth the flash of resentment Kilby could not have told. Nevertheless, when Sir Joshua spoke again, his voice was still genial, though decidedly grave.

"As you will, Mr. Kilby. I suppose it was foolish of me to expect that a police officer, machine-made and machine-controlled, would have any consideration for the good name of the dead. But why protest any further?... Well," he went on, leaning forward and speaking deliberately, "it was arranged that Mr. Hyde should call here on Monday afternoon to inspect a necklace, and purchase it, if we could arrive at an agreement... He rang the bell and I admitted him myself."

"Just a moment," interrupted Kilby. "Why were both your servants out at the time? Is it usual for them to go out together?"

Sir Joshua shrugged.

"You force me," he said, "to lay bare all my secrets. No, Mr. Kilby, it is very unusual for them both to have the same afternoon off. But even the best servants talk, and I was anxious to have the transaction carried out with as much secrecy as possible."

"I see. Please go on, Sir Joshua."

Sir Joshua moistened his lips and continued:

"I admitted Mr. Hyde, and conducted him to this very room. We lost no time in beginning business. I produced the necklace and spread it out on the table before me. Mr. Hyde came round behind the chair on which I had just sat down, and leaned over my shoulder, as though to examine the diamonds. Suddenly one of his arms twined itself round my neck, gripping it like a vice, and I felt a handkerchief pressed hard against my nose and mouth. Naturally, I resisted with all the strength at my command; but the chloroform, or whatever it was, soon overpowered me, and, just as I was losing consciousness, I felt myself being half-dragged, half-carried through that door into the next room." Sir Joshua indicated a door as he spoke.

"A very nerve-racking experience, Sir Joshua, and I sympathise with you. What next?"

Sir Joshua shuddered.

"The next, as far as I was concerned, was a painful return to consciousness, to find one of the servants undoing the ropes that bound me to the chair. When I had collected my scattered wits I realised that I had been in the other room, bound and unconscious, for several hours. I learned, too, that the necklace had disappeared."

Kilby looked sympathetic.

"Ah!" he said. "Truly a terrible experience, Sir Joshua. And did Mr. Hyde come provided with the ropes ready for use?"

Sir Joshua beamed.

"You will have your little joke, Mr. Kilby," he retorted, laughing. "Of course he didn't. But the next room, as you can see for yourself if you care to inspect it, is a kind of lumber room, and the ropes were there ready to his hand."

"How very fortunate—for him. By the way, I believe you mentioned a wife and daughter in your correspondence?"

Sir Joshua laughed outright.

"Just a little business touch, Mr. Kilby," he chuckled, rubbing his hands together. "Just a little business touch, nothing more. A buyer always thinks he's getting the certain bargain when the hard-up seller is making a sale unknown to his family. I confess I was hard up. I was very anxious to make a sale and—well, the wife and daughter were dangled as an extra bait. Mr. Hyde got more than the bargain he'd expected, though."

Kilby carefully scrutinised the crescent on his well-kept thumbnail.

"Can you describe the necklace, Sir Joshua?" he asked.

The other shook his head.

"Not very clearly, I fear. If it were a family heirloom, I suppose there would be drawings and a written description, photographs perhaps. But I must confess, Mr. Kilby, that there were no heirlooms of value in the family from which I have sprung. The diamonds that composed the necklace were bought by myself—one here, one there—and afterwards strung together. Perhaps you may wonder why I ever bought the stones. Well, I must lay bare another secret. I had meant that necklace to adorn the woman who had promised to become my wife. It was during the war years when luck seemed to be smiling upon me. And it was for the woman's sake that I consented to accept the title offered me. But—" Sir Joshua paused—"it was all useless. The woman jilted me in the end and—married an invalided officer with only one leg to stand upon."

Sir Joshua smiled grimly at his own subtle joke before he continued:

"After that I locked away the necklace. I felt that I never wanted to see it again. I didn't wish to be continually reminded of my folly. Nevertheless, until a few weeks ago, I felt that I couldn't sell it. Sentiment, I suppose... Now, Mr. Kilby, you will understand how I came to have the necklace in my possession, and why I am unable to describe it properly. It contained seventy-six stones of different sizes, and that's about all I can tell you... Is there anything else you would care to ask me?"

Kilby rose to his feet.

"There's just one more question," he said, handing Sir Joshua the photograph he had received from Inspector Parker. "This is a photograph of Mr. Hyde. You're sure he's the man who attacked and robbed you?"

Sir Joshua took only one glance at the photograph before springing to his feet.

"Good heavens!" he exclaimed, in apparent amazement. "I've been badly duped. And I owe the shades of the departed Mr. Hyde ten thousand apologies. The man who attacked me wasn't a bit like that picture."

Chapter 13

Kilby's Suspicions Are Aroused

As Kilby reached the outside of Hopeview House he was struck anew by the sinister aspect of the building and its inmates. Sir Joshua, after his first attempted rebuff, had treated him courteously enough, yet Kilby had the feeling that there was something about the man which repelled. Towards the end of the conversation there had appeared something peculiar about the eyes of the enforced host, something that he had seen more than once in the eyes of women driven by boredom or worry from one sensation to another.

"That man's a drug addict, or I'm a fool," he told himself. "I'd bet anything that he started to dope himself the moment I'd left the room."

Kilby would have lost his bet. Sir Joshua did not have recourse to the dope until he had first carefully composed a message.

Sam Grundy clanged the door to. Kilby glanced at the watch on his wrist as he made his way to the road.

"There's more than enough time for me to catch my train," he said to the taxi-driver. "Please drive me back to the Chief Constable's."

Kilby was determined to have a finger kept on the pulse of affairs in Donmoor, and the Chief Constable was the man to do it. He gave Major Walters an account of what had transpired at Hopeview House, and then said:

"I should be glad if your men would keep an eye on Sir Joshua and his visitors. Will you be good enough to give the necessary instructions, sir?"

The Chief Constable readily promised.

"When you mentioned Mr. Davis," he then said, "I had a hazy idea that I'd heard the name before. And you had hardly reached the pavement outside when I recollected that I had heard it from the manager of the British Bank."

"Yes," said Kilby, wondering what the other meant.

"It was Mr. Davis who asked the manager to have the notes traced."

The news was unintelligible to Kilby, for the notes had not been mentioned at the previous interview.

"I'm quite in the dark," he confessed. "And I am afraid I shall have to ask you to explain."

Then Major Walters commenced to explain. In as few words as possible, he told of how Mr. Hyde had presented a cheque at the British Bank and received in exchange sixty banknotes of £500 each; of how Mr. Hyde had returned later and paid £10,000 back into his account; of the diamond merchant's description of the keen bargain he had driven with Sir Joshua Jordan.

"Some of the details I have only just learned," went on the Chief Constable. "When I had recalled the connection in which I had heard Mr. Davis's name before, I hurried round to the bank, and while you were interviewing Sir Joshua I was catechizing the bank manager. Mr. Hyde mentioned one fact to that gentleman which may, or may not, be of importance. In the correspondence that preceded Mr. Hyde's visit to Hopeview House, Sir Joshua had made an attempt to describe the necklace. But the real thing was not a bit like what Mr. Hyde had expected to find. It was not inferior, but—it was quite different."

Kilby walked over to the window, and attentively regarded the traffic outside.

"Can you say whether Mr. Hyde showed the necklace to anyone?" he asked, coming back. "Did he show it to the bank manager, for example?"

"He didn't show it to him, so I think it's safe to assume that he showed it to no one. He didn't even tell the manager what it was like."

"And," said Kilby, "when I requested Sir Joshua to describe it, he couldn't. Do you know, sir, those diamonds, or the complete necklace itself, could be offered for sale in any jeweller's shop in the kingdom, and neither you nor I—nor anyone else, for that matter—would know a thing about it. I fear there isn't the slightest possibility of discovering the murderer by attempting to get on the track of the necklace... But you mentioned something about tracing the banknotes, sir?"

Major Walters then gave an account of the steps he had taken, and the discoveries he had made.

"Not that I did it all myself," he added. "Scotland Yard helped me. I didn't trouble to tell them why I wanted the numbers traced, or they'd have informed you, I dare say."

"Very likely. So the money was changed into various currencies. Nothing very original in that, I must say. I suppose you've followed up your discoveries by endeavouring to trace the francs and the dollars and all the rest of them?"

"No," replied Major Walters. "I did what I was asked to do, nothing more. I presume if they are to be traced the job will have to be undertaken by the various countries concerned?"

"I don't think so, sir. It isn't a case of the banknotes being changed by a person just going abroad. The fact that several currencies were selected proves that the person, or persons, who did the changing had no intention of leaving the country. And there must have been more than one person concerned in the transactions. No one person could have covered all the towns in your list in so short a time. No, the whole affair was simply a dodge to get rid of the incriminating banknotes as quickly as possible. But you may be sure they haven't held on to the foreign money. By now it's been changed back again into English notes. That kind of thing has been done before more than once. But what a pity that the bank manager allowed the affair to drop so quickly, sir! He ought to have asked you to get the numbers of the foreign notes from the various Exchange Bureaux. Some of them, at any rate, would have kept records."

"You think it's now too late?"

"Possibly no, probably yes. The gang—for I'm convinced there is a gang—has been allowed a rather long start. And time, in a case like this, is everything. That's why I say it's a pity the manager didn't have the affair investigated further."

Major Walters nodded his agreement.

"I see your point," he said. "But the manager, like me, was acting on instructions. Mr. Davis seems to be the man responsible for allowing matters to remain at a standstill. Now a rather peculiar aspect of the case has just occurred to me. Sir Joshua has admitted to you that it wasn't Mr. Hyde who robbed him. But, except his whole story is a fabrication, someone did. Have you formed any theory about the matter?"

"Hardly a theory, sir. But I've been thinking things over, and the only explanation I can see at present is that someone really did take the necklace whilst its owner sat bound and unconscious. Mr. Hyde, on the other hand, told the bank manager that he had paid Sir Joshua £20,000 for the necklace. Now, assuming that Mr. Hyde and Sir Joshua were not known to each other—and I really think that they weren't—it would have been a comparatively simple matter for a third person to impersonate both men in turn. The unknown third person, first posing as Mr. Hyde, dealt with Sir Joshua and took the necklace. Then, pretending to be Sir Joshua, he awaited the coming of the real Mr. Hyde, sold him the necklace, and pocketed the £20,000."

The Chief Constable made some crude sketches on a piece of pink blotting-paper.

"A very ingenious theory, Kilby," he observed, throwing down the pen on the table. "I can't see how a third person could have done it, though. To begin with, he would need to have had a pretty accurate knowledge of the correspondence that was exchanged between Sir Joshua and the diamond merchant. And it's the kind of thing neither of them would have proclaimed from the rooftops."

Kilby made an arch by placing the tips of his fingers together. It was a habit of his when he saw, or fancied he saw, a light shining through the darkness.

"No," he assented; "I don't expect either of them went around shouting about it. Yet there was one man who, in the ordinary course of his business, knew all about the proposed deal."

Major Walters started.

"You don't mean it?" he exclaimed.

"I do. What about Mr. Davis, the man who used to be Mr. Hyde's assistant?"

The Chief Constable sat in thoughtful silence for a considerable time.

"I shouldn't rely too much on that solution if I were you," he said at last. "You will probably find that Mr Davis was in London all the time the funny business was taking place."

But Kilby shook his head.

"You're wrong there, sir," he declared. "At the moment when Sir Joshua was being robbed Mr. Davis was not very far from here. He, himself, has admitted that he was in the Peak District."

On his way back in the train doubt crept into the mind of Inspector Kilby. As far as his information went, Jack Davis was the only third person who could have known beforehand of the intended visit of Mr. Hyde to Hopeview House. But did Davis know enough to enable him to carry out such a daring ruse as the double impersonation, to say nothing of the drugging and robbing of Sir Joshua Jordan? To have done so with any hope of success he would have needed to possess not only a knowledge of the proposed transaction, but an intimate knowledge of the routine of Hopeview House. In particular, it would have been necessary for him to be certain that he would not be interrupted by one or both of the male servants. Fortunately, or unfortunately, neither of them was in on that particular afternoon. But how could Davis have foreseen their absence?

A new thought struck Kilby. Were the servants accomplices? Had Davis bribed them to keep out of the way while he was carrying out his nefarious scheme? But Kilby quickly rejected the thought. Sir Joshua had told him explicitly that it was he, himself, who had sent the servants out of the way.

Furthermore, if Davis were the guilty person, why had he staged the robbery in Hopeview House? The banknotes seemed the final objective, and, surely, he could have obtained them earlier? But could he? Mr. Hyde had not had the money in his possession until he left the bank, and from there he had driven straight to Sir Joshua's in a taxi.

Then, suddenly, Kilby felt in the mood to curse his own stupidity. Like a fool, he had been reasoning as though Davis and Mr. Hyde were unknown to each other. True, Davis might have managed to carry out the first part of the scheme; but it would have been impossible for him to deceive his late employer, who knew him so well.

But—who else could it have been? Kilby had to admit that he could see no light anywhere. Further thought convinced him that Davis, if he were guilty, would have been an unmitigated fool to ask the bank manager to have the numbers of the missing banknotes circulated. Moreover, Davis himself could not have exchanged the banknotes for foreign money. Of course, he might be a member of the gang...

Another vital question occurred to Kilby. Was the person who had carried out the coup at Hopeview House also the murderer? If so, why had not the murder been committed in the house? The man who had been capable of drugging Sir Joshua, tying him to a chair, and robbing him, would surely have been able to overpower Mr. Hyde? But, instead of that, he had sold him the necklace for a sum much below its value. It was inconceivable that anyone should hand over the necklace to Mr. Hyde then, and, later, rush off to Highpen Tunnel and murder him there for the sake of the same necklace.

The slowing down of the train brought Inspector Kilby's tantalising reflections to an end. Glancing out through the window, he read the name of the station. Boxfield! Here it was that the stage must have been set for the murder, since all Mr. Hyde's travelling companions had entered at Boxfield.

The train stopped. A couple of passengers left Kilby's compartment, and three others entered. A few minutes later, as the train sped towards Highpen Tunnel, Kilby caught himself attentively regarding a man who occupied a corner seat. There was nothing remarkable about the man; Kilby's regard was simply due to the fact that this particular passenger was sitting on the right-hand corner of the seat, facing the engine. Mr. Hyde had occupied a similar position the moment before his untimely end.

Kilby closed his eyes, and immediately, in fancy, the compartment became peopled by those who had travelled from Boxfield on that tragic Monday afternoon. He, himself, was the only one who had no right to be there. And yet he was ousting no other passenger, for he was occupying the corner of the seat which Freda Lowe's attaché case had taken up.

He tried to visualise first Light-Fingered Freddie and then John Lofthouse committing the crime. But neither picture would materialise with any degree of clearness. Speculation was unprofitable. He opened his eyes. The man opposite was leaning back, and about eight or nine inches of the upholstery showed above the top of his bald head.

The whistle shrieked, and the train plunged into the tunnel. Though the darkness was impenetrable, Kilby still retained a mental picture of a face opposite; not the face of the bald-headed man, but that of Mr. Hyde, the murdered diamond merchant.

And then, sudden as the flash of the pistol that had ended the life of the diamond merchant, there flared across Kilby's brain a startling theory as to the manner in which the murder had been committed. A few moments later, however, when the train had rushed out of the darkness, he discarded the hypothesis as being too fantastic. Daylight had a chastening influence on the vivid imagination of Inspector Kilby.

He did not leave the train at Blackton, for he had decided to travel as far as Midtown and interview John Lofthouse. This decision he had arrived at before leaving Donmoor. His conversation with the Chief Constable, and a trunk call to Scotland Yard, had caused him to miss the train by which he had intended to return; but he had accepted the disappointment philosophically. After all, it gave him an opportunity to interrogate the bank manager and the man who had driven Mr. Hyde to Hopeview House. From neither of these, however, had he learned anything that promised to be of any use. The manager had merely confirmed what Major Walters had already told him, and the taxi-driver had been able to tell him nothing of what had happened at Hopeview House, except that he and Mr. Hyde, between them, had unbarred the heavy gates and driven right up to the front door. The driver had seen the door open in answer to Mr. Hyde's ring, but his position was such that he had not been able to catch a glimpse of the person who had opened it from the inside. And he had seen no other person when Mr. Hyde came out about ten minutes later.

Kilby was aware that his train left Donmoor at the same time as that by which Mr. Hyde had travelled on Monday afternoon. Probably the guard was the same. He determined to enquire as soon as he reached Midtown. Perhaps he could interrogate the guard as well as Lofthouse.

At Midtown he learned that his conjecture had been correct. And the guard was willing to talk. The man's narrative flowed smoothly along until Kilby interrupted him.

"Are you sure that Doctor Peters mentioned Blackton by name?" he demanded. "Perhaps he said 'the next station' or words to that effect."

"I'm quite sure," was the guard's emphatic reply. "From the way he spoke it struck me that the doctor himself was a Blackton man."

"Dashed funny!" was Kilby's unspoken comment. "One wouldn't have expected a Wimpole Street physician to name offhand such a comparatively unimportant station as Blackton. And what was he doing up here so far away from his usual practice? I must have Doctor Peters' records looked up."

Thus, by three different roads, three different men—Jack Davis, Constable Brent, and Detective Inspector Kilby—had begun to suspect Doctor Peters, the Wimpole Street physician.

Chapter 14

The Spent Cartridge

After breakfast that same morning Jack Davis went to a telephone box, rang up the solicitors of the late Mr. Hyde, and instructed them to make the necessary funeral arrangements. He and Miss Hyde, he informed them, would be in London for the funeral, but they were remaining in Blackton at the present.

In this he was acting as Connie's agent. Before he left her the previous evening they had discussed their future movements, and she had asked him to communicate with the solicitors and make known her wishes.

From the telephone booth, he hastened to Connie's rooms. As the landlady conducted him to the sitting-room, Connie opened the door and greeted him with:

"Oh, Jack, I'm so sorry you didn't get here a little sooner. Freda Lowe's just been and gone, and I should have loved you to meet her. I think she's a ripping sort.

"Connie, you darling, you're the only girl I want to—" began Jack when they had entered the sitting-room and closed the door. But Connie silenced him with an upraised forefinger.

"None of that!" she admonished with assumed severity. Then she went on more gravely: "There's more serious work to do, Jack. Have you been thinking things over during the night? Do you believe it will be possible to discover the wretch who—who murdered Dad?"

Jack seated himself beside her on the settee, and watched the shadow chase the sunshine from her face.

"Buck up, darling!" he counselled. "Worrying isn't going to help one little bit. I wish I could tell you that the murderer had been discovered, but I must admit I haven't the foggiest notion who he is."

"Hasn't the tracing of the banknotes helped you at all? Freda says that the notes ought to provide a clue, and she's ever so clever."

For a moment or two Jack did not reply, and when at last he did speak it was to ask a question.

"You told Miss Lowe what steps I had taken about the banknotes?"

"Of course I did. Freda's the kind of girl you simply can't keep anything back from. Moreover, as I've said, she's awfully clever, and she might be able to help us to puzzle things out."

"And I suppose you told her that we'd found Doctor Peters to be a fraud?"

"Naturally." Then the girl looked Jack straight between the eyes. "But surely you don't think I did wrong to mention it to her? Though I've known her only a day or two, I'm certain she's not the kind that would go around blabbing out other people's secrets."

Jack took Connie's hands in his.

"You little silly!" he cried. "Of course you didn't do wrong. I merely asked the question, that's all. Besides, I don't see how it could do any harm even if Miss Lowe did talk. But Doctor Peters worried me a lot during the night, darling. I cannot see his motive. And how did he manage to have a false professional card in his possession?"

"I suppose it belonged to the real Doctor Peters."

But Jack shook his head.

"You are forgetting, Connie, that there is no Doctor Peters; at least, there isn't one in Wimpole Street. Yet this man had a card, a false card. Obviously, it had been printed specially for the occasion. Now, a man who does that kind of thing has a very strong motive for his action."

"A very strong motive indeed," Connie agreed. She paused, reflecting, her gaze apparently following the intricate pattern of the carpet at her feet. "Do you know, Jack," she went on, "it almost seems as though he knew beforehand that Dad was—was to be shot, and he had the card prepared in readiness."

Jack's forehead corrugated in a puzzled frown.

"I'd been thinking something like that myself," he admitted. "But I finally rejected the idea. How could he possibly have known that such a thing was about to happen? Moreover, the card was unnecessary. As soon as he said that he was a doctor he was allowed to attend to your father. No credentials were asked for. It was only when he was about to leave Blackton that he presented the card, gratuitously. No one asked him for it; no one suggested that he ought to be detained."

"I know, Jack. I know. But we cannot ignore the fact that the card was printed specially for the purpose. Evidently, he didn't consider it unnecessary. Perhaps he foresaw the possibility of being asked to produce evidence of his professional status. Or perhaps... perhaps... Jack, I have it now. That card was intended to throw pursuers off his trail."

Jack dropped her hands and stared.

"I don't see what you're driving at, Connie," he said.

"You know, Jack, Doctor Peters was not a doctor."

"I'm afraid you are wrong, dear. True, he was not the doctor he pretended to be, but those people who saw him say that he carried the usual doctor's kit."

Connie, however, was not prepared to relinquish her theory without a struggle.

"The kit, like the card, was intended to deceive. It was—" She stopped abruptly and sprang to her feet. "Jack," she exclaimed, "I believe I see his reason for carrying the medical kit. It enabled him to travel alone with Dad—with poor Dad's dead body. The guard raised no objection. But would he have allowed it had he not been convinced that the man was really a doctor? I am almost certain he wouldn't."

Jack, too, was now on his feet.

"By Jove! Connie," he cried excitedly, "I believe you've ferreted out the motive for the whole elaborate scheme. He knew that your father would be murdered. And he knew that your father carried the necklace. Until now I was absolutely puzzled to account for its disappearance. I even searched the tunnel in the hope that I might find it there. And, no doubt, the police have left no stone unturned to discover its whereabouts. No wonder we couldn't find it. Connie,"—he lowered his voice—"the sham Doctor Peters robbed your father while he lay dead on the carriage seat."

Connie covered her eyes with her hands. In fancy, she saw the dead body being profaned by the ghoulish hands of the false doctor. Despite his many faults, Connie had loved her father well, and a great hatred of Doctor Peters suddenly welled up within her. The girl was not revengeful or cruel, but, at the moment, she felt that she could cheerfully stand by and watch Doctor Peters being torn limb from limb.

Jack removed her hands from her face and patted her on her shoulder.

"Don't, Connie," he begged. "That kind of thing isn't going to help."

The girl clenched her hands, and her teeth bit into her underlip.

"I know I am being silly, Jack. But—but it's not easy to behave otherwise. Weeping won't help to find the wretch, though. Jack, we've got to find Doctor Peters. And when we've found him we must make it our business to see that he hangs for the murder of Dad."

Although he was able to understand her feelings, the girl's vehemence surprised Jack, and he longed for the pleasure of burying his knuckles in the sham doctor's quivering flesh. Heroics, however, were out of place at present.

"Connie, dear," he advised, "we mustn't allow our feelings or our imaginations to run away with us completely. I believe Peters robbed your father. But he didn't kill him. He couldn't have killed him. Your father was dead when Peters entered the compartment."

Connie moved over to the fireplace and rested her elbows on the mantelpiece. Her back was turned to Jack, and he knew that she was making a final fight to overcome her emotion. Once on the tennis court he had seen her behave similarly when a lightning ball had struck her full in the face. After a few minutes of what must have been agony, she had smiled bravely and resumed the game. He knew she would do so now.

Presently she turned.

"You're right," Jack she said, smiling bravely. "I very nearly made a fool of myself. Of course he couldn't have killed Dad. But I'm sure he knows who fired the shot. His elaborate preparations show that he knew what was about to happen. And he wouldn't have known that much without also knowing the killer."

Jack nodded.

"I'm inclined to agree with you, Connie. By Jove!" he exclaimed, as a sudden thought struck him. "Can it be that he's one of the gang? Your father was convinced that there was a gang of daring jewel thieves somewhere in existence. Peters is probably one of them. By some means or other, they got to know that your father would be carrying the necklace, and they made their plans accordingly. Some other member of the gang was to fire the shot, and Peters was to pose as a doctor and remove the necklace while alone with the body."

There was silence for some moments, and then Connie asked:

"Which of the two was the other member of the gang?"

"You mean the two men who travelled in the compartment with your father?"

"Yes."

Jack frowned.

"That's more than I'm prepared to say, Connie. And I shouldn't like the job of having to fasten the guilt on either of them. If the police can't do it, I'm afraid I couldn't. If only we could find Peters though, the rest ought to be easy." He tapped the end of a cigarette against his case before he went on: "I fear it will be the very dickens of a job to find him. We've no idea where he is."

"Admitted, Jack. But, at any rate, we know where he isn't."

Jack pursed his lips and blew a cloud of smoke from between them.

"H'm!" he said. "There's plenty of places where we're sure he isn't. But you have some particular place in mind?"

"Yes, London."

She smiled, noting his bewilderment, but before she had time to explain Jack threw away his cigarette and thumped one palm with the other fist.

"I'm hanged, Connie, if that little head of yours doesn't possess a lot more grey matter than mine!" he cried. "You're thinking of that little piece of pasteboard with the Wimpole Street address?"

"Yes. And because it says that Doctor Peters is to be found in London you may be sure he isn't there."

"Of course. What a thickhead I must be! Even a fool would have thought of that at first."

"Thanks, Jack," said Connie pertly, her emotions now under complete control. "I thought of it first, so—" She left the sentence unfinished.

Jack laughed. Then there was a brief interlude, during which he endeavoured to convince her that the only sign of foolishness she had ever shown was in her determination to stick to such a worthless chap as himself. The method he adopted, however, might be calculated to strengthen her in her determination.

"Of course," he said, when they had become rational beings once more, "it's well known that London is the best place in the world in which to hide. Nevertheless, I think you are right. But, if he isn't in London, where is he? Would one be safe in assuming that he's at the other end?"

"You mean Donmoor?"

"Yes. As far as we know, London and Donmoor are the ends of the affair. And they were also the beginnings. I don't expect it would have been difficult for Peters to slip back to Donmoor." He withdrew a railway map from his pocket, and went on: "I got this last night. Wanted to look up Donmoor and Boxfield and a few other places." Moving over to a little table he spread out the map, while Connie followed and stood beside him.

"Here is Blackton," he said, indicating a spot on the map. "The railway line, as you see, runs south to Derwent Junction. But between here and the junction there are three or four stations, seemingly small ones. Now Peters might have got off the train at one of these intermediate stations and returned to Donmoor by the next available train. Or, from Derwent Junction, he could have gone east to Midtown and travelled to Donmoor from there."

Connie keenly scrutinised the network of lines that, like an irregular spider's web, ran up and down and across the map.

"I believe Doctor Peters to be a clever man," she observed at length. "And a clever man would do neither of those things. Had he got off at an intermediate station he would have been compelled to return through Blackton; and that is one of the things he would endeavour to avoid at all costs. He might be seen by someone here who would recognise him—a porter or the station-master, for example."

Jack nodded.

"You're probably right, Connie," he assented. "Then he went on to Midtown. I see that he could get to Donmoor from there without touching Blackton."

But Connie shook her head.

"He didn't go to Midtown," she insisted. "In the first place, he would naturally be anxious to leave the train as soon as possible without exciting suspicion. Without exciting suspicion, Jack! Remember, he stated openly in the hearing of the guard that it was his intention to catch a London train at Derwent Junction. Now, had he either got off at an intermediate station or gone right on to Midtown the guard's suspicions would have been aroused; therefore, Doctor Peters did what he said he would do: he alighted at Derwent Junction."

"And went on to London?"

"No. He didn't do all that he said he'd do. We've already decided that he didn't travel to London. Of course we may be wrong, but—well, if we keep placing obstacles in our own way we shall never arrive anywhere. We are assuming that he returned to Donmoor, so let us work on that assumption. Now look carefully at this map again. You will observe how the lines, at this particular section, form a triangle, the three corners of which are Blackton, Derwent Junction, and a large town called Hartby to the west of the junction. The L.M.S. lines form two sides of the triangle—Blackton to Derwent Junction, and Derwent Junction to Hartby. But—and this seems important—the third side is formed by a branch line of the London and North Eastern. From Hartby the North Eastern runs to Donmoor, via Blackton. Now, Jack, if I were in that man's place and wanted to return secretly to Donmoor, I should have gone from Derwent Junction to Hartby, and then from Hartby to Donmoor by the North Eastern."

Jack's gaze was concentrated on the map.

"But, Connie," he protested, "that brings us up against your own biggest obstacle. Had Peters done that he would have passed through Blackton, you know."

With both hands Connie vigorously ruffled Jack's sleek, black hair.

"You great big silly!" she taunted laughingly. "Can't you see that each railway system has a station of its own?"

Jack raised his arms to crush her to him, then dropped them to his sides. Observing the look in his eyes, Connie's suspicions returned with renewed strength. And Jack was uncomfortably aware that she suspected him. Yet, during their tender interlude some minutes before, both had managed to forget the circumstance that might part them for ever.

Meanwhile events, which demonstrated the truth of that trite aphorism that momentous effects often spring from apparently trivial causes, were taking place elsewhere. The cause was a rough-and-tumble fight between William Ernest Pardoe and another schoolboy. The effect was not apparent all at once.

After due formalities at the door, Bill Pardoe, senior, clattered into Inspector Parker's office. Bill's cap was in his hand, and he fidgeted uneasily. But in his eyes was a look that the inspector read as ill-suppressed pride. Not until Bill had explained, however, could Parker see any reason why the man should feel proud.

Bill Pardoe was indeed proud, inordinately proud, of his brainy son who had brought prestige to the family by winning a Minor Scholarship. Bill had yet to learn the bitter lesson that the day would surely come when that same son would not be proud of his father. Either William Ernest would take his parent in hand and endeavour to correct his speech, or, metaphorically, make of him the skeleton in the cupboard, a skeleton to be kept out of sight and hearing of the brainy one's youthful friends.

"Well, Mr. Pardoe, what is it?" asked the inspector.

A wide grin slowly spread across the rugged features of Bill Pardoe, as his nervousness fled before the geniality of the other.

"It's that there imp o' mine," he began with a chuckle. "'Im an' Ted Wilson's lad 'ad a reet-down good bust up yest'day. Nowt would do both o' the young devils but that they should start clinkin' one another. Ted's lad g'en our Will a clout in th' ear-'ole for summat or other, But our Will's got a punch in 'is fist an' a tidy candle in 'is lante'n, so 'e waits 'is chance an' lands wi' a beauty reet on Ted's lad's conk, an' then—"

"Which of them do you wish me to arrest, Mr. Pardoe?" interrupted the inspector, with a smile. "Or would you like both of them to cool their heels in the lock-up?"

The mere thought of so inglorious an end to such a royal battle horrified Bill Pardoe. It took him about five minutes to find a sufficient number of appropriate words in which to say so, but in the end the inspector contrived to steer him back to the object of his visit.

"Well, it's like this 'ere, sir," explained Bill. "In the scrimmage, our Will's jacket got mauled about a bit, an' when all the kids 'ad bin put to bed las' night the missus started to mend it. Summat dropped out o' one o' the pockets, an' when we see'd wot it was the owd girl said as how it wor' my duty to bring it along to you. It wor' a bit latish then, so I waited— But 'ere y'are, sir."

He held out his hand, and Inspector Parker beheld the spent cartridge from an automatic pistol.

Chapter 15

On the Trail

Though his hopes of success were none too rosy, Jack Davis determined to put to the test Connie Hyde's theory as to the movements of Peters after the murder.

His first duty was to discover whether Peters had been seen at Derwent Junction, and this part of the enquiry seemed to offer a ray of hope. He had already learned that the junction was a busy station at certain hours of the day. It naturally followed that the place would be well staffed. And Jack's own experience of travelling told him that the enquiries he was about to make would refer to what was practically the slackest hour of the day—too late for business people or shoppers to be going abroad, and too early for workers to be returning to their home, or pleasure-seekers to be leaving them.

There was at least the possibility that some member of the junction staff had observed Doctor Peters, whose glasses and spats and black bag and black garb would have made him sufficiently conspicuous for the observer to remember him.

Connie insisted on accompanying Jack; and Jack, well pleased, readily consented. After a run of about fifteen minutes, they found themselves on one of the platforms at Derwent Junction.

They went to the booking-office, where they found a short queue lined up outside the pigeon-hole. Curbing their impatience as well as they could, the two amateur investigators watched the human chain shrink in length, a length at a time, until they themselves were the only persons left in the booking-hall.

They stepped over to the pigeon-hole, and Jack, introducing Connie and himself, stated their errand.

The clerk threw an appreciative glance at the girl. Then he stacked up the tickets he had just received, and spread them out again on the counter. It was evident that he was undecided what course to adopt.

"I believe it's usual for the police to make such enquiries," he said at last. "But, in the circumstances,"—he glanced again at Connie—"I'll give you whatever help I'm able. Can you describe this Doctor Peters?"

"Not very clearly, I fear," confessed Jack. "I've never seen the man. But I've heard him described by people who have, and I'll do the best I can. Peters is of medium height and build, clean-shaven and fresh-complexioned, and he wears horn-rimmed glasses. On Monday afternoon he was dressed in a black suit, black patent shoes, and grey spats. I'm afraid that's the only information I can give you. Oh, by the way, I nearly forgot to mention that he carried a black bag—the kind that doctors use... well?"

The clerk tilted his head sideways and rubbed his chin, while Connie and Jack anxiously awaited his answer. So much might depend on what he had to say. But the answer, when it came, brought only disappointment.

"I'm sure I never saw the man," was the clerk's decided reply. "At that particular hour few people were booking, and I have no doubt that if I'd seen the man I should now be able to call him to mind. I can never look at horn-rimmed glasses without thinking of a certain American film-actor, and"—he smiled—"well, I didn't think of any film-actor, American or otherwise, on Monday afternoon."

Then Connie rose to the occasion.

"Of course," she said, smiling her most winning smile, "there's just the barest possibility that you may have seen him and forgotten. Now I noticed that each of those people who booked here a minute or two ago handed you a ticket, as well as his fare, in exchange for the ticket you issued to him. Is that the general custom at this junction?"

"The invariable custom, Miss Hyde. No one can book here without first handing in either a platform ticket or a ticket issued at some other station."

"Excellent. Now, there is reason to believe that Doctor Peters re-booked here on Monday afternoon. To do that he would have been compelled to produce a ticket bearing the name of the station from which he had travelled. Do you mind looking through your used tickets? Perhaps we might come across one that would give us a clue."

The clerk regretfully shook his head.

"Very sorry, indeed," he said. "The tickets handed in on Monday have already been sorted and forwarded to headquarters at Hartby."

Dispirited, they thanked the clerk, and strolled on to the platform.

"Seems a hopeless task observed Jack, a trifle grimly.

Connie moved in the direction of a seat,

"Let's sit down and think things over," she suggested.

"Wouldn't it be better to run over to Hartby and make enquiries there?" amended Jack.

Connie agreed, and he returned to the booking-office and purchased two tickets to Hartby. In exchange he handed over a certain sum of money and the two tickets that had been issued to him at Blackton.

The clerk's interest in the murder was now keenly aroused, and he engaged Jack in a discussion that lasted several minutes.

Meanwhile, Connie strolled along the platform towards the end by which she had arrived. She observed the barrier and, outside of it, a wooden structure, like a watchman's hut, that sheltered the official whose duty it was to issue free tickets to persons going on to the platform and to collect the used tickets from those going off it.

Observing Connie's approach, the porter on duty left his unpretentious office and stood waiting at the barrier with outstretched hand.

The girl did not misunderstand his action. Thinking she was about to leave the platform, he was demanding her ticket. Connie offered a smiling explanation.

"Sorry, Miss," grinned the porter. "Thought you were about to take the footpath to Little Faston. It's only a ten minutes' walk, and plenty of Little Faston people catch a train here, or leave it, as the case may be, for the service here is very much better."

Connie became suddenly alert. Plenty of people left the train at Derwent Junction and walked as far as Little Faston. She remembered Little Faston as the last station she had passed through a short time before. Doctor Peters had not gone near the booking-office here. But what was to prevent his leaving the platform and walking back to Little Faston? It would be such a simple method of throwing dust in the eyes of possible pursuers. His action would have excited no suspicion. The guard would have seen him leave the train at the junction, and there was no other person who would have been interested in his movements. From Little Faston he could have gone wherever he wanted to go. Of course, he could not have returned to Donmoor, direct, without passing through Blackton, but a man like Peters would have found it an easy matter to throw pursuers off the trail.

All at once, Connie realised that she and Jack had been far from thorough in pursuing their investigations. She now determined to take the intelligent-looking porter into her confidence.

The man listened attentively to what she had to say, and when she had finished he remained silent for a considerable time. Then he shook his head.

"I'm certain," he declared, "that the man you've described didn't come through this way. But, somehow, I seem to remember the black bag." He paused, and his brow wrinkled. "I have it!" he exclaimed. "After the London train had left, there was hardly anyone on either of the platforms—just a few women and one man. Before that, I'd noticed this particular man push a bag under one of the seats and then walk away from it. That's what drew my attention to him. But I'm afraid he's not much like the man you want, Miss. To begin with, he didn't wear glasses. And he wore no spats, either. Then you say that he was dressed in black. But the one I'm talking about was wearing a raincoat— Wait a minute, though! Yes, the man was dressed in black after all. I remember seeing the black trousers below the raincoat. And the patent shoes, too. I recollect saying to myself, when I saw his rig-out, that he looked like some sort of musician. Later, when he picked up his bag again and took a seat in the Hartby train, I decided in my own mind that he was off to play in one of the Hartby picture-houses or some place of the kind."

Connie thrilled with excitement. Even before the porter had finished speaking, she saw how easy it would have been for Peters to transform himself into the individual the man was describing. All he had had to do was to take off his glasses and spats, and don a raincoat. But he had been unable to conceal the black trousers, the patent shoes, and the professional-looking bag.

Thanking the porter, Connie turned and hurried back to the booking-office, from which Jack was just emerging. Breathlessly, she informed him of the discovery she had just made, and in a little while Jack was no less excited than she. In their eagerness they longed to be able to rush off to Hartby without another moment's loss of time. But they were compelled to wait nearly a quarter of an hour for a convenient train; and, by the time it rumbled in, the fine edge of Jack's enthusiasm was becoming slightly dulled.

"Mustn't be unduly elated because of one small victory," he counselled, as they took their seats. He had no desire to belittle the importance of what Connie had learned; but he realised that it was as ridiculous to be jubilant over one minor success as to be despondent because of a trifling reverse.

"Quite right," assented Connie. "But it's a victory, anyhow. And there's no knowing what we may discover at Hartby."

"Darling, I know you are hoping to discover that Peters purchased a ticket at Donmoor. But aren't you forgetting that he may have joined the train at any station between Donmoor and Highpen Tunnel?"

"No, Jack, I'm not forgetting that. And I shouldn't be surprised to learn that he travelled from Donmoor to some other station earlier in the day and waited there for Dad's train. If we can discover nothing at Hartby, I think we couldn't do better than to try every station between Donmoor and the tunnel, as well as Donmoor itself, of course... But where's the use of meeting trouble half-way?"

Jack, however, considered it better to be prepared for a possible disappointment.

"Even if we do find that a Donmoor ticket has been handed in at Hartby," he said, "there will be nothing to prove that it was ever in the possession of Peters. No doubt, dozens of Donmoor tickets are handed in at Hartby every day."

Connie watched a field and some placid cows rush past.

"Very likely," she conceded. "But I should think they are rarely used on this roundabout route. If we find that a Donmoor passenger travelled this way on Monday afternoon—"

She broke off as the train drew to a halt at a tiny station. A moment later they heard the cry of "Tickets, please!" and a railway official entered their compartment.

Jack handed over their tickets. The inspector carefully scrutinised the two pieces of pasteboard, then, still retaining them in his hand, prepared to leave the compartment. In a flash Jack realised what was taking place. The tickets were being collected here, instead of waiting until the passengers had left the train at Hartby. And the reason for the inspector's keen scrutiny was evident. Had the tickets been for a station beyond Hartby they would have been returned to the holders. Suppose this inspector had done the collecting on Monday? He would have looked carefully at the name of the station on every ticket...

"Just a moment, Inspector, please."

The official paused at the open door, and Jack spoke hurriedly, for he knew that his time was limited.

In the few moments that the inspector granted him, Jack learned that, to the best of the other's belief, no passenger holding a Donmoor ticket had travelled on Monday by the train mentioned. That particular train had been running merely from Midtown to Hartby, and most of the passengers were from Midtown, Little Faston, and a few other stations.

The inspector, however, was almost certain that he had seen a passenger answering to Jack's description of Doctor Peters. He could not say from what station the man had come, though, as he had already said, he was practically certain that it wasn't Donmoor.

The official banged the door. The train started, and Jack and Connie gazed at each other, hardly knowing whether to rejoice or lament.

At Hartby, they found the booking-clerks very busy, so they first interviewed porters, railway policemen, bookstall clerks, the station-master, everyone who might, by the remotest possibility, have seen Peters on Monday. But all their efforts were barren of result.

One fact, however, they did learn. In studying the map, they had concentrated so deeply on Blackton as the apex of a triangle that they had overlooked the obvious fact that a branch line of the L.M.S., running to the west of Blackton, connected Hartby direct with Donmoor. Thus it would not have been essential for Peters to make use of the North Eastern, as they had previously assumed.

Each fresh disappointment caused their spirits to sink a little lower. They—and, in particular, Connie—had allowed assumption to take the place of certainty. They knew that Peters had travelled from Derwent Junction on a train that passed through Hartby. But what proof had they that he had left it there? It was just as probable that he had travelled on to Crewe, or even to Holyhead.

At last the rush at the booking-office came to an end, and, thanks to Jack's urgent tone and Connie's charming smile, the head clerk invited them into his office.

But neither he nor any of the other clerks had any recollection of the wanted man. At Connie's request he placed several bundles of used tickets before them, each bundle being confined to a particular station. The Donmoor bundle was of considerable dimensions, and, as might be expected, nothing was to be learned from any of the tickets that composed it.

Wondering if there were anything further to be done, Connie absently picked up a bundle of Little Faston tickets and idly flicked her thumb along the top. Several times she mechanically repeated the operation; but a sudden exclamation escaped her, and then she deliberately examined the bundle, ticket by ticket.

"Were all these handed in on Monday?" she asked at length.

"Yes," said the clerk.

"And in this particular order?"

"Roughly, yes. But why do you ask, Miss Hyde?"

"There are seven of these tickets that strike me as peculiar," she cried, "very peculiar. The seven are together, and six of them can be arranged so that their numbers run consecutively. But the seventh—and it's in among the other six—makes a bad break in the series. There is a gap of—yes, of over eighty between its serial number and the lowest of the other six... Come on, Jack!"

She dragged the wondering young man towards the door. Then, aware of her lack of gratitude, she rushed back and thanked the amused clerk.

"What's stung you, old girl?" demanded Jack, when she had rejoined him.

"Why, can't you see?" she cried, forgetting, for the moment, her theory that Peters had come from Donmoor. "That seventh ticket must have been issued in the morning. Now, in ordinary circumstances, no one purchases a ticket until a few minutes before the departure of his train. But this one was purchased hours and hours before. And it was purchased by the man we're after. He was clever enough to foresee that enquiries would be made, and he took precautions. Ordinarily, no one would dream of associating him with a ticket bearing the name of Little Faston. Had I not accidentally noticed the number— But let's hurry back to Little Faston and make enquiries there."

At Little Faston it seemed as though luck were about to favour them. The clerk, while he could not be sure of the number, remembered issuing a ticket to Hartby on Monday morning. Of course, he was careful to explain, he had issued several tickets to Hartby, but there was something just a little unusual about the purchase of one of them, a fact which enabled him to remember the transaction.

"The ticket was demanded while I was busy issuing tickets for the 9.30 to Midtown," continued the clerk. "Now, the next train to Hartby wasn't due until 10.10, and I told the purchaser so. My information didn't seem to be appreciated though."

"And," put in Jack, "the purchaser was of medium height, and may, or may not, have been wearing horn-rimmed glasses. He wore black patent shoes, black trousers—"

"He didn't!" interrupted the clerk, with an amused laugh. "The 'he' was a 'she.' I didn't issue the ticket to a man, but to a rather good-looking young woman."

"Damn!" exclaimed Jack, and Connie never even thought of rebuking him.

Chapter 16

A Startling Revelation

O ld Dick, the potter, hammered the last nail into the lid of a stout little packing-case, then straightened his back and looked at his niece,

"Got the label ready, Freda?" he asked.

The girl handed him the label, and for the next few minutes he was busy affixing it to the top of the case. When this task had been completed to his satisfaction, he scrutinised the address, written in Freda's firm handwriting.

"Mr. John Smith, Jeweller," was the name he read; and the address was a certain number in Euston Road, London.

"I hope Mr. John Smith will find this lot as profitable as the last," laughed old Dick. "He ought to find it even more so. This case, as you know, holds some of my cleverest work."

"That remains to be seen, Uncle. One is never a reliable judge of one's own handiwork. And there's no need for me to remind you that the tiniest flaw can spoil what seems to be a perfect piece of workmanship."

Old Dick inclined his head.

"Quite true, my girl," he concurred. "But I know there's no flaw... You'll take the case to the station in the car, of course?"

"Of course. But, Uncle, what do you say to my having a good look round in old Lizzie? I could have the case despatched from whatever convenient station I happened to run across."

The old potter gave the matter his careful consideration.

"A very good idea, Freda," he agreed. "While you are getting ready I'll attend to Lizzie."

Freda ran into the cottage, and her uncle pushed the potter's wheel from in front of the door of the shed. The affair was mounted on little cast-iron wheels and was quite easy to move. Then, going to the back of the shed, he stepped into the car.

Dick started the engine and drove out to the gravel-covered square in front of the so-called garage. Then, first taking a good look round, he stopped the engine and dismounted. There was none of the usual backing and turning to be done, for it was a habit of old Dick never to drive straight into the garage after returning from a journey. All the necessary turning was done then, before he backed in the car between the wide doors.

The old man surveyed the car and grinned. And the reason for his amusement was fairly obvious. The body of the dilapidated vehicle was a music-hall joke, and the engine and other running parts were nameless. Yet—and perhaps this had something to do with his merriment—worn-out though the car undoubtedly appeared, it had never once failed him on any journey he had undertaken.

The girl reappeared, and old Dick placed the case in the back of the hybrid vehicle and covered it with a rug. The car seemed to belong to the period when a handle in front was an indispensable appendage. While Freda mounted to the driver's seat and thumped the lumpy cushions, old Dick caught the handle and jerked it round.

There followed a cough and a hiss, then silence. He repeated the operation many times, until at last the engine snorted violently and a shuddering vibration shook the vehicle to its smallest bolt. A rude boy, had one been present, would have openly jeered at the whole performance.

Dick came round from the front and stood close to Freda.

"A pleasant run, my girl," was his hearty wish. He had to speak loudly to make himself heard above the roaring and spitting of the engine. "Don't you wish," he added, grinning, "that you had your young policeman by your side?"

Freda pouted her lips and sniffed.

"Uncle, I do wish you wouldn't be so ridiculous!" she retorted.

The old man laughed outright.

"Ridiculous, am I?" he demanded in high good-humour. "Well, perhaps I am. After all, there's much better fish than young Brent. Take that chap Davis, for example. He's got brains, if you like. Was the first to discover that there's something shady about Doctor Peters. And he may discover a lot more yet. If he does, he'll soon make a name for himself. Freda, my girl, haven't you ever felt that you'd like to 'click' with Davis?"

"Miss Connie Hyde might have something to say to that," was Freda's guarded reply.

"Perhaps you're right," said old Dick. "It would be a mistake to quarrel with her."

Freda made a swift movement. The car lurched forward and crunched and rattled along the gravel towards the gateway that gave access to the road. Before she had reached the gate, however, her uncle shouted and ran forward. Freda stopped, and he quickly came up with her.

"Nearly forgot to tell you," he said, "that the tyre on the off back wheel is wearing thin in places. Of course, it's good for dozens of miles yet, but we'd better have it replaced before there's a burst-up." He handed her some notes. "Better get a new one while you're out. You're bound to run across plenty of garages on the way."

"Any particular make of tyre, Uncle?"

"The make doesn't matter. Get a serviceable one, that's all."

Freda nodded, and the car rattled off once more.

Inspector Kilby returned to Blackton that evening, feeling tired but cheerful. The chance remark of the guard had opened up a new avenue which he was determined to explore to the utmost of his ability.

Stepping on to the platform, he waited until the string of carriages had trundled out of the station. He had now an uninterrupted view, and on the sidings beyond the main line he could see the coach which was responsible for his presence here in Blackton. For several moments he remained undecided, then he turned on his heel and walked off the platform. He would again thoroughly examine every square inch of the compartment in which Mr. Hyde had met his death, but at present he felt too tired to undertake the task.

A walk of five minutes took him to the police-station, and in less than another minute he was sitting in the presence of Inspector Parker. Lighting a cigarette, he leaned back in his chair and stretched out his long legs with a contented sigh.

"I've had a very busy day, Parker," he observed, exhaling a cloud of smoke through his nostrils.

"Yes," replied Parker. "I can see that you look played out. But have you made any discoveries that compensate you for your fatigue?"

"I've made a few discoveries, Parker. Whether they are worth the trouble, however, remains to be seen. Let me tell you what I've learned."

Then Kilby recounted the results of his day's investigations, whilst the other listened. It was not without a serious effort that Inspector Parker kept his attention from wandering, for he was keenly anxious to discuss his own discoveries. And he had no doubt that these discoveries were quite as interesting as Kilby's.

In a smooth-flowing, conversational tone Kilby related all that he had heard from the Chief Constable of Donmoor and from the bank manager. And he gave an account of the steps which Jack Davis had taken to have the banknotes traced.

"Davis puzzles me," admitted Kilby. "Either he's had a hand in the affair or he's making a genuine effort to discover who murdered the father of the girl he loves. I shall have a talk with the young man at the first opportunity, and perhaps I shall then be able to decide whether he's black or white."

"I too, suspected Davis," said Parker, and the other did not seem to notice that he spoke in the past tense.

Kilby flicked the ash from his cigarette, then told of the peculiar manner in which he had been received by Sir Joshua Jordan. Parker really became interested as he listened to an account of the interview that had followed. He had heard the gist of the story before, of course, but it now seemed to take on a deeper significance. A knight drugged, bound, gagged, and robbed in his own home was not an everyday occurrence. And then the man who had committed that outrage afterwards to pose as Sir Joshua and sell the necklace to Mr. Hyde! No ordinary man could have carried out such a daring coup.

From Donmoor to Midtown was a big jump, but Parker soon found himself listening to what Kilby had learned from the guard of the train.

"When the guard told me," said Kilby, "that Doctor Peters had mentioned Blackton by name, I thought it seemed funny. It's rather unusual, you know, for a Wimpole Street physician to be found far away from London except when he's on a holiday. And Peters wasn't holidaying, for he carried his medical kit. When, in addition, he knows the district so well that he can give the correct name of a station of no particular importance without even pausing to think—well, one begins to wonder."

Parker nodded and smiled. The moment for his own revelation had not yet come.

"I questioned the guard still further," continued Kilby, "and learned that Peters got off the train at Derwent Junction. That was according to programme, however. The doctor had already stated his intention of catching the London express there."

"Yes," assented Parker. "He made the statement to me."

"From Blackton to Derwent Junction he travelled in the compartment immediately behind that in which the murder had occurred. All the other passengers had kept away as far as possible from the fatal compartment, but it seems to have held some sort of morbid fascination for him. He couldn't ride in the compartment itself, for the guard had locked it, so he rode as near to it as he possibly could."

"Perhaps," put in Parker, "he didn't want to ride in it. He had travelled in that compartment, remember, from the point at which the murder was discovered until the train stopped at Blackton... Just a moment, please." He struck the bell on the table, and a sergeant soon entered.

"Sergeant," said the inspector, "I believe Constable Brent is somewhere about. Will you please send him here."

"What's the idea?" asked Kilby when the sergeant had gone.

"If you don't mind, I'd rather you waited until Brent comes."

Kilby assented with a nod, and a few minutes later Police Constable Brent entered the room.

Parker made the necessary introductions and then said:

"Brent, will you tell Inspector Kilby all you know about the broken window?"

In as few words as possible the constable related what he had learned from his own observations and what William Ernest Pardoe had told him.

"H'm!" observed Kilby. "So the breakage had become worse by the time the train arrived at Blackton. There doesn't seem to be much in that, though. The shattered glass fell out on the way, I expect."

"I don't think so, sir. I did at first, but I don't now. The boy seems particularly sharp, and he's confident that the glass wasn't shattered—just a clean hole. Moreover, I've been back along the line and found the glass. Now, sir, it's my opinion that if it had fallen out because of the shaking of the train it would have dropped out a bit at a time, and I should have found a piece here and a piece there all along the line."

Kilby nodded.

"A very shrewd suggestion," he observed. "Well, wasn't that how you did find it?"

"No sir. I found several pieces, but they were practically in one heap."

"Ah! And what do you argue from that, Brent?"

"That the window was deliberately broken, sir; or, rather, that the breakage was deliberately enlarged."

Kilby rose to his feet and paced up and down the room. As a tired hunter forgets his weariness when he sights a promising trail so now Kilby's weariness disappeared as though it had never existed. After several turns, he stopped abruptly in front of the young constable.

"Brent," he said, "your inspector has told me that he rates your ability very highly. Now, I'm not given to flattery, but I should like to say that, from the little I've seen of you, I heartily agree with him. I mention this so that you will speak freely what is in your mind without the fear that your views will not receive the consideration they deserve."

Inspector Kilby was a thoroughly efficient officer, with not a spark of petty jealousy in his composition. He freely admitted that he made plenty of mistakes; and he was just as willing to concede that many of his successes were due not to his own cleverness but to the help he had received from others. Even his worst enemies could not say of Kilby that he battened on the brains of others.

"Now, Brent," he continued "who, in your opinion, broke the window?"

"Doctor Peters, sir."

Kilby started back and stared. It surprised him considerably to find that his suspicions of the doctor were shared by another. Quickly recovering his composure, however, he asked:

"And what makes you think it was he?"

Constable Brent paused for a few moments to choose his words. He knew that the theory he was about to advance might have far-reaching consequences, and he wished to formulate it as clearly as possible.

"No one else could have done it, sir," he replied at last. "Only he and the dead man were in the compartment when the second breakage took place."

Kilby nodded gravely.

"You must be right," he said. "Assuming that the breakage was enlarged after the train had resumed its journey, no one but he— But, of course, there's no need to assume anything of the kind. The glass you found on the permanent way is conclusive proof. May I go further, Brent, and ask why the doctor behaved like a mischievous boy?"

This time there was no hesitation about Brent's reply.

"Because, sir, he wanted it to be thought that the pistol was thrown from that compartment."

Inspector Parker now joined in the conversation.

"You remember I told you," he said to Kilby, "that Brent refuses to admit that the pistol we found in the tunnel had been flung through the window. He insists that it was thrown by someone standing somewhere near the mouth of the tunnel. I managed to convince him that the shot couldn't have been fired from outside, as he had at first supposed, but he sticks like a limpet to his theory that the weapon was thrown not from the carriage but from the ground."

Constable Brent smiled. One of the things Parker had always admired about the young constable was his refusal to feel abashed in the presence of a superior.

"It's rather more than a theory, sir," Brent quietly insisted. Then he explained to Kilby how he had arrived at his conclusion by the discovery of the little channel in the sand. Although Parker had already told him about it, Kilby listened attentively; and he was now convinced where, formerly, he had been sceptical.

Parker unexpectedly echoed Kilby's conviction.

"At first I was inclined to laugh at Brent," he confessed. "But now I know that he was right. How or when, or by whom the pistol was thrown into the tunnel, I don't know. But I do know that it wasn't flung through the broken window."

Kilby returned to his chair and sat down. It occurred to him that he was not the only one who had been making discoveries.

"Yes?" he said. The question was vague, but comprehensive.

"Kilby," said Parker, and this was the first time for him to address the other so familiarly, "we've been off the line all the time. Or, rather, we've been on a sort of side track. We've been puzzling our brains to discover how anyone of those people in the compartment could have fired the shot without the knowledge of the others. I had formed several theories, but none of them would satisfy me fully. And I'm not surprised now. Kilby, the pistol wasn't thrown through the window for the simple reason that it was never in that compartment at all—until afterwards."

Kilby planted his feet firmly on the floor.

"Then," he exclaimed, "Brent was right at first and the murder was committed by someone standing on the permanent way!"

"No. Brent was wrong. The shot was fired from the compartment immediately behind."

Chapter 17

Certainties and Conjectures

A silence that lasted several minutes followed Inspector Parker's startling announcement.

In obedience to his superior's nodded invitation, Constable Brent now seated himself. Parker sat back in his chair, noting with satisfaction the tense attitude into which his words had thrown Inspector Kilby.

"The shot fired from the next compartment!" exclaimed Kilby, breaking the silence at last. "Good God!" Relaxing his rigid attitude, he leaned forward. "Parker," he said, "there are moments when inspirations seem to come to us from Heaven knows where. But we're so hard-headed that, nine times out of ten, we brush them aside or trample them underfoot. Such an inspiration came to me this afternoon, but I was fool enough to laugh at it as the figment of an overwrought imagination. It was while I was passing through Highpen Tunnel. Darkness, as you know, helps to make one's imagination peculiarly acute. In a flash it occurred to me how easy it would have been to fire a bullet through the partition between the two compartments. Like the fool I was, though, I spurned the inspiration the moment I had emerged from the darkness... But are you sure that that's how it happened?"

"Quite sure. I have examined both compartments and found where the bullet entered the partition through the upholstery and came out at the other side. But I don't believe I should ever have made the discovery had I not been looking for it. Once I had found it, however, the hole on the victim's side was pretty plain. But the ragged edge had been smoothed back so carefully that a casual observer would have noticed nothing. On the murderer's side there was hardly a hole at all—just a dint in the tapestry, and the slightest suspicion of scorching."

"Shouldn't have been surprised if there hadn't been even a dent. A small high-velocity bullet fired through that kind of material often merely presses the strands aside and forces a passage between them without snapping even a single thread. When the strands have sprung back to their original positions there is nothing to show that a bullet had passed through."

Inspector Parker crossed his knees and apparently studied the toe of his shoe.

"Had I not seen it for myself," he said, "I should have thought it impossible for a bullet to pass clean through a man's skull after first penetrating the partition."

But Kilby shook his head.

"There's nothing wonderful in that, Parker. In fact, one of the disadvantages of the type of pistol the murderer used is in the tremendous speed of the small bullet it fires. The faster a bullet travels, you know, the cleaner will be the opening it makes; and there are cases on record of a bullet going clean through a man and leaving him practically uninjured. Of course, no vital spot could have been touched. Now, had the bullet we're talking about not gone through the partition first, Mr. Hyde would have stood a better chance of escape, for the wound would then have been much neater—no ragged edges, and probably a much smaller hole."

"But surely," objected Parker, "you don't mean to say that he would possibly have escaped if the murderer had stood behind him in the same compartment and fired?"

Kilby smiled and shook his head.

"Hardly that, Parker. He'd have had about an extra chance in a million, that's all. By the way, it's now pretty obvious why Peters took the trouble to break the window."

"Wish everything were as plain as that. His object was to make it appear that the pistol had been thrown through it. We'd already assumed that, of course; but it's now plain that his real motive was to pretend that the owner of the pistol had travelled in that compartment."

Kilby picked a piece of paper off the table and twisted it into a spill.

"Parker," he asked, "can you explain why it took so long to discover that the window had been broken?"

Parker stroked his chin and pondered.

"Yes," he said after a time, "I think I can. The window, as you know, was on the right side of the train, and I presume all the doors on that side were locked. When the alarm was raised and the train stopped, most of the people left their seats and got out. But they had to get out on the other side; and when they discovered that a murder had taken place they had no eyes for anything so trivial as a small hole in a pane of glass. At Blackton, the hole was much larger, I admit, but only the guard, and the station-master and I entered the compartment—by the door on the left, of course—and the dead man claimed all our attention."

"I see. A case of the greater obscuring the less. It was the bullet that broke the window in the first instance, of course?"

"I think there can be no doubt on that point. Whether accidentally or by design, Peters did not aim straight in front, but slightly obliquely. Bearing in mind the slanting course of the wound in the dead man's head, I took measurements in both compartments, and discovered that the point at which the bullet left the partition was a little nearer to the window than that at which it had entered on the murderer's side. The slant would have been just sufficient to allow the bullet to go through the window that's broken."

Kilby screwed up his spill and aimed it at the wastepaper basket.

"If his other actions weren't so damnably clever," he affirmed, "I'd be inclined to think that the murderer was a lunatic. Just fancy any sane man firing a pistol through the partition into the next compartment! Why, he might have killed anyone! Suppose that girl, Freda Lowe, had been sitting close to the window. Or suppose the slanting course of the bullet had been to the left instead of to the right. If it didn't actually kill the girl outright, it would certainly have had sufficient momentum to cause her serious injury."

The chair that held Constable Brent grated harshly. Parker, pretending not to have observed the constable's emotion, picked up a sheet of paper and passed it to Kilby. "The girl seems to have been in no real danger," he said. "Here is a rough sketch showing the disposition of the various passengers in the compartment. You will observe that the girl's attaché case kept her so far away from the window that a slant, even to the left, except it were a very sudden one, would have left her quite safe. But that doesn't excuse the murderer, of course. He couldn't have known that no one was sitting directly opposite to his victim."

"Perhaps not," remarked Kilby, rising to his feet. For some moments he stood swaying backward and forward on heels and toes, and then he said: "Shouldn't be surprised to find that the slanting course given to the bullet was deliberate. Peters was satisfied with one murder. Of course, he knew where the diamond merchant was sitting. He caught a glimpse of him at Donmoor or somewhere along the line."

"But Mr. Hyde might have changed his seat, en route."

Kilby laughed.

"So might this station change over to the other side of the road. Have you ever known a man to give up a corner seat, save, perhaps, to some damsel in distress? And even that's seldom done nowadays except the damsel happens to be particularly attractive."

They discussed that aspect of the affair still further, and then Kilby observed:

"One can now see why Peters was so anxious to travel as far as Derwent Junction in the compartment from which he had fired the shot. He wanted to conceal the mark the bullet had made in the tapestry."

Parker, however, did not agree.

"I don't think so," he said. "The mark was so small that whatever concealment was possible could easily have been carried out while young Pardoe was pulling down the chain next door. No, Peters was searching for something he hadn't had time to find before."

"Searching, Parker? What do you mean?"

Inspector Parker pulled open a drawer.

"This is what he was trying to find," he said, handing over a spent cartridge.

Kilby stared at the shell; then he stared at the local inspector.

"Parker," he said at last, with a whimsical smile, "I am beginning to wonder why you asked for the assistance of Scotland Yard. I am supposed to be helping you, supposed to be trying to solve the mystery. I'll admit, too, that I considered I was making some headway. But you are miles ahead of me. What I've managed to find out is mere child's play compared with the discoveries you seem to have been making."

Parker, however, refused to accept the compliment.

"Don't tempt me to steal the thunder that rightly belongs to a schoolboy," he replied. "I didn't make the discovery off my own bat. The expelled shell was handed to me here in this room by the father of young Pardoe. And the boy found it in the railway carriage—in the compartment from which we now know the shot to have been fired."

Kilby whistled.

"Found in that compartment!" he repeated. "When Parker?"

"While the train was travelling between the tunnel and Blackton. You may remember that the guard bundled all the so-called witnesses into that compartment after the murder had come to light. Well, the boy found the cartridge where it had rolled under the seat. According to his father, the youngster found it by the merest accident, for it was almost completely hidden by the heating apparatus."

Kilby's face bore a puzzled expression.

"But why," he asked, "was not this brought to you sooner?"

"Retaliation!" A slight frown marred the symmetry of Parker's features. "I offended the mighty William Ernest, and this was his method of punishing my temerity. At first he withheld it with the idea of solving the mystery himself; but when he found that the puzzle was beyond him he decided to hand over the clue to me. Just at the wrong moment I spoke to him sharply, and—well, there you are. And the worst of it is, we can't give the young beggar the chastisement he deserves. I should only make a laughingstock of myself if I were to attempt to have him taught the error of his ways."

Kilby nodded.

"You can't very well collar and cuff him," he said, smiling. "Anyhow, we mustn't forget that he's helped us considerably. He's prevented Peters from finding the empty shell; and that must have caused the worthy doctor no small amount of worry. Had Peters been able to recover it we should still be working under the delusion, you know that the shot had been fired from the other compartment. In fact, it's doubtful if we should ever have been able to discover the truth."

"Yes," assented Parker, after a thoughtful pause, "we certainly owe the young imp a debt, whatever his intentions may have been. It was he, too, who showed us that the window had been broken twice. If his inquisitive eyes hadn't—"

"Just a minute, Parker."

Kilby suddenly grasped the telephone, rang up the exchange, and asked to be put through immediately to Scotland Yard.

"Parker," he said, turning to that astonished official, "just scribble the doctor's address on a piece of paper, will you?

"Send some men at once to 99A, Wimpole Street to arrest a man known as Doctor Peters!" he was soon shouting into the transmitter. "Don't lose time over a warrant or any other formality. Haste is everything. Ring me up again the moment the job's been carried out."

He put down the instrument and returned to his seat.

"Let's take things easy until we hear from the Yard," he said. "I can't concentrate my mind on anything till I learn that the arrest has been made."

But he wasn't allowed to take things easy for long. In a very short time he was again summoned to the instrument. Picking up the receiver, he was prepared to learn that the arrest had been made in record time. But the voice at the other end soon dashed his hopes to the ground.

"There must be some mistake," was the message carried to him along the wires. "There's neither a Doctor Peters nor a 99A anywhere in Wimpole Street."

"Damn!" was Inspector Kilby's forcible comment. To Parker he said:

"Both name and address are false. Peters has stolen a march on us. I was a fool, though, to have anticipated otherwise."

Inspector Parker moved over to a cupboard and returned with a bottle and three glasses.

"A good stiff whisky-and-soda seems to be the only suitable answer to that," he said. "Brent, bring the siphon, will you?"

Differences of status were forgotten or ignored, and in a short time the three men were drinking to the toast of: "Doctor Peters." But on Kilby's suggestion they held their glasses in their left hands.

"You gave it as your opinion this morning, Parker, said Kilby, when three cigars were well alight, "that it was young Pardoe who opened the carriage window last night. Have you found out whether it was really he?"

"I've discovered that I was wrong. It wasn't the boy. His father told me—and I have no reason to doubt his word—that the boy wasn't out after seven o'clock last night. He stayed in doing his homework, and when he had finished that he went to bed. Soon afterwards the boy's mother found the expelled shell."

Kilby's fingers strayed towards each other.

"Then," he declared with conviction "the man who opened the window and entered the compartment was Doctor Peters. It shows how desperately anxious he was to recover that shell. He must have known that it wasn't there or he would have found it on the way to Derwent Junction, yet, as a forlorn hope, he had another look for it last night. His over-anxiety may well be his downfall. You see, Parker, how he's given himself away, don't you?"

For a few moments Parker neither moved nor spoke. Then he shook his head.

"I don't quite see what you mean," he confessed.

"Why, if the man examined the compartment last night, as I'm convinced he did, it's pretty certain that he doesn't live in London. We already know that he doesn't reside in Wimpole Street, and I think we can safely go a step farther and assume that no London address would find him." He paused before continuing: "Of course, after all, that's only conjecture. It may be that it was a confederate who made the search last night." He drained his glass and set it down. "And it was probably Peters or a confederate who threw the pistol into the tunnel. One can now understand the absence of fingerprints on the weapon, for, of course, there was no hurry in disposing of it, and gloves were used. Oh, by the way, you're quite sure that this empty shell belongs to the pistol?"

"Yes." Inspector Parker again opened the drawer and withdrew the pistol. "See for yourself," he said, removing the clip from the butt of the weapon. The pistol contained a six-shot magazine. One cartridge was in the chamber, and four were in the clip. Parker snapped the empty shell into one of the vacant spaces. "See for yourself," he repeated.

Kilby soon assured himself that all the cartridges—the full ones and the empty one—were identical in every particular.

Handing back the pistol, he took a notebook from his pocket and glanced through its contents. Now and then he pencilled an addition to what was already written.

"The fog has lifted considerably," he observed, as he put the book away. "It's still pretty thick, though. Knowing how the murder was committed, however, ought to enable us to penetrate the mystery. Let's see how much we know for certain, and how much is merely surmise. We have at least two facts to prove that the shot was fired from the compartment behind that in which Mr. Hyde travelled—the marks made by the bullet in the tapestry, and the expelled shell. That Doctor Peters fired the shot is, however, only conjecture. But, no! It's more than that. Had another person used the pistol he would not have left the shell for the boy to find. But Peters hadn't had sufficient time to make the necessary search. After smoothing over the tapestry and giving a hasty glance round for the cartridge, he found it necessary to hurry to the next compartment and take charge of the dead body. You see, if he'd delayed, and there happened to be another doctor on the train, he might never have had the opportunity to travel to Blackton alone with the murdered man. And that, I fancy, would have wrecked the whole carefully-planned scheme. He would have been unable to conceal the bullet-hole in the tapestry on Mr. Hyde's side, and he would have been compelled to leave the window as it was. More important still, there would have been no chance to rob the dead body, in which case, of course, the murder would have been worse than useless."

"To which category," asked Parker, "does the robbery of the body belong—fact or conjecture?"

"Conjecture, naturally. But the conjecture is so strong that it almost amounts to certainty. If the motive were not robbery, then the murder would have been absolutely pointless. I'm sure you were right in your theory that the necklace was inside the tobacco pouch. And I'm equally certain that Peters abstracted them both."

He paused for some moments, then went on:

"He had the pistol in his pocket all the time. But I cannot see when or how he got rid of it. Did he return later and throw it inside the tunnel? Or did he pass it on to a confederate with instructions where it was to be placed? Now, who could have been the confederate, assuming that he had one? It couldn't have been Light-Fingered Freddie or the Midtown publican, so—" He broke off abruptly, and then exclaimed: "Parker, you say that Davis was hanging around this district that day. Davis had just been sacked... and the will was about to be altered. I shall really have to have a serious conversation with Jack Davis tomorrow."

But when he sought the young man on the following morning, he was informed that both he and Connie Hyde had left Blackton by an early train.

Chapter 18

Kilby Receives a Lesson

"She looks a dashed fine girl," remarked Inspector Kilby. "We must really stop and have a word with her, Brent."

Police Constable Brent, suspecting that he was being chaffed, stole a surreptitious glance at the Scotland Yard officer. But he failed to detect even the flicker of an eyelash.

They had just left Jack Davis's temporary lodging, and were walking back towards the police-station, when they saw Freda Lowe approaching with her usual athletic stride. George had not spoken to her since that unforgettable moment when their lips had clung together. He ardently wished that this present meeting were more private; but he couldn't very well ask Inspector Kilby to play the part of a loyal 'gooseberry' and go in search of a tobacconist's shop.

Freda called out a cheery "Good morning!" and halted. Kilby saw at once that his decision to speak was unnecessary: the girl would have stopped even if it had been his desire to go on.

"Found the birds flown, haven't you?" she enquired, after a short desultory conversation.

"Birds!" repeated Kilby, with a smile. "I'm a detective, not a bird-catcher," he flippantly added.

"Same thing. You spread the net, and the foolish naughty birds are soon inside it. Isn't that so, Mr. Kilby?"

"Only the foolish ones, Miss Lowe. And most of the naughty ones are wise. But, no doubt, you have some particular birds in mind?"

Freda nodded and smiled.

"I mean Connie Hyde and Mr. Davis, of course. You're just coming from Mr. Davis's place, aren't you?"

"Yes, that's where we've been."

"And I," said the girl, "am coming from Connie's. But I found that she had gone."

"Same here." Kilby's smiling eyes looked straight into the clear blue ones of the girl. "Perhaps, Miss Lowe, they are two of the wise birds."

"Just listen to how he twists my innocent remark," laughed Freda, addressing her remark to the silent Brent. "I can see that I shall have to be careful what I say. Don't you think so?"

Brent nodded.

"Uncle all right?" he asked. He was painfully conscious that the question was totally inadequate to the occasion; but the young policeman, like many another in similar circumstances, was experiencing the tongue-tying effects of the presence of his lady-love in conjunction with that of a third person. If only Kilby were not there things would be so different, he told himself. One would not then be obliged to weigh every word one said. A free rein to heart and tongue was all that would be needed.

"Uncle's in the pink," answered Freda. "But his pottery has been sadly neglected of late. He will keep worrying his poor old head over the murder."

"But why should he worry?" put in Kilby.

The girl smiled and shrugged her shapely shoulders.

"Perhaps worry isn't the right word," she amended. "But he keeps puzzling his brains, trying to find a solution to the mystery. I expect he's particularly interested in this case because I happened to be on the scene. But, apart from that, he loves tackling mysteries—crime mysteries. Hasn't George or Inspector Parker told you?"

Kilby nodded before Brent could reply.

"I believe one or other of them did mention it," he admitted. "But, of course, there's nothing unusual in your uncle's interest. Most people have a sneaking regard for criminals."

"Uncle's interest is more than just ordinary curiosity," Freda insisted, as though anxious to separate the old potter from the common ruck. "He's what's generally called a student of crime. Do you know," she went on, again turning to Brent, "he agrees with you about the broken window. And he also agrees that it must have been Doctor—Doctor—oh, yes, Doctor Peters who broke it."

Kilby laughed, whilst Brent looked as uncomfortable as he felt.

"There you are, Brent," said Kilby. "Your deductions confirmed by a keen student of crime! What more could man desire?" His banter concealed the thought that love had gone to Brent's tongue as well as to his head.

Freda's gaze travelled from one man to the other.

"Have I said too much?" she asked in mild dismay. "Have I given away—?"

She stopped. Kilby finished her question before answering it.

"Given away Brent? Not at all, Miss Lowe. No one could possibly blame him for discussing the affair with such a charming confidante. And as for your uncle—well, Miss Lowe, I've heard so much about him that I have no doubt I should find it both pleasant and profitable to discuss the murder with him. The official mind, you know, is apt to become stereotyped, whereas your uncle's brains are free from the trammels of routine."

"What!" cried Freda like a highly-delighted child. "You really mean it? Uncle will almost go off his head with joy. Why, for days both he and I have been fishing for this very thing, but George and his inspector were both too cautious to nibble. Let's go to him at once before you have time to change your mind."

Kilby smiled at her eagerness. "Let's," he agreed.

Three abreast, they walked along towards the potter's cottage. As they passed the North Eastern station, Kilby stopped as though he were about to make some remark. But, obviously thinking better of it, he resumed the journey without a break in the general conversation.

Police Constable Brent was feeling in a happy mood. His fear that Kilby would blame him for discussing the murder with an outsider was a thing of the past. Was not Kilby himself about to do the very same thing?

From the gate they saw old Dick sitting before his wheel at the open doorway of the shed. Freda ran on in front.

"Uncle," she called gaily, in tones loud enough for the other two to hear, "take off your hat and bow nicely to the gentlemen. Here's the famous Scotland Yard detective come to talk to you about the tunnel murder. You did a good stroke of business when you agreed with Constable Brent about the broken window. I'm sure that's what persuaded Mr. Kilby to do you this honour."

The potter rose to his feet, picked up a piece of sacking, and commenced to rub the clay from his hands. Freda moved off towards the door of the cottage, and Brent, in obedience to an almost imperceptible nod from Kilby, followed her.

"Delighted to meet you, Mr. Kilby!" cried old Dick, advancing with outstretched hand. But, before Kilby had a chance to grasp it, it was quickly withdrawn. "Too dirty to touch yours," explained the potter, a genial smile on his wrinkled old face. "But I hope you'll take the will for the deed."

"Certainly," replied Kilby. "However, I don't want you to imagine that I'm too fastidious to touch clay. As a boy I loved to play with it, and clay-modelling was the lesson I liked best at school. But I was never able to realise my ambition to model something on the wheel: the school wasn't fortunate enough to possess one."

Old Dick again laughed.

"A pretty plain hint," he chuckled. "You want to try your skill now? All right, then. See if you can do this."

He set the wheel in motion, picked a lump of clay out of a zinc bin, and threw it with unerring aim right on the center of the rotating disc.

"That's called throwing or centering, he explained. If the clay isn't centered properly to start with, you can't expect to turn out a symmetrical vessel. Like to have a shot at it?"

Kilby smilingly accepted the good-natured challenge. Taking off his coat, he rolled up his sleeves. Old Dick handed him the lump of clay which he had just removed from the wheel.

Inspector Kilby's first efforts at 'throwing' were no better and no worse than those of most amateurs. His first throw might have been intended for the outer circumference of the wheel, so accurately did it stick there. The second was slightly better, and after about a dozen attempts he was able to centre with a fair degree of accuracy.

"Not so easy as it seems, eh?" grinned old Dick. "But you haven't done at all badly. Had enough, I suppose?"

"Not half enough," replied Kilby with perfect truth. Already the fascination of the potter's wheel had gripped him, as it grips all who try to use it, and, for the moment, he forgot the object of his visit. "I wish you'd let me try to make something."

"Want to fly before you can even walk, eh?" chaffed the old potter. "As you will. But on your head be the consequences. Well, here goes. Watch carefully."

A water-tight trough surrounded the horizontal wheel, and in the trough was a small enamel bowl, half-filled with water. When the clay had been centred, old Dick dipped his hands in the water and then placed the tips of his bent fingers together. Next he brought his wrists towards each other until the fleshy pads at the base of the thumbs were touching. Within the rough circle thus formed by his hands he enclosed the rapidly revolving clay.

"Now watch closely," he counselled again.

What followed was like a conjurer's trick. With a steady motion, the old potter raised his hands until they were several inches above the wheel. Then he gave a sudden twist to his right hand, turning it palm downwards. For a fraction of a second he held it thus, then he removed both hands and took his foot off the treadle.

On the wheel reposed a truncated cone, perfectly smooth and perfectly symmetrical.

Kilby's gaze wandered from old Dick to his handiwork and back again.

"Is this," he asked, "an example of the potter's art, or is it pure sleight of hand?"

The mild sensation he had created obviously afforded the potter a considerable amount of pleasure, and he laughed so loudly that the sound of his laughter reached the ears of those inside the cottage.

"Why, that's as simple as falling off a stool," was his cheery reply. "But it's very important. The truncated cone is the foundation, so to speak, of many examples of the potter's art. Like to try your hand at it?"

Kilby nodded, and the other removed the cone from the wheel and squeezed it into a shapeless lump. "Here you are," said Dick passing it over.

When Kilby had finished with the clay, some ten minutes later, it shape was very little better than when he had begun. As a relief map showing mountains and valleys, it might have passed muster, but it was a hopeless failure as a cone. True, it was broader at the base than at the top, but its sloping sides were ridged and indented, without any regard to symmetry.

Kilby looked up, to find an expansive grin on the old potter's face.

"Don't be too disgusted with yourself," said the old man encouragingly. "Every beginner finds himself in the same fix. He doesn't know the correct amount of pressure to apply with his hands, or how to apply it evenly. That, however, soon comes with practice."

"May I hope that you'll allow me the necessary practice?" Kilby suddenly asked; "not now, of course, but some other time."

For an instant old Dick seemed to hesitate, but only for an instant.

"It would give me much pleasure," he answered courteously. "Come whenever you like. I may say, however, that you are the only person I have ever allowed to touch this wheel. But—well, it isn't every day one is privileged to tutor such a famous detective."

Disclaiming the adjective, Kilby proceeded to rub off some of the clay that had collected on his hands.

"Come and wash them," invited the potter. "There's a tap at the other end of the shed."

But Kilby shook his head.

"I wouldn't wash them for worlds," he said. "Inspector Parker is a bit of a sceptic, and he'll never believe that I've been engaged in making pottery unless my hands bear the sign of my labours."

"Can't help his troubles," insisted the other good-naturedly. "You've got to wash them. That is," he added, "unless you are prepared to offend Freda by refusing refreshments. That's why she skipped off so quickly, you know. Like me, she doesn't mean to let pass the opportunity of entertaining a real live detective. Of course, it's still too early for lunch; but if you were to go inside the cottage now I have no doubt you would find Brent engaged in the very homely duty of helping Freda to draw corks and arrange biscuits in such a way that a few look like a lot."

Kilby was about to offer a courteous refusal, when he remembered that he had not yet discussed the tunnel mystery with the old man.

"It's really too kind of you and your niece," he said. "But I'm not such a fool as to deprive myself of the pleasure."

"Good. Then let's get ready. The tap's over here."

He led the way to the back of the shed, and stood beside Kilby while he washed his hands at the tap. Kilby was about to use a towel that was hanging on a nail when he found a brush pushed into his hands.

Better use this," advised old Dick. "Clay under the nails is neither comfortable nor pleasant to look at."

Kilby thanked him and used the nailbrush. Old Dick, who merely used a piece of sacking on his own hands, watched him use the towel when the scrubbing was finished.

"Plenty of room here, I see," observed Kilby, as he turned down his shirtsleeves and surveyed the end of the shed in which they stood.

Near the corner on the left were several petrol tins; whilst at the other corner stood two sheets of corrugated iron, placed lengthwise and arranged at right angles to each other. Between the petrol tins and the sheets of iron stood the mongrel motor car, its radiator facing the doorway.

The tolerant smile that Kilby bestowed on the ancient vehicle did not escape the keen eyes of the old potter.

"Not so bad as she looks," he remarked, grinning. "True, she does rattle a bit; but she goes at any rate."

"At any rate!" echoed Kilby, with a grin that matched old Dick's. Then he moved closed to the corrugated iron.

"My furnace," explained the other, indicating a brick-and-mortar structure inside the improvised barrier. "The iron's used to keep sparks from getting near the petrol."

The sheets were merely propped against each other, and, as he spoke, he pushed them apart and allowed them to drop flat on the floor.

Then he pointed out how the furnace worked. Kilby was an interested listener while Dick showed and explained the draught and the damper, the muffle, the spyhole, the temperature cones, and other items of interest. But Kilby observed other things. He noted, for example, that that corner of the shed was constructed of bricks, whereas the rest of the shed was made of wood. That, of course, was to obviate the risk of fire. And he noticed a little heap of ashes that had fallen from, or been raked out of, the furnace. He had observed it particularly, because the ashes had blown about a little while the old man was manipulating the arrangement that regulated the draught. He moved slightly forward, and his knee brushed against the wall of the furnace.

Pulling a handkerchief from his pocket, he proceeded to flick the dust off the knee of his trousers. But he held the handkerchief so carelessly that it dropped on the heap of ashes.

Bending down, he picked up the handkerchief and nonchalantly returned it to his pocket.

Chapter 19

The Forced Staple

"Well, what's your latest discovery?" asked Freda, when she and Brent had reached the cosy sitting-room of the little cottage.

George smiled and shook his head.

"Nothing much," he replied. "But let's try to forget the affair for a little while. You may be sure that your uncle and Inspector Kilby are doing more than enough talking for the lot of us."

Now that he had Freda to himself, George wanted to discuss something more agreeable than a sordid murder in a dark tunnel. Moreover, a slight tightening of Kilby's lips while he signalled to him to follow the girl could only mean an injunction to keep his mouth shut. Evidently Kilby had decided to maintain secrecy even in the presence of such trustworthy persons as old Dick and his niece. But, then, was not secretiveness an obsession of Scotland Yard? Yet Kilby's avowed intention was to discuss the mystery with the old potter...

Freda nodded, as though glad of an excuse to shelve an unpleasant topic. Thereafter, for some time, they talked only of themselves; their conversation was frequently punctuated by a silence that was even more pleasant than speech.

The sound of old Dick's ringing laugh reached them from the shed, and they broke apart. Rather, Freda disengaged herself as though the laugh were a signal.

"We're forgetting the others," she said, rising to her feet and commencing to bustle about. "Uncle's sure to make Inspector Kilby stay for refreshments. You may help me if you like, George."

Old Dick's conjecture was there and then proved correct, for the young constable really did draw corks and arrange biscuits. Freda, however, could have done the job much more quickly herself, George's efforts proving a continual source of distraction.

When Kilby and the old potter entered the room their eyes were greeted by a shining array of bottles and glasses.

"What did I tell you?" laughed old Dick. "Freda would never have forgiven you if you'd refused to come in. Well, Mr. Kilby, what's your favourite poison? Sorry we can't offer you champagne or a cocktail, but there's port and Scotch. What do you say to a whisky-and-soda?"

Kilby and the old man had a whisky-and-soda each; and Brent had a port because Freda was having one.

It was Freda who poured the drinks. When the two guests were seated, Old Dick begged to be excused while he changed his jacket. He went into another room, and some minutes elapsed before he returned.

Freda glanced at her uncle, then smiled behind her hand at Kilby. The second jacket was hardly more presentable than the first, and the change had obviously been made merely as a concession to convention. Kilby smiled back, as though appreciating the joke as well as the compliment.

When the empty glasses had been drained and set down, Kilby produced his cigarette-case.

"A cigarette, Miss Lowe?" he invited. "Or is it that chocolates are your usual dissipation?"

"A cigarette, please," she replied, reaching over and taking one. "I detest chocolates."

"Miss Lowe made me so interested that I felt I had to see you," said the inspector to his host, when three cigarettes and a pipe were sending clouds of smoke floating about the room. "She tells me that you are a keen student of crime and are trying to solve the tunnel mystery. Well, so am I; and since we are both in the same boat it occurred to me that we ought to pull together—provided you are willing, of course."

"Willing!" ejaculated old Dick. "Why, nothing could possibly give me greater pleasure. And I'm sure I need hardly mention that I consider it an honour to be privileged to discuss the matter with a man of your attainments."

Kilby inclined his head.

"Well, to begin," he said. "Perhaps it will be better if I first summarise the facts in my possession. Afterwards, with the various details fresh in our minds, we ought to be able to talk things over more intelligently."

Then, beginning with the correspondence that was exchanged between Mr. Hyde and Sir Joshua Jordan, he rapidly outlined a summary of many of the known events that had preceded and followed the murder. Constable Brent, who was an interested listener, observed that several minor details were omitted altogether, perhaps because they were too trifling. Some facts were just mentioned and passed over, whilst a few others were emphasized. The young constable was quick to notice that nothing was mentioned which the potter could not be presumed to know already, and he was now fully convinced that Kilby meant to disclose nothing that could safely be kept in the background.

"I think we are all agreed that it was the doctor who broke it," said old Dick when the broken window was mentioned.

Kilby nodded.

"There can be little doubt of that. And it's pretty clear that he meant the world to believe that the pistol was thrown through the window while the train was still in the tunnel. But it's difficult to estimate the extent of his guilt or complicity. We now know that the weapon was not thrown through the window at all. But how did it get to the spot where we found it? Brent says that it was thrown by someone standing near the mouth of the tunnel. But by whom? The doctor could hardly have done it, for we know that he continued his journey on the same train."

Old Dick carefully studied the matter.

"No," he agreed at last. "The doctor couldn't have done it. It almost seems," he went on, after another thoughtful pause, "as though Peters had a confederate."

"That's what I've been thinking, Mr. Lowe. But how was the weapon passed on to the confederate? And who passed it on?"

"It could have been passed on in one way," replied the potter; "and only in one way, as far as I can see. The moment the alarm had made the guard stop the train, all the passengers left their seats and gathered round in a crowd. The trick could have been done then. In the excitement it would have been an easy matter for someone to slip back and throw the pistol where Brent afterwards found it. The train stopped quite close to the tunnel, you know."

"By Jove!" exclaimed Kilby. "That's a very plausible theory. While everything was in a state of confusion, Peters quietly handed the gun to someone standing conveniently near."

There was a whimsical twinkle in the potter's eyes.

"You forget," he said, "that the doctor had no gun to hand over. He came straight on the scene from some other carriage, and almost immediately proceeded to see whether he could do anything for the murdered man. After that he didn't leave the compartment until Blackton was reached."

Kilby shrugged his shoulders.

"Of course," he conceded. "How stupid of me!"

The potter smiled. Kilby had dropped in his estimation.

In Brent's opinion, Kilby was either engaged in the vulgar practice of leg-pulling or was allowing the conversation to take its present course in the hope that some shrewd observation of the old potter might serve to shed light on what was a very real mystery. Kilby had just agreed that the doctor had never had the pistol in his possession. Yet Brent knew Kilby's real opinion to be the exact reverse.

"Anyhow," said Dick "the murderer is far more important than the accomplice, if, indeed, Peters was really an accomplice. In your opinion, Mr. Kilby, which of the two men did it?"

"You refer to the two men who travelled in Mr. Hyde's compartment, of course? Really I must confess that I'm not yet able to fasten the guilt on either of them. Light-Fingered Freddie was unable or unwilling to give me any helpful information. And yesterday, just after it had opened for the evening, I visited the Red Reynard, where I stayed for nearly an hour. Nothing that I saw there gave any indication that the proprietor was the kind of man we are after. True, I saw several betting-slips being passed; but backing horses—even illicit backing—is very different from a carefully-planned murder. Before I left, I engaged Mr. Lofthouse in conversation. He told me, or seemed to tell me, all he knew, which was very little. He mentioned the flash he had seen, and he was positive that it hadn't had its origin in the compartment in which he was travelling."

"Very puzzling," said the potter. "Very puzzling, indeed. But if the publican fired the shot, he'd naturally do all he could to mislead you. On the other hand, he may be right. Lightning plays strange pranks, and a flash may have entered the tunnel. But, then, how is it no one saw the flash of the pistol? Again, if he's right in saying that the flash was not in his compartment, there's the likelihood that it came from the fire-box of the engine. Have you enquired whether the fireman did any stoking while he was passing through the tunnel?"

"No, I haven't," answered Kilby. "That's another point I've missed."

The old potter knocked the ashes out of his well-seasoned pipe, and proceeded to refill it.

"I saw in this morning's paper," he casually remarked, "that all who travelled on that train on Monday, particularly those who were in compartments near that in which the murder was committed, are requested to communicate with Scotland Yard, with you here at Blackton, or with the nearest police-station. You were the instigator of that appeal, I presume?"

"Yes. And a similar one was broadcast by the B.B.C. last night before listeners were taken over to the Regal for dance music."

"Very ingenious!" smiled the potter, a mischievous twinkle in his eyes. "Of course, the murderer will now have no option but to come along and tell all about how he did it."

Kilby, too, smiled.

"I'm not quite so sanguine as that," he confessed. "But there may be someone who saw or heard something that might be useful to us. For example, if the pistol were really handed to an accomplice in the crowd, someone may have observed it. It's your opinion that that's what took place, isn't it?"

"Can't see any other explanation, Mr. Kilby. The murderer got rid of the weapon while the doctor was examining the body. If only we could discover the person to whom the pistol was passed, we should have found a valuable clue."

Kilby flicked the ash off his cigarette.

"Even without that knowledge," he said, "there's still a clue. Perhaps, not exactly a clue, but, still something to work on. I don't believe the weapon was placed in the tunnel until that night or early next morning. Now, the person who placed it there doesn't live far from this locality. I'm confirmed in this opinion, because on the night before last there was a peculiar happening which couldn't possibly have been the work of a total stranger. Someone entered one of the compartments of the coach that's in the sidings."

Kilby's unexpected announcement surprised the silent Brent. Brent had come to the conclusion that it was Kilby's policy to reveal nothing that could safely be concealed, but now he realised that he must have been mistaken. Because he had had no hand in making the discovery, Brent himself had kept this matter a secret.

The old potter's eyes opened to their fullest extent.

"Someone been in one of the compartments last night!" he exclaimed. "No need to ask which one, eh?"

Kilby smiled.

"That's where you are wrong," he said. "It wasn't the compartment one would naturally expect, but the one immediately behind."

The information seemed to take old Dick completely by surprise.

"Good heavens, man!" he ejaculated. "That sounds like the action of a madman! What possible motive could anyone have in entering that compartment?" the old potter asked.

"Please ask me another," replied Kilby with a shrug. "Anyhow, here are the facts."

The potter listened with rapt attention while Kilby related how he had discovered that someone had been tampering with the carriage window. But before the recital had come to its natural conclusion, old Dick sprang to his feet in a state of obvious excitement.

"Are you sure that it was putty the fellow used?" he demanded abruptly.

Kilby sat thoughtful for a moment or two.

"Well, no," he admitted at last. "I can't say I am sure. But I assumed that it was putty."

"It wasn't!" declared the potter with conviction. "It was clay—potter's clay—my clay!"

His words caused a mild sensation in the breasts of Freda and Brent. Kilby, however, was outwardly calm.

"What makes you say that, Mr. Lowe?" he quietly asked.

"Because my shed was broken into that night. The doors are usually fastened with a hasp and padlock, and yesterday morning I discovered that a staple had been forced during the night and afterwards loosely replaced in its original position. I had a good look round, but couldn't discover that anything was missing, so I concluded that it was the work of one of those muffled youths whose sole idea of enjoyment seems to be confined to rough horse-play and the destruction of property. Now, however, it's pretty obvious that the burglar helped himself to some of my clay. Come and see the door for yourselves."

Leaving Freda inside, the three men went out to examine the door of the shed. A brief examination was sufficient to show that, as the potter had said, a staple had been forced and afterwards replaced without being hammered in. Kilby even observed in the woodwork a dent that had obviously been made by the end of some instrument that had been slipped through the opening of the staple and used as a lever. This dent seemed to have been made comparatively recently.

"Wonder what he used to do the forcing with?" said Kilby aloud. As though searching for a possible instrument, he moved round the corner of the shed and along by the end. He even turned the next corner, thus bringing the back into view. There he stood for some moments looking along the gravel path that led to the back door of the cottage, but he saw nothing to suggest a means by which the staple had been forced.

"Thought he might have dropped it somewhere about," he said to the potter, who had accompanied him. "But, evidently, he took the implement away with him. The mark in the door looks as though something like a poker had been used."

They retraced their steps to the door of the shed.

"Well, Mr. Kilby," asked the potter, "what do you make of things now?"

"I'm more than ever convinced that only a man who lives in this neighbourhood could have taken some of your clay the other night before going down to the railway sidings."

Old Dick inclined his head.

"Seems the only explanation," he agreed. "By the way," he went on, "couldn't you manage to get hold of a piece of the clay that was used on the window?"

Kilby did not immediately answer. After a few moments, he said:

"I've got hold of a piece already."

"Good! exclaimed old Dick. "Then, Mr. Kilby, you had better take a piece of my clay with you and compare the two."

"A very sensible suggestion, Mr. Lowe. And I thank you for the offer." A faraway look came into his eyes, and some moments elapsed before he continued: "We mustn't make the mistake of confining this neighbourhood to too small an area. Donmoor's not so very far away, and I consider that it ought to be included."

"Yes? But why Donmoor?"

"Because that's where Mr. Hyde obtained the necklace, seemingly the cause of the whole trouble. Donmoor ought to provide us with a good starting-place for our next line of investigations. And I have the feeling that Sir Joshua Jordan didn't tell me all he knew. I think the best thing I can do is to take the afternoon train to Donmoor, and see whether I can induce Sir Joshua to speak out."

"Mightn't be a bad idea," old Dick assented.

Soon afterwards, Inspector Kilby and Police Constable Brent took their departure, the potter expressing the wish that they would soon pay him another visit and let him know what progress was being made. Brent took a hasty farewell of Freda at the cottage door.

Mothers-in-law, though they cannot be ignored, are seldom respected. But a man always likes to be able to feel proud of his father-in-law or uncle-in-law. Brent was no exception.

"Well, sir," he ventured, as he walked along by Kilby's side, "what do you think of Mr. Lowe?"

"I think he's a very, very clever man, Brent," answered Kilby, hurrying along.

Kilby was hurrying because he wished to lose no time in sending a message to the Chief Constable of Donmoor.

Chapter 20

A Knock-Out Blow

There was really no mystery about the early-morning departure of Connie Hyde and Jack Davis. They had left Blackton to attend the funeral of the girl's father, whose body had been conveyed to London by motor-hearse the previous day.

When the funeral was over, they attended the reading of the will, to learn, as they had expected, that, save for a few minor bequests, everything had been left to Connie.

Later, Jack discussed the terms of the will with the keen-faced, bespectacled lawyer, while Connie went to confer with the servants. Jack explained how death had prevented the proposed altering of the will, and then asked:

"Would such a will have been legal? I fancy I've heard someone say that a will which forbids a person to marry can be set aside by the Law Courts."

The lawyer removed his spectacles and polished them with a silk handkerchief.

"The will would have been perfectly legal," he said. "If it were to stipulate that Miss Hyde should remain a spinster all her life, it could have been set aside. But that had not been Mr. Hyde's intention. The new will, had he lived long enough to make it and have it properly executed, would simply have contained the proviso that she was not to marry you under pain of being disinherited. It would have left her free to marry whomsoever else she pleased, and Mr. Hyde would have been perfectly justified—I mean legally justified—in making such a will. I make no comment on the moral right or wrong of the affair."

"Then," said Jack somewhat bitterly, "I had a very strong motive for murdering him."

The startled lawyer made a clever catch, and thus prevented his spectacles from clattering on to the polished surface of the table.

"God bless my soul!" he exclaimed. "What a peculiar observation! You're not joking, Mr. Davis? Because if you are..." The unfinished sentence conveyed in no unmistakable terms the lawyer's opinion of such an ill-timed joke.

"No. I'm not joking. Apart from the questionable taste of such misplaced levity, the affair's far too serious for that. But I am sure there's no need for me to remind you that in a case where direct proof of guilt is missing the question of motive is regarded as all-important by the police. I believe the Blackton inspector already suspects me. And I shouldn't be surprised if the Scotland Yard man thinks likewise."

"Pooh!" said the lawyer, after he had keenly scrutinised Jack's grave face. "You shouldn't let that worry you. Surely you can convince the police that you had no hand in the affair."

"It's not so easy as it sounds. On the afternoon of the murder I spent several hours alone among the Derbyshire hills. But I can't prove it, for, as far as I know, not a soul saw me. As likely as not, the police will assume that I was at the tunnel and will take steps to prove their assumption. And I shouldn't be surprised if they succeeded. Many a man has been convicted on circumstantial evidence before now."

"True. But only when the evidence left no room for doubt. And in your case there seems to be a very strong element of doubt. What do you propose to do about it, though?"

"As far as I can see, there is only one thing for me to do, and that is to endeavour to discover the murderer. Already I am working on a clue that promises to lead somewhere."

The old lawyer held out his hand.

"I wish you the best of luck," he said. "And permit me to offer you a final word of advice. Don't allow your imagination to magnify mole-hills into mountains. If the police really thought that you were in any way responsible for the murder, you would not be sitting here with me now."

They rose to their feet, and Jack picked up his hat. After thanking the lawyer for his kindly words of encouragement, the young man went in search of Connie.

Fifteen minutes later, they were on their way to St. Pancras, for it was their intention to return to Blackton and remain there until the mystery was solved, or until all hope of its solution had been abandoned.

Mr. Hyde's place of residence was not far from the British Museum, and, as they had plenty of time at their disposal, Connie and Jack decided to walk to St. Pancras.

Deep in conversation, they strolled along Gower Street, towards Euston Square, where they turned to the right. But, although their conversation was engrossing, Connie was able to devote an occasional glance to the shop windows along Euston Road. Not far from Euston Station, she abruptly stopped, and gripped Jack by the arm.

"Seen something that's taken your fancy?" he smiled, allowing himself to be pulled towards the window of a jeweller's shop.

Contrary to Jack's expectation, it was not an article of personal adornment that had claimed the girl's attention. One window of the shop contained a glittering array of jewellery of all descriptions; the other was devoted to household articles, mainly silver or silver-mounted—cases of cutlery, cruets, dishes, bronzes, bowls, and dozens of other articles that were useful or ornamental. But all the objects were not silver, or even silver-mounted. There were many examples of the potter's art that did not have to depend for their beauty on the addition of a precious metal.

It was to this window that Connie steered Jack, and her gaze was concentrated on a particular vase.

"What do you think of the design, Jack?" she asked.

"Beautiful," he answered, after a short scrutiny. "Beautiful—but horrible."

The design showed two intertwined serpents, their free heads upraised as though preparing to strike.

"Yes," she agreed, "it is rather horrible. But do you think it's rare?"

"Can't say, old girl. But I don't remember ever having seen anything quite like it before—not on a vase at any rate. Why do you ask, though?"

"Because I've seen the design before. Rather, I've seen something very much like it, though not quite. In the other design the fangs were protruding from the open mouths of the serpents. Here, you will observe, the fangs are not showing. Jack," she went on, "I saw the other design on a vase at Mr. Lowe's—the old potter's, you know. Freda showed me round the cottage the other day, and I noticed the vase while she hastily opened and closed a cupboard door."

Jack laughed.

"But, darling," he said, "what are you so mighty serious about? This vase is exposed for sale, and anyone who is willing to pay the price can have it. No doubt the Blackton potter bought the specimen you saw."

"I don't think so. A potter doesn't usually buy pottery. Moreover, Freda started to talk about the vase when I mentioned that I'd seen it, and she declared that the design was her uncle's and had never been used by anyone else."

Jack looked dubious.

"It looks none too original," he objected. "Anyhow, it wouldn't be very difficult for someone to copy the old chap's design—or the other way round."

The proprietor came to the door, and they moved away; but not before Jack had glanced at the name above the door.

"John Smith!" he said, when they had got beyond earshot of the man at the door. "If features are anything to judge by, he spelt his name differently in the past."

They arrived at St. Pancras with several minutes still to spare, so they sat on a seat which happened to be close to a heap of parcels and boxes that were being carried off the platform to the railway delivery van.

"Good gracious!" Connie suddenly exclaimed. "Another reminder of Blackton and our friend, the potter!" She pointed to a stout wooden box which the removal of a parcel had just exposed. "I saw that box at Mr. Lowe's cottage."

Jack's smiling eyes regarded her excited face.

"You are simply wallowing in mystery, Connie," he chided. "One box is very much like another of the same size, and how in the world can you tell whether you have ever seen that particular one before?"

"I can, because of those rings," she replied with conviction.

On one side of the box were two concentric circles that had been burned into the wood, seemingly by the red-hot ends of two hollow cylinders of different diameters.

Jack was able to move over and glance at the address on the box before a porter came up and carried it away.

"There's some sort of connection, right enough," he said, somewhat ambiguously. "That box was addressed to our friend John Smith, back on the Euston Road."

Connie remained silent for some moments, and then she broke into a sudden laugh.

"Jack," she confessed, "you were right when you said that I am wallowing in mystery. But this little mystery is cleared up now. Freda Lowe told me that a London jeweller disposed of some of her uncle's best work. That vase we saw in the window was really made by the old potter. And we've just seen another consignment about to be delivered. John Smith, the Euston Road jeweller, must surely be the man to whom Freda alluded."

"And now there's no reason why intertwined snakes and concentric circles should keep you awake tonight, darling."

They had tea on the train, and, when they had lighted cigarettes, Jack asked:

"Connie, dear, do you mind if I ask you to continue the journey from Derwent Junction alone?"

Connie removed her cigarette from between her lips and blew the ash off the tip.

"Why, Jack?" she presently enquired.

"Because I should like to make further enquiries at Hartby. We cut short our investigations, you may remember, when we picked up the false clue in connection with the tickets booked at Little Faston. How full of hope we were as we rushed back to that station!"

"Yes, Jack. And how like a pair of burst bubbles we felt when we learned that it was a girl who had purchased the suspected ticket! But what good do you expect to do by going to Hartby again?"

"I don't believe there's anything further to be learned at the L.M.S. station. But there's the North Eastern, you know. Have you forgotten your first theory that Peters had returned to Donmoor by that line?"

"No, I haven't forgotten. But why can't you wait till tomorrow, Jack?"

"Because the longer I wait, dear, the more difficult will be my task. Peters may have been observed by someone, and I want to get hold of that someone before the doctor's appearance has faded from his memory."

Rain had commenced to fall since their departure from St. Pancras, and for some minutes Connie seemed to be watching the raindrops pattering against the windowpanes.

"Jack," she said at last, "I'm going with you to Hartby."

"You are not," retorted Jack with blunt kindliness. "You've had a very trying day, darling, and are badly in need of some rest. Now, Connie, old girl, don't insist. If you do I shall simply postpone the visit to Hartby."

Realising that he meant to be firm, Connie reluctantly gave way. Truth to tell, she was really physically tired, and her nerves were so jangled that only a good sleep could put her right again.

"It's possible that you may have some visitors before I get back," said Jack as the train neared Derwent Junction. "Inspector Parker or the Scotland Yard man may come along asking questions, and if they do—well, dear, I leave it to your discretion to put them off as best you can. Try not to give anything away, for we must endeavour to see this thing through ourselves.

Connie smilingly promised to curb her chattering propensity, and soon afterwards the train drew in at Derwent Junction. Before this, however, they had bidden each other good night, in the usual lovers' way.

"I know I shan't see you again until morning," said Jack. "Even if I get back from Hartby in good time, I shan't disturb your rest, so don't expect me, but go to bed."

At Hartby North Eastern Station Jack Davis was unable to learn anything that promised to throw light on the movements of the man he sought. He described the doctor to porters and various officials, but none of them had seen him, or, if they had, they had forgotten.

The only information the booking clerks could give him was that the clerk who had issued tickets at the Donmoor window on Monday afternoon and evening was now off duty. Jack obtained this man's address, and set off to interview him.

His labour was in vain, however, for the clerk, though he received him courteously, could tell him nothing about the pseudo-doctor.

Dispirited, he walked back towards the North Eastern station, intending from there to travel to Blackton. One slender hope still remained, he told himself. On the morrow he would go to Donmoor—and to all the stations between Donmoor and Highpen Tunnel, if necessary. Perhaps at one of those places he might find someone who had seen Peters on Monday afternoon, or, better still, since Monday afternoon.

With no very firm foundation, Jack still doggedly stuck to his theory, or, rather, Connie's theory, that Doctor Peters belonged to Donmoor or to somewhere in its vicinity.

He turned up his coat collar, for the rain was coming down in a soaking drizzle. Dusk was falling, and numerous street lamps winked into sudden brilliance. Walking close to the edge of the pavement, he had almost reached the station when a motor car coming from behind dashed past between the kerb and a crawling tram-car. A shower of muddy water splashed him, and, instinctively, he cast a quick glance at the cause of his unwelcome ablution.

He was too late to catch a glimpse of the driver's face, for the car was already some yards in front; but the car itself caused him to come to an abrupt halt.

It was the car that had nearly knocked him down outside Donmoor a few days before.

All Jack's senses were immediately on the alert. Though there was no reason whatever why a car should not have been seen at Donmoor one day and at Hartby a few days later, and though there was not a scrap of evidence to connect the car or its driver with the murder of Mr. Hyde, yet Jack's suspicions were instantly aroused.

A hundred yards ahead, the car swerved across the road, and took a turning on the right. Without pausing to reflect that the chase seemed utter madness, Jack suddenly determined to follow the vehicle.

Luck was with him. When he reached the road on the right, he saw that it was narrow and unfrequented. The tracks of only one set of tyres showed on the road, and he was quick to note that the studs of one of the tyres formed the well-known swastika design. Though the car was out of sight, it ought to be easy to follow it, provided its destination was some part of Hartby.

The street lamps enabled him to follow the trail, and fifteen minutes later he was standing outside a pair of large iron-studded doors set into a high limestone wall overshadowed by dripping trees.

The doors were securely fastened. But Jack soon discovered, further along the wall, a little door that was only latched. It squeaked as he pushed it open, but nevertheless he ventured through and closed the door behind him.

It was terribly dark, but he dared not risk striking a match. After a time, however, his eyes grew accustomed to the darkness, and he was able to discern the large pile of a building some distance in front. His ears took in the sound of the drip-drip from the trees, and once he fancied he heard a slight rustle behind an adjacent shrub.

"Only the wind," he tried to convince himself.

He moved cautiously forward. When he had passed the shrub, he heard the rustle repeated behind him, and he suddenly wheeled round.

But he was too late. Something descended on his head with a dull thud like a stick beating on a feather pillow.

Chapter 21

Footprints

D espite his plain hint to the old potter, Inspector Kilby did not travel to Donmoor by the early afternoon train.

On his return to the police-station, he immediately rang up the Chief Constable of Donmoor and asked for certain assistance. Then he filled in a telegraph form, addressed it to Stoke, and requested Inspector Parker to see that it was taken to the local post office without delay.

His next procedure was even more significant. He rang up Scotland Yard, and was soon in communication with the Assistant Commissioner.

"What's the idea, Kilby?" asked General Norman, when he had listened for some time. "You want us to send a wireless message to New York asking the authorities there to wireless back all the information they can about the notorious jewel-thief, Abraham S. Power, commonly known as 'Abie, the Mole'? But I was under the impression that Abie's activities had ceased some years ago."

"His activities seem to have ceased in the States. But, sir, he got his nickname because he's so sleek and works underground. In my opinion, he controls the gang that's working England now. We've got his record in the Index, you know, but it's rather sketchy, and I should like something more elaborate. Will you ask them, sir, to wireless Abie's photo as well, if they can manage it?"

"I'll do what I can, Kilby. Any developments in Blackton yet?"

"That's more than I'd care to say, sir. I've found some clues, of course, but I can't say yet whether they'll lead anywhere."

The Assistant Commissioner said Goodbye, and Kilby was about to put down the telephone when he heard the voice at the other end shout:

"Hello! Are you still there, Kilby?" Kilby signified that he was still ready to listen, and the voice at the other end went on: "I'd nearly forgotten to tell you that we came to a dead end tracing those banknotes. Several of our men have been on the job, as well as the local police from a number of counties, and there seems to have been little difficulty in picking up the trail of most of the notes. Unfortunately, however, all the different trails were soon lost again, because, in some cases, notes whose numbers were unknown came into the possession of some member of the gang. In other cases, valuable stones were purchased, and we are now up against a stone wall, with no chance of getting to the other side."

"Have you," asked Kilby after a thoughtful pause, "been able to get a description of the persons engaged in the various transactions?"

"Very unsatisfactory descriptions, Kilby. We have been able to establish the fact that at least three men were concerned, but in each case the description would suit anyone of ten thousand different persons. The only thing that seems certain about the affair is that a well-organised gang is at work."

"Abie, the Mole's gang," remarked Kilby, and then the conversation terminated.

Thereafter the two inspectors spent a considerable amount of time reviewing the case from every conceivable angle.

"One thing is now absolutely clear," said Kilby, "and that is that we are up against a clever gang of scoundrels. Such being the case, I think we can safely rule Jack Davis out of the affair. Of course, I still want to have a talk with him, and I shall make it my business to see him as soon as he gets back from London. Did I tell you that he and Miss Hyde went to London this morning to attend the funeral? He left word with his landlady to that effect. Miss Hyde, however, doesn't seem to have been so frank, for her friend, Miss Lowe, was obviously surprised at her absence."

"Funny," observed Parker. "I thought the two girls were very fast friends, considering the short time they had known each other."

Kilby smiled, but he made no reply.

"I suppose," went on Parker, seeing that the other did not mean to say anything further about the girls, "Light-Fingered Freddie and Lofthouse, the publican, may also be ruled out of the affair?"

"I don't know, Parker. We can safely assume that neither is a ring-leader, but either may be an accomplice."

At this point Parker broke the thread of the conversation by saying:

"While you were out this morning no fewer than seven Blackton people called here in answer to your appeal. I asked them to call back later, and I fancy I can hear one of them outside now."

"Not a bad response, Parker. And before I went out I had nearly the same number of telephone calls. But let's hear what the visitor has to say."

During the course of the next twenty minutes the seven people were interrogated, for Parker had mentioned the approximate time at which they were to return, and each was dismissed with a word of thanks.

The last person had hardly left the room when a telegram, addressed to Kilby, was brought in.

Kilby's face was devoid of expression as he tore open the buff envelope and read its contents. And not even a mind-reader could have read his thought as he handed the communication to Parker.

"This is from Stoke," he said—"from the managing director of Dean and Durham's pottery works."

The telegram briefly stated that Richard Lowe had been manager of a certain branch of the works until three years before when he had retired, to the regret of all who knew him. Soon afterwards he and his niece, Miss Freda Lowe, had left Stoke for an unknown destination.

Kilby laughed at the bewilderment on Parker's face.

"Surprises you, eh?" he enquired jokingly. "But it's only a sample of the Yard's thorough methods. I determined to find out all I could about every one who was even remotely connected with the crime, and as the potter's niece was in the compartment with Mr. Hyde I decided to verify the old chap's account of the life he lived before he came to Blackton. As you can see for yourself, this reply to my telegram proves that Richard Lowe and his niece are above suspicion."

Parker handed back the telegram, and suggested lunch. But Kilby shook his head.

"I am expecting a call from Donmoor at any moment," he explained, "and I must be here when it comes. Perhaps, though, you wouldn't mind letting me have some sandwiches in here."

The sandwiches were brought in and consumed; but Major Walters had not yet rung up Kilby. As the quarters chimed from a neighbouring church clock, it became obvious that Kilby was growing worried.

"The best-laid plans of mice and men..." he quoted sententiously. Rising to his feet, he thrust his hands in his pockets and commenced to pace up and down the room.

"Parker," he said, coming to a sudden halt, "I had an inspiration a day or two ago, but I was foolish enough to reject it. today I had another inspiration, which I determined to put to the test forthwith. I'm very much afraid it's been a false one, for—"

Just then there came a peremptory whirr from the telephone bell.

Kilby grabbed the instrument and clapped the receiver to his ear. For several moments he listened, and all Parker heard was an occasional exclamation or a question that conveyed no meaning to him.

When he had returned the receiver to its stand, Kilby sat down, leaned his elbows on the table, and stared at an ink-stain that disfigured its otherwise spotless surface. But he did not see the stain, and the tapping of his bridged fingers against one another seemed purely mechanical.

Presently he rang up the local telephone exchange and put some questions to the operator. But the frown with which he received the answers showed that they were unsatisfactory.

"Get me Victoria, 7000, please," he snapped.

He was soon in communication with Scotland Yard and giving instructions.

"Please get it done at once," he said, his request sounding like an ultimatum. "Ring me up again the moment you've found out."

Fifteen minutes later, during which time he managed to interview two more persons who had travelled on the ill-fated train on Monday afternoon, he was again listening to a voice from Scotland Yard.

"Can't be traced," said the invisible speaker. "The call was put through from a public telephone box near Russell Square."

"Damn!" snapped Kilby, forgetting that he was speaking into the transmitter.

"That's what I say, Kilby," came the laughing retort from the receiver.

Kilby was forced to echo the other's laugh.

Inspector Kilby steered the car through the Boxfield traffic and was soon out on the main Donmoor road.

There was a straight stretch in front, with very little traffic, and Kilby decided to test the capabilities of his borrowed car. He watched the indicator dance about and move upward, and at last he exclaimed:

"Sixty, Brent! This car wasn't made on the day God created crawling things."

"No, sir," agreed Brent with a grin. "She's a racing type, you know."

"So I see. You're used to an automatic, I suppose?" he added, flying off at a tangent.

"Yes. Think we shall need it, sir?"

In defiance of the law he was supposed to uphold, Kilby cut in between a heavy lorry and an approaching motorcycle.

"I hope not, Brent. But it's as well to be prepared. Sir Joshua might turn nasty if he's stroked the wrong way. And I shall probably ruffle his fur today."

After his second conversation with Scotland Yard, Kilby had decided to carry out the suggestion he had made to the old potter. Parker had offered the use of his fast little car, and Brent was being taken as a necessary precaution. Reaching Donmoor without mishap, they drove straight to the office of the Chief Constable. Kilby left Brent in charge of the car, while he, himself, jumped out and dashed up the half-dozen steps that led up to the office door.

When he returned, he gave Brent no indication of the nature of his errand, or its results.

"We'll garage the car, Brent," was all he said. "Then we'll go on foot to Hopeview House."

When they arrived at the gates of Sir Joshua's house, Kilby did not attempt to make use of the ordinary means of admittance. Instead, he walked along close to the wall for some distance until he reached a spot where a tree inside the grounds thrust out large overhanging branches.

"We ought to be able to get over here," he said. "I fancy the gates can be overlooked from one of the upstairs windows, and I don't wish to advertise my presence just yet. There's a little investigation I should like to make before announcing myself to Sir Joshua."

Waiting until no passer-by was in sight, for Kilby did not wish to be hampered by misplaced curiosity, they managed to climb up and clamber over the ten-foot wall. They found themselves in a wilderness of trees, shrubs, and tufted grass.

"Let's make for the drive," whispered Kilby. "Now, Brent," he said in the same cautious tone, as they caught sight of the drive between the trunks of two large trees, I want you to use your eyes and see if you can find any indication that anyone has been hiding around here within the last week or so."

Moving parallel to the drive and in line with each other, they steadily approached the house, keenly scrutinising the ground round the trees and shrubs as they advanced. But when the forbidding front of Hopeview House became visible, they were compelled to stop.

Kilby beckoned, and they quietly retraced their steps.

"Nothing on this side," he said, when they had got well away from the house. "Let's try the other."

At a point which they were sure could not be overlooked from the house they crossed the drive, and continued the search. This time their labours were quickly rewarded.

About midway between the house and the gates, and about half a dozen yards from the drive, was a large pine tree whose lower branches almost sprawled on the ground. As is usual with trees of this kind, the ground around it was bare of grass, but covered with a carpet of needles. On the side farthest from the drive the needles had been considerably disturbed, thus exposing many bare patches of moist earth. On these bare patches two different sets of footprints were plainly discernible.

"Just as I suspected," muttered Kilby, suppressing with difficulty his jubilant tone. "It occurred to me that it would have been much more sensible to rob Mr. Hyde of his money before he reached the house than to allow him to enter it and purchase the diamonds. How fortunate—or unfortunate—that he didn't walk from the gates as they had anticipated... Now I feel in a position to interview Sir Joshua. I think we'd better get back to the road."

He turned and moved off. But when he had gone a few paces, he became aware that Brent was not accompanying him. Wheeling round, he saw the young constable on hands and knees, his downbent face hardly a foot above the ground.

Kilby returned.

"What is it?" he asked in low tones.

Brent pointed to a set of footprints.

"Look at these, sir," he said. "You will notice that the impression is much deeper on the outside than on the inside."

Kilby, too, bent down.

"So it is, Brent," he concurred. "Those footprints were made by a man with bandy legs."

"That's what I thought, sir," said Police Constable Brent.

At a convenient spot they re-crossed the drive and moved towards the road.

"We'll go back the way we came," suggested Kilby. "Better open the gates from the outside in case they are under observation."

It was well that they took this simple precaution, for presently they discovered that the gates, including the wicket-gate, were locked or bolted on the inside, and, had they walked up to the house after their discovery of the footprints, it would have immediately become apparent to the inmates of Hopeview House that the wall had been scaled.

Kilby pressed an up-to-date bell-push which he found set into the wall high above the reach of mischievous boys.

After a long wait, they heard footsteps clumping towards the gates. Bolts were undrawn, a key grated in a lock, and the wicket-gate reluctantly swung open.

"What the—" began Sam. Then he stopped. "Oh it's the gentleman from Scotland Yard," he went on, more amiably. "Want to come in, sir?"

"That's why I rang," replied Kilby. "Sir Joshua all right?"

Sam's eyes looked like two points of burnished steel.

"Of course 'e is, sir," he said. "Why shouldn't 'e be all right?"

"Why shouldn't he!" echoed Kilby, stepping forward.

The gate—it was more like a door than a gate—clanged shut. Sam then took the lead, and this time the inspector and the constable walked boldly towards Hopeview House.

Muttering to himself, Sam conducted them to the room in which Kilby had previously interviewed Sir Joshua Jordan. As soon as they had entered, he closed the door behind them.

Sir Joshua attempted to rise to his feet. But the effort was obviously too much for him, and, with a groaning "Oh, my God!" he sagged back into his chair. His face was sallow and emaciated, and below his sunken eyes were blue-black rims. Kilby, who knew the symptoms, saw that Sir Joshua was suffering from the severe mental and physical depression that all too surely follows the temporary exhilaration induced by the taking of drugs.

"Sir Joshua," said Kilby, "I've called to ask you a few more questions if you'll be good enough to answer them."

"Oh, go to the devil!" was Sir Joshua's irascible rejoinder. Kilby smiled, in no way offended, for he knew that excessive irritability is inseparable from the confirmed drug-taker.

"I've come to ask you some more questions, Sir Joshua," he repeated. "I'm not quite satisfied that you told me everything last time."

"Oh! clear off and be damned to you and leave me alone!" It was not the nature of the question that disturbed the drug-addict. He was simply filled with an intense weariness of body and mind, and speech of any kind was a torture. All he desired was to be left alone to slump in his chair; and had a loaded pistol been held to his head it is doubtful if he would have raised his hand to brush it aside.

"If you will only answer a few questions I shall take my departure and leave you in peace."

Purposely, Kilby kept on using practically the same words, for he was well aware that few things are more maddening than unpleasant reiteration.

"For the sake of a little peace, I will answer anything, say anything. But not now." Sir Joshua's speech was frequently punctuated by a groan or a gasp. "Dammit! man, can't you be reasonable? Can't you see that I'm in no fit condition to be bothered now? But come back later when I am myself again and I'll tell you everything. Yes, everything, for I'm heartily sick of the whole damned affair. I've been in hell ever since that cursed diamond merchant came here."

"I want you to speak now," persisted Kilby.

The door was thrown open and a man hurried into the room.

"Did you call, sir?" asked the intruder, who was obviously a servant. "I thought I heard you." He approached Sir Joshua, and passed something to him.

Sir Joshua wasted no time in answering. The back of his hand was near his nostrils, and he was sniffing with semi-demented energy.

In a moment a sparkle began to show in his eyes, and Kilby realised that Sir Joshua, in his drug-induced paradise, would cheerfully defy him. He would have to leave Hopeview House, defeated for the present, and return later.

His gaze wandered from Sir Joshua's face to the servant's, which was distorted by a wolfish snarl.

Then his gaze dropped lower, and he started so violently that the other retreated a step.

The servant's legs were bowed like a jockey's.

Chapter 22

Sudden Death

The three men seated round the table were hardly conscious of the clamour and clatter that came in through the open window from the busy street outside.

"Do you really mean to say," asked the Chief Constable in reply to a statement made by Kilby, "that Sir Joshua is deeply implicated?"

"I do. I've had my doubts almost from the first, but now I am sure. To begin with it seemed peculiar that both servants should be out on that particular afternoon. Of course, Sir Joshua explained their absence by saying that he sent them out so as to keep the sale of the necklace a profound secret, But we know it wasn't a secret. The servants were concealed behind the pine tree ready to pounce on Mr. Hyde as he walked past. You may be sure that he would never have been permitted to enter the house had he left the taxi outside the gates."

The Chief Constable nodded, but remained silent.

"You will observe," went on Kilby, "that the gang had a very intimate knowledge of the proposed transaction. Mr. Hyde came all the way from London, yet no attempt was made to molest him until he had arrived at Hopeview House. They knew it would be useless, for the diamond merchant had informed Sir Joshua that he would withdraw the money at the British Bank here in Donmoor. Only Sir Joshua could have passed on that information, for I'm certain that Mr. Davis has no knowledge of the gang. And why should Sir Joshua refuse beforehand to accept anything but banknotes? He wouldn't have anything to do with Mr. Hyde's cheque, although he must have known that it would be duly honoured. As I see it, the problem resolves itself into this: the gang meant to have the money, but Sir Joshua was merely the decoy and was to appear as though he had engineered a perfectly legitimate transaction."

Major Walters gravely stroked his chin.

"But suppose, as you say, that Mr. Hyde had been attacked by the men lying in wait?" he objected. "The grounds were Sir Joshua's, and suspicion would probably fall on the owner."

"It doesn't follow, sir. The robbery could easily have been put down to footpads. Brent and I, you know, scaled the wall today. Well, what we did, others could do equally easily. Moreover, on Monday afternoon the wicket-gate was neither bolted nor locked. But the large gates were barred and bolted, though not locked. Mr. Hyde and the chauffeur, you may remember, unbarred them themselves after they had entered by the small gate. I suppose Sir Joshua thought it might look too suspicious if they were locked, though, doubtless, he made the mistake of assuming that Mr. Hyde, when he discovered that the large gates could not be opened from the outside, would have been satisfied with opening the smaller one and walking up to the house. But to return to what I was saying: footpads could easily have entered the grounds, and the attack, had it taken place, would have been classed as the work of some lawless unknown persons. In that case it is extremely doubtful if the footprints would have been allowed to remain behind the tree for us to identify. But the attack failed to materialise, consequently they assumed that the grounds would not be inspected and so made a very bad blunder."

"Then the supposed attack on Sir Joshua inside the house never took place?"

Kilby leaned back and crossed his knees.

"I'm rather inclined to think it did. Sir Joshua described it so convincingly that I believe it actually took place. But it was a sham attack, staged so that he would not be obliged to rely on his imagination when describing it afterwards. You know how likely one is to trip up when discussing in detail a purely imaginary event. Of course, he wasn't really drugged or knocked unconscious, but it's my opinion that the whole farce was gone through for the sake of realism."

For a few moments Kilby seemed to be listening to the roar and rattle of the traffic outside, then he continued:

"The servants, who were really accomplices, having gone through the pantomime of binding their master—and, of course, releasing him—went out and took up their stand behind the tree, while Sir Joshua prepared to receive Mr. Hyde, should he happen to call. Probably they were astute enough to foresee the possibility of the hitch that actually occurred. What really happened afterwards is already known. Mr. Hyde drove up to the house, was admitted by Sir Joshua, and, after some haggling, the necklace was purchased for £20,000. It was Sir Joshua, of course, and not an impostor, who received the money."

The Chief Constable frowned in perplexity.

"Seems inconsistent, somehow," he said. "If Sir Joshua is a member of the gang, and was willing to allow an attack to take place in his grounds, why wasn't Mr. Hyde attacked inside the house instead of being sold a necklace at less than its real value?"

"Because suspicion had to be diverted from Sir Joshua and Sir Joshua's house. As I've already said, sir, footpads could be blamed had the attack been made outside. But inside was altogether different. The taxi-driver was outside the front door, you know, and, if he couldn't have helped his fare, he would at least have been an important witness. Moreover, the gang could afford to let the necklace go, for they had decided to get it back again, even though its recovery meant murder."

"Don't think I am trying to pick holes in your theories," said Major Walters, "but I can't see even now why Sir Joshua should have parted with the necklace for less than its actual value. The gang could have got the whole of the £30,000 as easily as they got back the diamonds."

"I don't think so, sir. Had the sale not taken place, Mr. Hyde would have taken all of the money back to the bank. Somehow the gang foresaw that he would risk carrying the necklace to London, but not the notes. Besides, it would have looked very suspicious if Sir Joshua were to refuse to sell after bringing Mr. Hyde all the way from London."

Major Walters inclined his head.

"I see your point, Kilby," he conceded. "But I've still got a pebble to throw in your cogs. The sale having been completed, why should Sir Joshua afterwards deny it and use all that bunkum about drugging and impostors and such like?"

Kilby considered the matter for a considerable time.

"That's rather a poser, sir," he confessed. "Probably his idea was to show that the person who overpowered and robbed him was in league with the diamond merchant's murderer. By throwing suspicion on another he was, naturally, diverting it from himself. Nevertheless," Kilby added, "I'm not quite satisfied with that explanation."

"Perhaps the necklace was insured, sir," suggested Constable Brent, who had not previously taken part in the present discussion.

"Well, I'll be—dashed!" exclaimed Kilby. "What a fool I was not to have thought of that! I must get the Yard to make enquiries at once. But wait! If Sir Joshua took out an insurance policy he probably did it locally. May I use your phone, sir?"

"Certainly," said the Chief Constable, reaching for the Directory. "Perhaps I can help you to find the numbers you want."

Kilby rang up the local superintendents of two insurance companies, to learn that neither had ever heard, officially, of Sir Joshua's necklace. But he was more successful when he spoke to the representative of the Providential Assurance Company.

"Yes," answered the superintendent, as soon as Kilby had introduced himself and stated his requirements, "less than a year ago Sir Joshua took out a £30,000 policy on a diamond necklace. Already he has paid three quarterly premiums. I am able to give you this information without having to refer to books, for the matter has given our company considerable worry during the past few days."

"Ah! Sir Joshua has sent in a claim, then?"

"Yes. And the claim has presented us with a pretty problem. Of course, the murder, while we naturally regret it, is no actual concern of ours. But the loss of the necklace is a different matter. Everything hinges on when and where the robbery took place. If the necklace was taken from Sir Joshua by force, I suppose we are liable. But if the sale took place and Mr. Hyde carried away the stones with him—well, naturally, our responsibility ended the moment the transaction was completed. Our own investigators are busy working behind the scenes; but if you can give us any information likely to be helpful we shall be immensely grateful."

Kilby promised to give all the help in his power, and then asked:

"Didn't Sir Joshua inform you that he was about to sell the necklace?"

"Oh, yes. And he promised us that he would endeavour to get the purchaser to take over the policy. We were agreeable—we had to be. Naturally, we couldn't forbid him to sell what was his own. Had

Sir Joshua been unknown to us we should have insisted on being represented at the sale, but—well, we didn't insist."

"Wonderful the virtue there is in a title!" laughed Kilby. Then he thanked the superintendent and rang off.

"Twenty thousand from Mr. Hyde," he remarked in slow, reflective tones, "thirty thousand from the insurance company, and the necklace back again! Jove! Had everything developed according to plan, they would have made a pretty haul!"

Although Constable Brent had attentively listened to the audible part of the telephone conversation, yet his brain had been working busily in another direction, and, when Kilby had given a full account of what the superintendent of the Providential had said, he asked:

"How did the murderer know that Mr. Hyde had the necklace, sir?"

The young constable met the steady gaze of two pairs of eyes, without lowering his own.

"What exactly do you mean, Brent?" demanded Kilby.

"Well, sir," explained Brent, "it is your theory that if Mr. Hyde had walked up the drive he would have been attacked there and robbed of the £30,000. Had that happened, he would never even have seen the necklace. Yet the murderer seems to have known that the attack planned for the outside had failed. How did he know that? Or is it that the murder was committed just to make sure, sir?"

Kilby drummed a devil's tattoo on the arm of his chair.

"I hardly think so, Brent. The pistol shot silenced Mr. Hyde's tongue, of course. But, no; that wasn't the reason. There would have been no need to keep him from talking if he never entered the house. Now, wait a moment... Why, of course! I see it now, Brent. Mr. Hyde's death served two useful purposes. In the first place, it enabled the gang to recover the necklace; and, in the second, it left Sir Joshua free to claim the insurance money. He daren't have done that if Mr. Hyde were alive to state that he had purchased the necklace from Sir Joshua."

"But," put in the Chief Constable, "Mr. Hyde did talk. He told the bank manager all about it."

"I know. That, however, was one of the things the gang couldn't possibly have provided against. And it's fortunate for us that he did speak. Had he driven straight to the station, as the gang probably anticipated, we should be completely in the dark as to what actually took place in Hopeview House."

"But all this," objected Major Walters, "doesn't dispose of Brent's question: how did the murderer know what had really taken place?"

Kilby thrust his hands in his pockets and paced up and down the room. Presently, he returned to his seat.

"I have no doubt that the man who called himself Doctor Peters was the murderer," he said. "And it's possible that Peters was somewhere about in Donmoor that day. A signal, or a sign of some kind, may have been arranged beforehand by which some other member of the gang was to let him know what had happened. After receiving the signal, he took the same train as Mr. Hyde, and committed the murder in Highpen Tunnel."

The Chief Constable shook a doubting head.

"I made all possible enquiries, as you asked me to," he said; "but no one at Donmoor Station, or anywhere else in the town, seems to have seen the doctor."

Kilby nodded.

"I merely mentioned it as a possibility," he reminded the other. "But I'm more inclined to believe that Peters caught the train further south. Of the passengers who travelled on that train, I have seen several and spoken to others on the telephone, yet not one of them had observed the elusive doctor until he came forward professionally just after the murder. On the other hand, many of them declared that they had seen Mr. Hyde. I have even spoken with one of the five passengers who travelled as far as Boxfield in Mr. Hyde's compartment. Mr. Hyde was the last to enter the compartment at Donmoor, consequently he was unable to choose his seat; but as soon as the other five proceeded to get off at Boxfield he moved over to the fatal corner without loss of time. Now, if several people observed Mr. Hyde, I am sure that the doctor, had he also been a passenger, would not have escaped everyone's notice."

"Where, then, in your opinion, did he join the train?"

"At Boxfield, the station before Highpen Tunnel. And luck seems to have favoured him, for I believe he had a compartment to himself. At any rate, no one who travelled in the compartment behind Mr. Hyde's has come forward in answer to my appeal."

It was now the Chief Constable's turn to rise. Moving over to the window, he partly closed it, and stood there for some time looking out. Then, remaining where he was, he turned and faced Kilby.

"And I suppose," he said, "Doctor Peters got on the train with the fixed determination to murder the diamond merchant?"

"Sounds terribly cold-blooded when you put it like that, sir," replied Kilby. "Nevertheless, I believe it is true."

The Chief Constable strolled back to the table.

"But we are still up against the difficulty presented by Brent's question," he persisted. "Had the robbery taken place outside, it would have been policy to leave Mr. Hyde alive, for then, of course, the insurance money would not have been claimed. But it would have been vitally necessary to silence him for ever if he had bought and paid for the necklace. Now, how was Doctor Peters, miles away at Boxfield, to know which course to follow?"

"Provided arrangements were made beforehand, he could have been let known in a dozen different ways. However, my belief is that the wires were used—either telegraph or telephone."

"Telegraph," suggested Major Walters, after a thoughtful pause.

"You are probably right. Sir Joshua wouldn't be likely to use his own phone, for fear of subsequent enquiries. Of course, he could have rung up the doctor from a public telephone box. I wonder, though. Unless Peters had a phone of his own in Boxfield, he couldn't receive the message without attracting a certain amount of notice. A telegram would be more simple. No need for me to remind you, sir, that it is quite a common practice to send a telegram to a passenger, in care of the station-master of a particular station." He glanced at his watch. "What about seeing the Donmoor postmaster, sir? We might be able to find out whether a telegram has been sent. And a personal interview will be more satisfactory than ringing him up. We have plenty of time, for it would be useless to make another call on Sir Joshua just yet."

"We are probably giving ourselves unnecessary trouble," went on Kilby, as they walked towards the post office, "for Sir Joshua is almost certain to confess everything. Nevertheless, it's as well to leave no stone unturned."

Their enquiries at the post office took much longer than they had anticipated, but in the end their patience was rewarded. They learned that, at 3.20 on Monday afternoon, a telegram had been handed in at the sub-post office in George Street, not far from Hopeview House. The telegram was addressed to Thomas Jones, care of Station-master, Boxfield, 3.52 train.

"Slump in shares," was the brief message.

In ordinary circumstances the telegram would have excited no special comment, for, on the face of it, it was obviously a business communication between business friends, or between a broker and his client. Kilby, himself, would have passed it by as unworthy of notice had he not been actually looking for something of the kind. But, in the light of the knowledge he already possessed, the coincidence was too striking to be ignored.

"Here's what we want, sir," he exclaimed, holding out the copy of the telegram.

"Slump in shares," read the Chief Constable. "Code, I suppose?"

"Hardly that, sir. Just an innocent-looking, prearranged message, meaning murder. Its opposite might be 'Boom in shares—' or it might be—just anything. Merely a matter of prior arrangement. And Thomas Jones was, of course, the name which Peters temporarily adopted. The station-master at Boxfield will probably be able to verify that point. I must make it my business to see him on my way back to Blackton."

Back in the office, some minutes later, the Chief Constable picked up a railway timetable and turned over some leaves.

"I'm afraid that was a genuine message after all," he said. "The 3.52 runs in the wrong direction."

"Just an extra clever touch," replied Kilby. "They hoped that a telegram handed to a man ostensibly travelling north on the 3.52 would never be traced to Peters going south by the 4.10."

Next moment Kilby glanced at his watch and remarked that it was time for him to return to Hopeview House.

"I shall probably be able to induce Sir Joshua to speak now," he said. "The exhilarating effects of the drug which the bandy-legged servant handed to him will have worn off by this time. But he will not yet have sunk into the depressed state in which I found him a few hours ago. If only he will speak—and I think he will—I have no doubt that the entire gang will be in our hands."

He picked up his hat, and, accompanied by Brent, was about to leave the office when the telephone bell rang.

The Chief Constable picked up the receiver, and Kilby paused. Some instinct warned him that he ought to remain.

"Good God!" he heard Major Walters exclaim a moment later. "Kilby, Sir Joshua Jordan has died suddenly. He was found dead in his study about fifteen minutes ago."

Chapter 23

The Poisoned Needle

"Who's speaking to you, sir?" cried Kilby, as he strode over to the Chief Constable's side.

"The station-sergeant from King Street police-station. He's been ringing up every few minutes for the last quarter of an hour or more. Do you want to speak to him?"

Kilby nodded and took the receiver from the other's hand.

The information the sergeant had to impart was very scanty. About fifteen minutes before, he had received an urgent call from Hopeview House; and someone speaking in an agitated voice had told him that Sir Joshua had just been found lying dead on the floor of the study. After sending off two men to take charge at Hopeview House, the sergeant had rung up a doctor. Thereafter, until the present moment, he had remained at the telephone, calling up the Chief Constable's office at frequent intervals.

"Let's go at once," said Kilby to Major Walters.

Followed by Constable Brent, they hurried to the garage where Inspector Parker's car had been left, and in a few minutes they were tearing through the streets of Donmoor. The gates belonging to Hopeview House stood wide open, for they had been opened to let the doctor's car through, and Kilby hardly slackened speed as he steered between the massive pillars and zigzagged dangerously along the winding drive.

In the study they found the body of Sir Joshua sprawled on the floor near the chair in which Kilby had seen him seated such a short time before. Kneeling beside the body was a pursy-looking little doctor, who rose to his feet when he saw the officers of the law.

"Dead without a doubt," he fussily asserted, as though someone had stated otherwise. "Been dead for well over an hour, I should say."

The Chief Constable nodded to Kilby, who thereupon took direction of affairs.

"Have you formed any opinion as to the cause of death?" he asked.

"Can't say with certainty. But it looks like heart disease."

"H'm!" was Kilby's sole comment, his glance travelling round the room.

Standing in a corner by themselves were Sam and the bandy-legged individual, their expressions strained and anxious-looking, whilst near the door were the two constables whom the sergeant had sent to take charge.

Kilby's gaze returned to the huddled heap on the floor, to the contorted face which clearly showed that Sir Joshua had died in extreme fear or in terrible agony. For several moments he stared at the distorted features, then, pulling a tape measure from his pocket, he proceeded to take some measurements. This task completed, he motioned to the two constables.

"Lift it on to the couch," he said, indicating the inanimate heap that had so recently been a sentient human being.

The body was laid on the couch, and then Kilby undid some of the clothing and searched for marks of violence. But when he had completed this part of his investigations he had to admit to himself that death seemed to have occurred from natural causes. Nevertheless, he had the feeling that Sir Joshua's life had been brought to an untimely end, either by his own hand or by another's. He moved over to the servants, who still stood apart from the others.

"Which of you found him?" he asked.

"I did, sir," Sam answered. Despite his nervousness, Sam seemed painfully anxious to talk. Obviously, his idea was to create a favourable impression. "Ted 'ere was ge'ttin' some tea ready," he went on, indicating the other servant, "an' 'e says to me, 'Sam,' 'e says, 'you go an' see whether the master's all right. 'E was lookin' a bit dicky when I seen 'im last.' Well, sir, I kem in 'ere, as Ted 'ad asked me to, an—well, sir, you can see what I seen. Sir Joshua was lyin' on the floor, just as you seen 'im yourself, an' I knew at wanst as 'e was a goner. Then off I runs to the phone an' calls up the slops—I mean the police, sir."

"Ah! I see. Must have been a dreadful shock for you. You have no idea, of course, what caused your master's death?"

The question was addressed to both servants, and it was Ted who took the responsibility of answering:

"Heart disease, sir. Didn't you hear what the doctor said, sir?"

"Oh, of course," said Kilby, quick to note that Ted's mental equipment seemed far superior to that of his fellow servant.

Kilby reflected for several moments. He was firmly convinced that everything was not as it ought to be; yet there was nothing in particular to which he could point and say, "This indicates foul play." But Sir Joshua had died when there was a strong possibility that he could be persuaded to confess, and the fact seemed ominous.

He stepped over to the fireplace, lighted a cigar, and placed both hands on the mantelpiece. He could control his thoughts far better with the living and the dead shut out of sight.

He raised one hand to his cigar—and discovered that he had left a clear impression of the hand on the mantelpiece. And then he became aware that the mantelpiece and everything on it had remained undusted for a very long time. But, no, not everything. Near one end was a bronze figure of Britannia which was spotlessly clean, in strange contrast to the layer of dust that coated the remaining ornaments. At the other end was a second bronze exactly similar to the first in shape and design, except that the features and draperies of Britannia were almost obscured by a coating of dust.

Perhaps, though, one of the bronzes had recently been dusted. It was quite likely that Sam or Ted had begun dusting operations on the mantelpiece and been called away before he had well commenced.

Kilby could have asked, but he preferred to find out for himself. He picked up the dusty Britannia and saw, as he had expected to see, a clean disc on the mantelpiece where the base of the bronze had rested. Then he picked up the other, and his eyes sparkled. Here there was no circular patch free from dust, but merely a circle where the projecting rim of the bronze had rested. Inside the circumference of the circle there was a thick layer of dust.

The bronze had recently been put down on the dusty mantelpiece,

And now he remembered that when he was in this room some hours before his subconscious brain had registered the impression that there was something unsymmetrical, something lop-sided, about the arrangement of the ornaments. Now he knew what had been responsible for that vaguely-defined impression. Two hours ago there was only one bronze figure on the mantelpiece. Now there were two.

He suddenly wheeled round, to find Ted's screwed-up eyes glaring at him malevolently. But Kilby was quick to notice that fear leavened the malevolence.

"Well?" he snapped.

Ted swallowed hard. "Well, sir?" he echoed with an ill-concealed snarl.

"Has anyone been here today?" demanded Kilby, for his thoughts had sped far from the room in which he stood. "Any visitors called before the—before your master's sudden death?"

"Yes, sir."

Kilby bristled. "Ah!" he exclaimed. "Who?"

"You, sir. You and—him." Ted nodded in the direction of Brent.

Kilby felt a tingling about the muscles of his right fist, but he merely smiled.

"How witty!" he said, with cutting sarcasm. "And who were the others?"

"There wasn't no others. Just you and him, I tell you."

"And the boy with the parcel," interjected Sam.

Kilby glanced from one servant to the other. Sam fidgeted uneasily; but Ted now seemed quite unperturbed, and his face was as expressionless as a slab of cheese.

"Tell me about the boy," invited Kilby, his gaze concentrated on Ted.

"How was I to know that you'd call an errand-boy a visitor?" demanded Ted in aggrieved tones. "If people would only say what they mean... Anyhow, soon after you'd left, a boy delivered a parcel. That's all. There was a bronze in the parcel, and it's on the mantelpiece there just under your nose." In Ted's opinion, politeness was a sure sign of weakness or inferiority, and he was determined to let Kilby see that he was neither weak nor inferior. "Sir Joshua ordered it the other day to replace the one he broke accidentally a week or two back: he was messing about with it, and accidentally broke off the fish-spear business."

The explanation seemed quite feasible; nevertheless, Kilby was far from satisfied with it.

"Who took in the parcel?" he asked.

"I did, sir," replied Ted in more amiable tones. "It was done up in brown paper, and, not knowing what was inside it, I took it in here to Sir Joshua himself."

Further questions elicited the information that Ted had returned to the kitchen after he had handed the parcel to his master. Later, Sir Joshua's bell had summoned him to take away the paper and crinkled cardboard in which the Britannia had been wrapped. Ted had burned these without troubling to ascertain whether they bore the name or address of the sender. That, declared Ted, was all he knew about the affair.

Kilby turned again towards the mantelpiece and puffed savagely at his cigar. He itched to take Ted's neck between his hands and wring it as one wrings a fowl's, for he knew that the bandy-legged wretch's apparent frankness was merely the cloak in which he covered his low cunning.

Again he picked up the two bronzes and placed them side by side. Except that one was clean and the other dirty, they made a perfect pair. But when he turned them upside-down, he observed a slight difference in their bases. Save for the rim, the base of the older bronze was quite flat; but near the centre of the base of the other was a raised disc about the size of a shilling. Hardly realising what he was doing, Kilby pressed this raised piece with his finger.

As though it were an apple containing a wasp that had stung him, Kilby threw the bronze to the hearth-rug, and the others were amazed to see him snatch the cigar from his lips and press the end hard against his first finger. Not until an agonizing sweat was pouring down his forehead and the smell of the burning flesh rankly permeating the atmosphere of the room did Kilby remove from his finger the red-hot end of his half-smoked cigar.

Ted threw a startled glance towards the door, but the two constables had returned to their post. His glance sped towards the window, and

Brent strolled over in that direction. Then the owner of the bowed legs shrugged defiantly and thrust his hands in his pockets.

The bronze figure still lay on the rug, Kilby picked it up by the helmet and handed it to the Chief Constable.

"Will you be good enough to look after this for the present?" he asked. "And be careful how you handle it, sir."

Then he took hold of the lifeless right hand of Sir Joshua and examined it with the help of a powerful magnifying-glass. On the pad of the thumb he detected a tiny puncture.

They were back again in the Chief Constable's office, Sir Joshua's study having been locked and a constable placed on guard, and the two servants, despite their protests, securely lodged behind bolts and bars at the King Street police station.

"May I have a drink, sir?" requested Kilby. "And let it be a good stiff one, please."

Major Walters produced a decanter, a siphon, and glasses and then poured a generous measure of whisky. Ignoring the siphon, Kilby drained the spirit at a gulp.

"Ah!" he exclaimed with evident relief. "That's better."

A doctor who had been summoned by telephone—for Kilby had taken an instant dislike to the pursy individual who had examined the body of Sir Joshua—now hurried in, and Kilby showed him his damaged finger.

"It probably needs to be treated only for a burn," he explained. "But it's as well to be on the safe side, Doctor. I accidently pricked it with a poisoned needle, and attempted to cauterise it immediately afterwards, hence the burn."

The doctor looked curious, but, professional reticence triumphing, he asked no awkward questions.

"You are sure is was poisoned?" asked the Chief Constable, when the doctor had completed his ministrations and taken his departure.

"It was poisoned without doubt, else why should the needle have been there at all? And I'm equally certain that the poisoned needle was the cause of Sir Joshua's death. I shouldn't be surprised, though, if the post-mortem reveals heart disease, for it was probably some subtle poison that directly affected the heart."

Kilby poured some more whisky, and then filled his glass to the brim with soda.

"I'm probably doing a foolish thing," he said. "But I never felt more in need of it, and I am pretty certain that the cigar effectually disposed of the poison. Now, sir, will you give me a full account of that intercepted message?" he added, settling himself comfortably in a chair."

Major Walters carefully selected a cigarette, tapped the end on his case, and struck a match.

"The moment I received your instructions from Blackton," he began, "I advised the telephone exchange here not to put through any call to Hopeview House until they heard from me again. Then I called on the postmaster, and got him to promise that if a telegram came for Sir Joshua, or one of Sir Joshua's servants, it would immediately be sent to me. After that I hurried to the telephone exchange.

"No call had come through for Hopeview House since I had rung up the exchange, so I decided to wait. I gave instructions to the operator, and took the seat and the cigarette she offered me.

"The waiting was painfully tedious, but at last the call came. The girl waited for a few moments, then, telling the caller that he was through, she handed the receiver to me. The voice at the other end demanded to know whether I was Sir Joshua, but he was careful not to give his own name. And I daren't ask for it, lest my enquiry should arouse the other's suspicions.

"Copying Sir Joshua's voice as well as I could—for I had previously spoken with him a few times—I informed the speaker that I was the person he wanted. Then I received the message intended for Sir Joshua. It was such a peculiar message that I had great difficulty in restraining my desire to demand what it meant.

"'Joshua the second,' said the voice. Just that and nothing more.

"To me, the message sounded absolutely meaningless; or, rather, it was a message that seemed to admit of various interpretations. 'Joshua,' obviously, was the first name of the person whose place I had temporarily usurped; but what did 'the second' mean? Was there a second person named Joshua? Or was a date meant?—or the number of a drawer or shelf or door? You can imagine, Kilby, how bewildered I felt, and my face must have expressed my bewilderment, for I caught the operator smiling.

"'My good girl,' I said, 'can you tell me what "Joshua the second" means?' I spoke on a sudden impulse, merely as an outlet to my feelings and without the slightest hope that she would be able to enlighten me.

"But I take off my hat to that girl. 'Perhaps the second chapter of the Book of Joshua,' she answered without an instant's hesitation. I have since learned, by the way, that the girl is a Sunday-school teacher, and I'm sure that her liking for cigarettes doesn't make her teaching one bit less effective. Had she known that Joshua was the name of the person who was supposed to be receiving the message she would, I daresay, have been as muddled as I was; but I had given her only the telephone number of Hopeview House, therefore 'Joshua the second,' conveyed only one meaning to her. Fortunately, it was the right one.

"I must confess that my knowledge of the Bible is rather rusty, and the message was still as meaningless as ever. But I hurried off home and scared my wife out of her wits by demanding the family Bible. I believe she thought that I had developed a sudden attack of religious mania. Anyhow, Kilby, I looked up the second chapter of Joshua, and found that it was mainly concerned with spies. Then I saw the meaning of the message. Sir Joshua was warned to be on his guard against spies. You, I take it, were the spy?"

"Yes," assented Kilby, "I was one of the spies. Probably you were the other."

The Chief Constable's face bore a puzzled frown.

"But how," he asked, "could you have known beforehand that the message which you asked me to intercept was about to be sent?"

Kilby indulged in a quite smile.

"I didn't know, sir," he replied. "I just guessed it."

A casual remark made by the Chief Constable some minutes later set Kilby on another trail. They were talking of the murder of Sir Joshua, and Major Walters said:

"The gang were afraid that he would squeal, so they took effective steps to silence him."

Then Kilby sat bolt upright.

"Jove!" he exclaimed. "That reminds me! When we were going through the copies of the telegrams that were despatched from, and received at, the post office one of them struck me as being rather funny. Of course, I didn't connect it with our present enquiry, but—well, it was peculiarly worded, to say the least of it. Now, let me see if I can remember the exact words. Something about rats squealing... I've got it, sir. 'Cornered rats always squeal' was what the telegram said. And I believe it was a telegram received at Donmoor. I haven't time at present to look into the matter myself, for I must soon return to Blackton, but I should be very glad if you would investigate the matter, sir, on the off-chance that it may have some relation to the murder."

The Chief Constable promised, and, later, he also gave the assurance that he would endeavour to trace the boy who was said to have delivered the parcel at Hopeview House.

When they were in the car, ready to return to Blackton, Kilby told Brent that he would first drive as far as Hopeview House and take measurements of the footprints found behind the pine tree.

But when they had arrived at the spot he found that the footprints had been obliterated and carefully raked over.

"One up for Ted or Sam," he muttered grimly.

Chapter 24

The Brass Stud

As consciousness slowly returned to Jack Davis he had the uncomfortable feeling that inside his head there was something which raced round and round at a terrific speed. And the motive power that drove this dreadful Something was a man whose face he could not see, but whom he knew to be Doctor Peters.

Gradually, the fog began to clear from his brain. His head ached abominably, and he attempted to raise his hand to his temple to ease the pain. Then the fog lifted considerably with the realisation that his hands were bound behind him.

A few moments later he became aware that he was half sitting, half lying on the back seat of a swiftly-moving motor car. His eyes soon became accustomed to the gloom of the interior, for, although no lights were on inside the car, the rain had cleared outside and a watery moon was speeding across the storm-swept sky. On the opposite seat was a burly individual, whose flashing eyes seemed to be aiding the moon in lighting the semi-darkness of the car.

Jack closed his eyes and endeavoured to recall recent events. His brain now functioned fairly rapidly, and he was able to recollect his enquiries at Hartby railway station, his visit to the booking-clerk's private address, his pursuit of the car with the swastika-marked tyre, his discovery of the car's destination, his stealthy advance in the direction of the gloomy-looking house, and after that... oblivion.

Again he opened his eyes and looked about him. The car in which he was being forcibly carried away was large, smooth-running, and luxuriously upholstered; and Jack had no hesitation in concluding that it was not the car he had tracked through the streets of Hartby.

"What the devil does all this mean?" he demanded at last of the man who was obviously his guard.

The brawny guard said nothing, but his actions were significant. In one hand he held up what looked like a large handkerchief; the other gripped a revolver.

Jack attempted to renew his protest, but the other brandished the gag.

"Shut up, will you!" he growled. "If you don't..." The prisoner's imagination was allowed to complete the threat.

Jack Davis was no fool. He knew that while he was bound it would be madness to attempt to resist or to call out, so, biting his lower lip, he held his tongue.

He was now able to review events in their proper perspective, and it galled him to think that he had failed just at the moment when success had been almost attained. Without doubt, he told himself, he had managed to track Doctor Peters to his lair. But of what use was that, now that he had fallen into the doctor's hands? Perhaps it was the sham doctor himself who now sat within a few feet of him. But, no! His guard was rugged and broad-shouldered, and he had been told that Peters was only of medium build.

He wondered why he was being thus spirited away. Evidently no serious harm was intended to him. If they meant to put him out of the way for good, it hardly seemed likely that he would have been allowed to leave that house in Hartby alive. But a disturbing thought suddenly occurred to him, and he felt a cold sweat ooze through the pores of his forehead. The gang could not be expected to know that he had discovered the Hartby house more or less accidentally. Probably they suspected that he had made important discoveries which he must never be allowed to reveal. And they would be likely to assume that he had taken the simple precaution of informing someone else that it was his intention to pay a surreptitious visit to the house that evening. Thinking thus, they daren't have taken the risk of murdering him on the spot. But was it not highly probable that he was now being taken to some place where the murder could be carried out without any risk of discovery?

Whither was he being taken? he asked himself. To Donmoor? He looked through the window in an endeavour to recognise objects or landmarks outside. But all he could see was a blur of hedges rushing past. Later, as they passed through a town, his knowledge of his whereabouts was just as vague. Even familiar scenery seems quite unfamiliar when viewed at night through the window of a swiftly-moving car.

At last, however, knowledge came to him. They were rushing through a well-lighted village, and the road ran parallel to the railway line. Still looking through the window, Jack observed several telegraph poles fly back to meet him in rapid succession. He was quick to note from the arrangement of the cross-pieces which carried the wires that he was not being taken north, for, when he was travelling with Connie a few hours before, he had observed, more or less subconsciously, the side of the poles to which the cross-pieces were affixed. A few minutes later, a scudding cloud left the face of the moon clear, and the moon's position in the heavens confirmed his opinion that he was going in the direction of London.

Towns and villages flew past, with brief stretches of country in between. At last they were on the outskirts of London, though Jack failed to recognise it. The taciturn guard withdrew a bottle from his pocket, uncorked it, and held the large handkerchief over its mouth. Then he tilted the bottle.

Jack's struggles were brief and ineffectual. He endeavoured to shout, in the hope of attracting the attention of some passer-by, but his cry was strangled at its birth. The chloroform quickly took effect, and he lay helpless as the car proceeded at a greatly reduced rate through the streets of London. He was quite unconscious of the fact that the car finally came to a standstill, and that the driver and the man who had been his guard helped him out of the car and into a house.

A police officer witnessed the scene from a distance. But he smiled, shrugged his shoulders, and resumed his beat. The duties of the ordinary policeman are too arduous to permit of his interfering when he sees a helpless 'drunk' being assisted home by a couple of kindly-disposed friends.

"Looks as if the Byng boys haven't stamped out all the secret night clubs," he muttered, glancing at his watch and noting the time.

Little sleep came to Connie Hyde that night. Though weary in body and mind, she sat up until nearly midnight, hoping that Jack would call to tell her the result of his enquiries at Hartby. True, he had warned her that he would not call, but she had the feeling that if he made any important discovery he would run in, if only for a minute, to let her know about it.

In the end, she decided that Jack would not come, and, reluctantly, she decided to go to bed. But sleep was slow to close her eyes. And when eventually she did sleep she was troubled by restless dreams in which Jack Davis and Doctor Peters largely figured.

She arose in the morning, still tired and unrefreshed. On her breakfast plate, when she went downstairs, she saw a letter, and she eagerly tore open the envelope.

Her spirits sank still lower. The letter—it was hardly more than a note—was from Freda Lowe and had been written to bid her au revoir. Freda and her uncle were leaving Blackton for a few days on a visit to Mr. Lowe's sister, who was seriously ill. The note, written the night before, went on to say that they would be leaving early in the morning, therefore there would be no time for Freda to call round to Connie's before they departed. But it was Freda's hope to return before long and renew a friendship which she dearly cherished.

Freda's sentiments about the dearly-cherished friendship found a strong and clear echo in Connie's breast. Apart from Jack, Freda was the only real friend she had in Blackton; and she was selfish enough to wish that old Dick's sister had chosen a more fitting time in which to fall ill.

While she toyed with her breakfast, Connie's thought reverted to Jack, and she wondered how soon he would come. But the minutes passed, the quarters chimed outside, and still Jack Davis failed to appear.

At half-past ten she came to a sudden decision. She would go to the house in which Jack lodged and put an end to her suspense.

What might be called a Council of Three was deliberating in Inspector Parker's office. But there was one of the members who was hardly conscious of the proceedings.

Constable Brent had also received a letter that morning from Freda Lowe; and, save that it was couched in somewhat warmer terms, it was very little different from the note which had so depressed Connie Hyde.

For the first time in his career Brent was finding Duty conflicting with Inclination. To concentrate his thoughts on a sordid murder was extremely difficult when the girl he loved, and whom he had hoped to meet today, had left Blackton for a vaguely-defined period of time. 'A few days' was such an elastic term. And suppose the girl's aunt grew worse? Suppose death took place? Why, it might be weeks before he saw the girl again. Freda had not said whether she meant to write before her return. And she had furnished him with no address to which he could write. No wonder his mind was far from the business now under discussion.

At last, however, he forced himself to give his attention to what was being said. Kilby was briefly recapitulating a long list of facts, some of which were known to have a direct bearing on the crime, some that were doubtful. Most of the facts were already known to Brent, but it was when Kilby broke fresh ground that he forced his wandering attention away from Freda Lowe.

"...I asked Major Walters to intercept any message that might be sent to Hopeview House," Kilby was saying. "Well, Parker, a message was sent all right. But Sir Joshua never received it, although the sender was under the impression that he did. The warning was cryptic—simply a reference to a certain chapter in the Bible—but Major Walters, with the help of the telephone girl, was able to discover that it was intended to put Sir Joshua on his guard against spies—against me, in fact. That warning message was sent from London."

"From London?" echoed Inspector Parker. "Then the leader of the gang is there?"

Kilby, however, shook his head and smiled.

"I hardly think so, Parker," he said. Then he went on to give an account of the two visits he had paid to Hopeview House the previous day. "I am almost certain that I could have got Sir Joshua to make a clean breast of the whole affair had it not been for the servant called Ted," he continued. "Sir Joshua had reached the stage where he would willingly have put ropes round the necks of his dearest friends, if for no other reason than to get rid of me. But Ted who must have been listening outside the door, came in at the critical moment and handed his master some dope under my very nose. Ted killed all my hopes of hearing Sir Joshua's confession."

"Was it Ted," asked Parker, "who also killed Sir Joshua?"

"That's more than I'm prepared to say. But, without doubt, he knew what had caused his death. And I'm inclined to believe that he knew Sir Joshua was dead before Sam found the body. The poisoned bronze was on the mantelpiece, and it's hardly likely that Sir Joshua placed it there after the needle had pricked his thumb. I don't think he would have had time to leave his chair and do it, even if he'd wanted to. My opinion is that Ted knew what was about to happen as soon as he received the parcel at the door—perhaps even sooner."

"You're sure he did take in a parcel?"

Kilby nodded.

"Yes. As you know, I had a long conversation with Major Walters on the phone early this morning. Well, he succeeded in finding the boy who delivered the parcel at Hopeview House. The boy, however, was able to throw no real light on the affair. A slouch-hatted man had stopped him in the street and given him a shilling to deliver the parcel—which he did, to a man answering Ted's description. To the boy, the shilling was far more important than the giver, for all he could say with certainty was that the unknown man's hat was pulled well down over his eyes, and that he wore a raincoat.

"But to go on: Ted took in the parcel and left Sir Joshua to undo it. Or he may have undone it himself, and afterwards burned the brown paper and crinkled cardboard. That point, however, seems immaterial. Ted may even have spoken the truth when he informed us that his master had ordered the bronze a few days previously. But I have no doubt that he knew that the bronze which arrived bore the poisoned needle at the base. And it's equally certain that precautions were taken to ensure that Sir Joshua would prick himself. Ted may have deliberately jabbed the unfortunate man's thumb against it. Or a note may have been enclosed which induced Sir Joshua to press the raised centre of the base. Again the point seems immaterial. If Ted did not actually murder his master, he was an accessory, and consequently equally guilty of murder. But the difficulty, of course, will be to prove his guilt."

"Then there's no doubt that Sir Joshua was killed so as to ensure his silence?"

"No doubt whatever. At first they warned him—or thought they warned him—to be on his guard. But it seems pretty obvious that the leader soon afterwards decided that the warning would be useless. It was known that Sir Joshua was addicted to drugs, and so could not be trusted. The only safe method was to close his lips for ever."

Parker stuffed some tobacco into the bowl of his pipe and struck a match.

"But how," he asked, "could the leader of the gang have known that Sir Joshua had ordered a bronze to replace the one which he had accidentally broken?"

"Sir Joshua may never have ordered it, in which case the bronze, when it arrived, must have come as a surprise. On the other hand, if he really did order it, Ted's complicity is even more certain. It was he who informed the leader that his master was expecting a bronze. Anyhow, the poisoned needle killed Sir Joshua. And Ted's part seems fairly clear. Assuming, for the moment, that he did not actually kill his master, we may take it for granted, I think, that he went into the study and found his master dead. Then he removed all traces of the crime. If a note had been enclosed, he burned it. And he picked the deadly bronze off the floor and placed it on the mantelpiece. Quite a clever hiding-place, too, if he'd only taken one simple precaution. Had he dusted the mantelpiece and the other ornaments on it I should have noticed nothing unusual, and the secret of Sir Joshua's death would probably have remained a secret for ever."

"Seems a fortunate coincidence," said Parker dubiously; "fortunate from the gang's point of view, I mean, that Sir Joshua should be in need of a bronze."

Kilby smiled.

"The gang doesn't have to rely on coincidences, Parker. But advantage is taken of them as they arise. And, in this case, what seems a coincidence may actually be nothing of the kind. We don't know that it was Sir Joshua who broke the bronze a few weeks ago. It may have been Ted who did it thus creating the coincidence. Moreover, had they found it impracticable to use the bronze with the poisoned needle, they could have disposed of Sir Joshua in anyone of a dozen other different ways. And now I can foresee another objection you are likely to raise. Within a few hours after he had showed signs of confessing, Sir Joshua was dead. The time, you will probably say, was too short for the leader to be informed of what had transpired during my visit, and for elaborate plans to be made for silencing the would-be traitor. I agree. But, in common parlance, Sir Joshua's number was already up. Had I never paid that visit, Sir Joshua would have died just the same. He was a drug-addict, and not to be trusted once he had come under suspicion. And now to resume: when Ted had obliterated, as he thought, all traces of the crime, he grew exceedingly cautious. It was probably then that he stole out and obliterated the footprints behind the pine tree. That done, he very cleverly allowed Sam to discover that their master was dead."

But Parker had another objection to raise.

"Why," he asked, "do you fix on Ted as the guilty one? It may have been Sam."

"No. Sam hasn't the brains. He's the kind that could safely be relied on to bludgeon one from behind; but where cunning is needed Ted's the man. There's another fact that points to Ted's complicity. Soon after the intercepted telephone message, a peculiarly-worded telegram was received at Donmoor. 'Cornered rats always squeal' is what it said. The cornered rat was Sir Joshua. Major Walters has succeeded in discovering the person to whom the telegram was addressed—a frowsy woman living in a frowsy Donmoor street. He has interviewed the woman, and, although she tried all kinds of evasions, he established the fact that she is Ted's wife. The message was for Ted, of course; and Ted's business, you may be sure, was to see that Sir Joshua met the fate of all cornered rats—before he had the time to squeal. The bronze was the means used to accomplish that end."

There was silence for several moments, and then Kilby produced an envelope, from which he shook a discoloured brass object on to the table.

"What do you think it is, Parker?" he asked.

Parker picked up the little object and scrutinised it keenly.

"Looks like the top part of a press-stud belonging to a glove," he said.

Kilby smiled.

"It does, Parker," he agreed. "Or... a tobacco pouch."

"Mr. Hyde's, sir?" exclaimed Brent, now thoroughly aroused.

"Exactly, Brent. That little piece of brass was once part of the murdered man's pouch."

Chapter 25

The Photograph

A knock sounded on the door, and Kilby replaced the little object in the envelope.

"Miss Hyde wishes to see you, sir," said the constable who opened the door.

Although the remark was addressed to neither inspector in particular, it was Kilby who gave the curt order:

"Show her in, please."

Extreme agitation was depicted on Connie Hyde's face as she hurried in. Parker rose to his feet with the intention of offering her a chair, but the girl had eyes only for Kilby. Moving swiftly to his side, she cried out with a gulp:

"Mr. Davis has disappeared. I've come to you to—to—"

The features of Parker and Brent expressed the surprise they felt, but the girl's announcement seemed to leave Kilby unmoved. Rising slowly to his feet, he presented his own chair.

"Won't you sit down, Miss Hyde?" he invited.

Connie, however, ignored his invitation. Gripping the chair by the back, so as to still the violent trembling of her hands, she again attempted to speak. But Kilby cut her short.

"Miss Hyde," he said, "I should have thought that you were too level-headed to act like an hysterical schoolgirl!"

The reprimand stung Connie. Biting her lip, she increased the strength of her grip, until her knuckles stood out white. But her hands were now steady. Her flashing glance swept over Kilby's smiling face, and what she saw there made her lower her gaze.

"Thanks, Mr. Kilby," she said, immediately sitting down. "That was just what I needed."

Kilby continued to smile.

"Yes," he replied. "I thought a little jolt would do you good. Forgive my seeming rudeness. And now we can talk things over quietly. You say Mr. Davis has disappeared? Begin at the beginning, and tell me all about it."

But, although her emotions were now well under control, Connie dreaded to waste valuable time by going back to the beginning. Instead, she told of Jack's decision to leave her at Derwent Junction the previous evening and go over to Hartby to make enquiries about Doctor Peters at the North Eastern station.

"Why the North Eastern, Miss Hyde?"

"We thought it possible that Doctor Peters had gone back to Donmoor from there. As far as we could learn, he hadn't booked on the L.M.S., so Jack—Mr. Davis—decided to try the other station."

Kilby moved over to the side of the room, and brought back a chair to replace the one he had given the girl.

"Miss Hyde," he said, when he had seated himself, "you have just made use of the expression 'gone back.' Now, to say that Peters had gone back from Hartby implies that he must have been there. Have you any reason for thinking that the man was ever in Hartby?"

"We know that he went there after the murder." Connie's voice carried conviction, and the three men listened, absorbed, as she went on to relate how Peters had been seen twice—first, at Derwent Junction; and afterwards on the train itself just before it reached Hartby.

For some moments after she had finished, Kilby's face still bore the same absorbed expression.

"There seems to have been a great deal of method about your enquiries," he presently observed. "But what gave you the idea, in the first place, that Peters had gone to Hartby?"

"Guesswork. Well, no; it was hardly that. We reasoned that he had not gone on to London, therefore it was natural to assume that he had returned to Donmoor. When we had studied a map and seen that Hartby is served by two different railway systems, both of which also serve Donmoor, well, we thought we'd better make enquiries about Hartby to begin with."

"Hartby's certainly a strategic point," conceded Kilby. "One who wishes to hide his movements has only to go there by the L.M.S. and leave by the North Eastern, or vice versa. And then, of course, there are the roads. But the same thing applies to Blackton, you know. Days ago, when I was passing the North Eastern station here, it occurred how easy it would be to mask one's movements, or lay a false trail, in Blackton. It really struck me as an ideal place for that kind of thing... Anyhow, Miss Hyde, I must congratulate both you and Mr. Davis on a clever piece of work. I, too, have been trying to get on the trail of Peters, and I must confess that you have succeeded where I have practically failed. I only wish you had seen fit to confide in me before it was too—"

He stopped abruptly.

Fear again gripped Connie by the heart.

"You don't think anything has happened?" she cried; "anything serious?"

Kilby shook his head.

"Wish I could tell you that, Miss Hyde. But I hope not. Parker," he asked, turning to the local inspector, "what size is Hartby?"

"Oh it's quite a large place. Let me see." Parker went to a bookshelf and consulted a book of reference. "Population's over 120,000."

"Phew! exclaimed Kilby. "A man missing, or in hiding, would take some finding in a town of that size. Without something definite to go on, he'd be almost as difficult to lay hands on as the proverbial needle in the bundle of hay." His hands sought his pockets, and, rising, he began to pace about the room. Presently, observing the distress on Connie's face, he returned to his seat.

"Miss Hyde," he said gently, "I shouldn't worry if I were you. It's not unlikely that Mr. Davis made some important discovery last night, something that needed to be followed up at once. Perhaps he again got on Peters's track and found it necessary to rush off after him without waiting to inform you. If no better course occurs to me, I shall go over to Hartby and endeavour to pick up the young man's trail. And I shouldn't be surprised if it were to lead to Peters. Meanwhile, will you tell me everything that happened to you two yesterday from the time you caught the early morning train at Blackton. Don't leave out anything, even though it may seem quite trivial. You may have been under observation by Peters or one of his accomplices, and it's important that I should be familiar with every movement you made."

Apart from one or two intimate details, such as the manner in which she and Jack had bade each other good night, Connie omitted nothing in telling her story. The recital occupied a considerable amount of time, but Kilby listened to the narrative with rapt attention.

"Parker," he exclaimed, before the girl's tale had come to its natural end, "I now know who it was that sent the telegram to Ted's wife and attempted to warn Sir Joshua by telephone!"

Parker made no reply. But his brain functioned rapidly. The girl had mentioned John Smith, a Euston Road jeweller. She had also spoken about bowls and bronzes and a vase with a peculiar design. A bronze had been responsible for the death of Sir Joshua Jordan. And the two messages received at Donmoor had been sent from London. Parker convinced himself that he saw light at last. John Smith, without doubt, was the leader of the gang. Nothing could be clearer.

Kilby's interjection had broken the thread of Connie's narrative, and, for some moments, the ticking of a clock on the mantelpiece was the only sound that broke the silence of the room.

Presently Kilby reached for the telephone, rang up Scotland Yard, and, among other instructions, asked to have enquiries made about a message received by the Euston Road jeweller about noon or early afternoon of the previous day.

Kilby put down the instrument, and the conversation drifted back to the enquiries which Connie and Jack had made at Derwent Junction and Hartby.

"You had no real foundation," asked Kilby, "for thinking that the doctor had come from Donmoor on the day of the tragedy?"

"No; it was merely surmise. Dad was returning from Donmoor, and we thought it likely that Doctor Peters had joined the train there. We made enquiries about Donmoor tickets, but the booking-clerks were unable to help us."

"You set them a rather difficult task, Miss Hyde. Anyhow, you happen to have been wrong about Donmoor, although I must admit that your reasoning was sound. I suspected that Peters joined the train at Boxfield, and on my way back here yesterday the Boxfield stationmaster confirmed the truth of my suspicion."

"We, too, thought of Boxfield," said Connie. "But we considered it less likely than Donmoor. We were wrong, of course. And it wasn't our only blunder. We thought we had made a wonderful discovery at Hartby when we came across a Little Faston ticket with the wrong serial number—had been obtained in the morning, but not used until the evening. We felt sure that it had been purchased by Doctor Peters so as not to disclose the actual place from which he had come; but when we rushed back to Little Faston we discovered that the suspected ticket had been purchased by a young woman."

Kilby's fingertips strayed towards one another.

"H'm!" he said. "Purchased by a young woman! And not used until six or seven hours later! Seems unusual!"

"Don't know that it's so very unusual," put in Parker. "Monday is rent-dodging day, you know. On Monday many of the women go for trips, and it's commonly called 'Dinah's day out.' Probably this woman we're talking about stayed at home part of the day to do the weekly washing, but made sure of her ticket before the rent-collector called. Rent-dodging's quite common in Blackton, and I shouldn't think Little Faston is any different."

"But," objected Kilby, "we are talking of a woman who is young, and therefore not likely to be one of the rent-dodgers. I believe these two investigators were right. Peters could easily have asked a young woman to obtain the ticket for him. He foresaw that an attempt would be made to trace him, and was wily enough to prepare for it beforehand."

"But," said Parker "if he belongs neither to Donmoor nor Boxfield, why couldn't he have handed in a ticket that had been purchased at either of those places?"

"You forget that Sir Joshua lives—or lived—at Donmoor, and enquiries had to be diverted from there. And enquiries at Boxfield would be likely to reveal the fact that Peters had been handed a telegram by the stationmaster there."

A few minutes later, Kilby was answering a call from Scotland Yard.

"Dash it!" the other heard him exclaim, when he had listened for a moment or two. "Another of those confounded public boxes!"

He banged down the instrument and then turned to Connie.

"Miss Hyde," he said, "I was hoping that that call might help me to discover the whereabouts of Mr. Davis. But the tactics of the enemy seem to have provided for every contingency. Nevertheless, I would still advise you not to worry. I have the feeling that the young man is all right, and I shall do all in my power to find him. Should you hear anything, you will let me know, of course?"

Connie accepted his words as a polite dismissal, and, thanking him, she took her departure. She was now feeling less worried, but she wished there was something which she could do instead of remaining inactive in a state of suspense. If only she could confide in Freda Lowe they might, between them, be able to think of something that could be done. But Freda would be away from Blackton for some days.

In a thoughtful frame of mind, Inspector Kilby took a walk with Constable Brent. Feeling like a chess player who sees many possible moves on the board, he found it difficult to decide which piece to play. Each move gave a promise of success, but it also held the threat of disaster. His opponent was exceedingly skilful, and a wrong move might mean that the game was irretrievably lost. As he walked along, Kilby silently studied every aspect of the game, carefully weighing his chances of success or failure.

Speaking not a word to his companion, he strolled past the North Eastern station and on towards the cottage of the old potter. Presently, he was level with the gate, and he looked up towards the cottage in the expectation of seeing old Dick sitting by his wheel at the open door of the shed. But old Dick was not there, and the doors were shut.

Kilby stopped, and though his gaze was still directed towards the cottage and the lean-to shed, his expression seemed to indicate that he was seeing something much farther away.

At last he turned to the young constable.

"Brent," he said, "at the back of my mind when I set out, I had the idea of talking things over with old Dick, for his opinions are well worth serious consideration. But it looks as though the old chap isn't in. He isn't at his wheel, anyhow. Shall we go to the cottage and see if we can dig him up?"

Brent had no alternative but to disclose his bittersweet secret.

"'Twould be useless, sir," he replied. "Both he and Miss Lowe have left."

"Ah!" Kilby's voice and face were expressionless. "Left did you say, Brent?"

"Yes, sir. Mr. Lowe's sister is seriously ill, and they have gone to visit her."

"One of the corporal works of mercy, isn't it, Brent? And when do they propose to return?"

For a moment, Brent was inclined to resent what seemed like impertinence. But he quickly decided that Kilby was really anxious to consult old Dick about some particular problem that puzzled him. Had not Kilby expressed the opinion that the old potter was a very clever man?

"In a few days, sir," answered Brent, determined to conceal nothing. "They left early this morning. I received Miss Lowe's note by the first post today."

"What a pity! As I've already said, I should like to talk things over with the old chap. But you'll be writing to one or the other of them of course?"

"The note was evidently written in a hurry, sir, and no address was enclosed." Kilby was quick to observe that the other did not offer to show him the so-called note, and he smiled. Obviously, the epistle contained some tender passages that were intended only for Brent's eyes.

"Standing here reminds me about the garage doors having been forced," went on Brent, as though anxious to give a slight turn to the conversation. "I suppose, sir, you haven't done anything to find out who did it?"

"No, Brent, I've done nothing. I didn't need to do anything, for I know who wrenched out the staple... Now you'll want to be asking me why the person who did it hasn't been arrested. But all in good time, Brent; all in good time... Now, let's be getting back."

When they had almost reached the police-station, Kilby demanded with startling suddenness:

"Brent, supposing you found yourself caught in a quicksand, what would you do?"

Wondering whether the question were a peculiar kind of joke, the young policeman keenly scrutinised the other's face. But when he observed Kilby's grave expression, he replied:

"I know what I ought to do, sir. But I'm afraid I should do the reverse."

"And what ought you to do?"

"Keep perfectly still, sir."

"Quite right, Brent. If you struggle in quicksands, the chances are a thousand to one that they'll drag you down. But if you have the common sense to keep quiet, you'll be all right until help comes along. And if there's no help to be expected, you stand a good chance of extricating yourself if you only work quietly and carefully enough. But let me repeat it, Brent: the man who struggles in a quicksand is inevitably doomed."

Brent was quick to see the underlying meaning of the fanciful illustration.

"You mean, sir...?"

"I mean, Brent, that the murderer, the double murderer, is finding himself in the quicksands. And he has started to struggle..."

At the police-station, a special messenger from Scotland Yard handed Kilby a bulky envelope.

In a moment the envelope was slit open, and from among several typewritten sheets and fingerprints Kilby pulled out a photograph that showed the head and shoulders of a bearded man.

"'Abie, the Mole,'" he flung over his shoulder to Inspector Parker.

For several minutes he studied the photograph, the frown on his brow deepening every moment. Presently, he took up a sheet of paper and covered the lower part of the picture, so that only the face was showing. A fraction of an inch at a time, he slid the paper upwards. At last even the nose was hidden. Then a cry of satisfaction burst from Kilby.

"Know him?" asked Parker, craning over the other's shoulder.

"Yes. I recognise the eyes. I've met 'Abie the Mole,' before."

"You have!"

"Yes, Parker. I only hope this photograph wasn't wirelessed too late."

Chapter 26

The Affable Jeweller

C onstable Brent left the room to perform some specified duty, and then Kilby related the history of 'Abie the Mole,' as far as it was known. Several times, in the course of his narrative, he referred to the typewritten documents which had been compiled from the information received from New York. And Abie's history was recorded pretty extensively, for General Norman, not satisfied with the radio alone, had used the Transatlantic telephone to converse with Captain Morgan, Chief of the detective department of the New York police.

"Incredible!" exclaimed Inspector Parker, when the other had finished.

"Seems so, Parker. Nevertheless, it's true."

"You have no doubt that Abie is the leader of the English gang?" Parker spoke as though his own doubts were giving him trouble.

"No doubt whatever. And it was Abie himself, in the guise of Doctor Peters, who planned Mr. Hyde's murder and carried it out. The same might be said of the death of Sir Joshua Jordan, although in this case, Abie kept more in the background. Now, Parker, let me think for a minute."

But Kilby, hands in pockets, spent several minutes pacing up and down the room before finally returning to his seat.

"Parker," he said then, his tone grim and unyielding, "I fancy I can now see the whole thing from beginning to end. Some day you will hear the complete story, but there's more important work to be done now. My knowledge of how the deed was done will be of little avail until Abie, or Peters, has been laid by the heels."

Parker left off examining the photograph to ask:

"Aren't you afraid that Peters will clear off altogether?"

"I believe he will eventually make the attempt. But I'm hoping he won't succeed. All the ports and aerodromes are being carefully watched. And the Euston Road jeweller is being kept under observation."

"A short time ago," said Parker, "I thought that the jeweller was the head of the whole affair.

"He's only a cog in the wheel, Parker—an indispensable cog, I grant you, but Abie's the hub round which the jeweller and all the other cogs revolve, each performing his own allotted task. To go on: Abie will be clever enough to know that he cannot leave the country at present, therefore he'll decide to go into hiding for a time. And he'll hide in London. That's why I'm so hopeful of digging him out. London is no longer the secure hiding-place it was supposed to be a few years ago; but even the cleverest criminal still deludes himself with the idea that it is. We'll run a fine comb through London, and, except he's unusually lucky, Abie will get caught in the teeth." Kilby laughed grimly. "Funny metaphor, Parker, isn't it? Fancy using a comb to catch a mole!"

Parker, however, was still doubtful.

"You'll have considerable difficulty in recognising him even if you should come across him. I see New York says Abie's disguises are so many and so clever that no one is quite sure which is the real Abie."

"True, Parker. I anticipate a difficult task. If Abie were a real American his accent would betray him. But he's what's commonly called a Cosmopolitan, and his accent is perfect—rather, he has no accent at all. His accomplishments are many and varied. Apart from possessing an extensive knowledge of obscure poisons, he is an expert shot. And he is so skilful with his hands that he can make them do almost anything. Nevertheless, as my American friends would say, I have a hunch that I will get him. Sooner or later he's bound to give himself away. There's his mania for thrills, you know. Any sport, or game, or pastime—call it what you will—that has a thrill in it simply fascinates

Abie. Perhaps that's why he has become such a daring criminal. But strangely enough, it is only where crime is concerned that he plays an active part. At other thrilling events he is merely an onlooker. New York says that he would brave any danger to watch speed-mad motorists dashing wildly round the track. Now, Parker, perhaps you will be able to see wherein lies my hope of capturing him. Dirt-track racing provides thrills in plenty, and one or another of the meetings will be certain to lure Abie from the hole into which he has slunk."

A smile of comprehension slowly spread across Parker's face.

"You'll watch the Dirt-track meetings?" he asked.

"That's what I propose to do, Parker. In addition, of course, London will be combed, as I've already said."

"But," objected Parker, his smile fading, "there's still the difficulty of Abie's various disguises. You might be standing beside him and fail to recognise him."

"I'd know his eyes among a million pairs. Moreover, he has a peculiar habit, of which he is probably unconscious. Most of us have one or two funny habits, you know. His is to scratch the crown of his head with the first finger of his left hand, while his little finger pokes up into the air... But I've already wasted too much time in talking. Parker, are you acquainted with any of the Hartby police?"

"Superintendent Broadwood is a personal friend o' mine."

"Good. Perhaps you wouldn't mind seeing him and trying to learn something about young Davis. Frankly, I haven't much hope of your success, but it's as well to leave no stone unturned."

Parker readily promised, and then Kilby said that he would take an hour's walk by himself before returning to London to begin the search for 'Abie, the Mole.'

Kilby's walk, however, occupied considerably more than an hour, and, when he returned, his first action was to wash his hands and face and brush his clothes, for his appearance was exceedingly grimy. Nevertheless, he seemed to be in excellent spirits, and, after eating a hearty meal, he caught the next train to London.

Kilby was too familiar with traffic jams to take a taxi from St. Pancras, so he hurried to the Underground and made all possible speed to Scotland Yard. It would have been much more convenient to call on the Euston Road jeweller first, but he was keenly aware of the danger of taking a false or premature step. And before he was two minutes in the presence of the Assistant Commissioner he was glad that he had managed to curb his impatience.

"After you had rung us up," said General Norman, "we made all the enquiries we could, and, as you were informed, we learned that John Smith had been called up yesterday from a public telephone box in Hartby. Of course, it was impossible to trace the call further than that."

Kilby nodded.

"Yes, sir," he agreed. "Abie, by the way, seems to have his head screwed on very securely."

"You are sure that Abie's at the bottom of that affair, Kilby?"

"Quite sure, sir."

Then Kilby once more related the story he had told Inspector Parker, and again he was listened to with rapt attention, in spite of the fact that the listener already knew much of what he was being told. Kilby even went further and disclosed his theory as to the exact manner in which the murder had been engineered and carried out. And he advanced the theory as though it were not a theory but an established fact.

"Sounds almost too ingenious to be true," observed the general. "I daresay you are right, though. By the way, Kilby, I think I can tell you where young Davis is to be found. Late last night, a constable on duty in the Euston Road observed an apparently drunken man being carried into a house by a couple of men, seemingly friends of the 'drunk.' The constable was too far off to see them with any degree of clearness, and he is unable to point out with certainty the house into which the helpless man was taken. However, he is quite positive that the incident took place quite close to the jeweller's shop, if not actually at the shop itself. To my mind, there can be no two opinions about the meaning of the occurrence. Davis had to be put out of the way because he was becoming too troublesome."

"That's about it, sir. The young man stumbled on some clue at Hartby, and, in doing so, he was unlucky enough to stumble on someone belonging to the gang. I should love to know what it was that he discovered, and I think, sir, I couldn't do better than pay a visit to Mr. John Smith."

General Norman grinned.

"The name's a guarantee that you can easily pump him," he said.

Though he was feeling far from amused, Kilby, too, laughed.

"Better take charge of these, sir," he said, taking several diamonds from his pockets and placing them in a heap on the table. "I've already explained how I got them."

When Kilby entered the jeweller's shop, the proprietor was affability itself. Rubbing his palms together, in the fashion that seems inherent in all shopkeepers, he courteously demanded his visitor's pleasure.

On his way from Scotland Yard, Kilby had debated with himself whether to reveal his identity at once or to pose as a would-be customer. Finally, he had decided to be guided by the nature of his reception and by the appearance of the jeweller. John Smith's agreeable manner now induced him to temporise.

"There's a vase in your window that I should like to examine," he said.

"Certainly, sir. Do you mind describing it?"

Kilby didn't mind. "That's an easy matter," he replied. "You seem to have only one of its kind, and it's rather uncommon—blue, with red serpents."

"Certainly, sir," repeated the other. "I know the one you mean. Just a moment, please."

He moved over to the window, opened a sliding partition, panelled in frosted glass, and took down the vase from its plate-glass stand. On his way back, he stepped on a little knob that projected above the level of the floor behind the counter.

"Here you are, sir," he said, handing the vase to Kilby. "A beautiful piece of workmanship. Just inspect it and see for yourself."

Kilby turned the vase round about and upside-down, and then concentrated his attention on the intertwined serpents. He had expected to find that the design was merely a transfer, or a stencilling, but in this he was mistaken. His expert eye quickly assured him that he was gazing at a genuine hand-painting. Obviously, the man who had made and painted the vase was too much of an artist to be satisfied with mechanical methods.

"A lovely piece of work," agreed Kilby.

A genial smile was on the jeweller's face.

"Very fine indeed, sir. I observed that you examined the base. Looking for the maker's name, I suppose?"

Kilby's reply was non-committal.

"I understand that's where is usually to be found," he said. "Who's the artist, may I ask? I fancy I've seen an example of this kind of work somewhere else."

The jeweller's hesitation was so slight that it would have passed unnoticed by one less alert than Kilby.

"There's no secret about it, sir. That vase was made by a retired potter who now lives at a place called Blackton. I manage to dispose of all of his best work for him. In fact, sir, I could find purchasers for treble the amount; but the supply is limited... You've no intention of buying this, of course."

The statement—for it was not a question—took Kilby by surprise.

"Why do you say that?" he asked.

The jeweller rubbed the tip of his hooked nose and laughed.

"Because you praised it, sir. No man praises the thing he's attempting to buy. He leaves that till afterwards."

At that moment John Smith looked very much like an honest man of business who scorned to use the ordinary wiles of the salesman in disposing of the fruits of his friend's hobby. The man's plausible manner, however, did not succeed in deceiving Kilby. He was still convinced that it was the smiling man before him who had sent the two messages to Donmoor. And he had no doubt that John Smith knew all about the present whereabouts of Jack Davis. Then it struck him that the jeweller did not seem anxious to effect a sale. Naturally, that convinced Kilby that he ought to buy.

"You are wrong, Mr. Smith," he said. "The vase has taken my fancy, and I should like to purchase it. Name your price, and, if it isn't too exorbitant..."

Mr. Smith stated a price that seemed quite reasonable, and the vase changed owners.

While the purchase was being wrapped up, Kilby again referred to the peculiar design, and was informed that the Blackton potter seemed partial to red serpents. He did not confine himself to that design, however, but often used birds, or fruit, or flowers.

"I told you," said Kilby, "that I have already seen a vase resembling this. As far as I remember, though, the other design showed the serpents with protruding fangs."

The jeweller lowered his eyelids and considered.

"Yes," he said. "I believe I have received and sold a few like that." But he did not seem sufficiently interested to ask where Kilby had seen the other vase.

Kilby's keen eyes had already surveyed the shop, but he had to admit to himself that everything connected with it seemed to indicate a genuine business establishment. The shelves were well stocked, and he could detect nothing to justify his suspicion that the jewellery business was a camouflage for something infinitely more sinister. Behind the counter, and almost opposite to the front door, hung a red curtain that obviously concealed a door leading to a room at the back of the shop. Kilby would have given much to be able to open this curtained door and explore whatever lay behind it. But he had not the legal right; and he felt it inadvisable to give the Press an opportunity to come out with its glaring scare headlines about another alleged high-handed action on the part of Scotland Yard. There seemed nothing further that he could do, yet he hesitated to take his departure.

"Yes," he said, as though speaking to himself, "I'm sure I have seen a vase like this before. I wonder where it could have been...? Oh, I've got it now! It was at a night club."

The jeweller said nothing, and Kilby was compelled to widen the rather crude opening he had made.

"Talking of night clubs reminds me that a friend of mine saw a belated reveller being helped home about midnight last night. It was in the Euston Road, too—not far from here."

The pleasant smile vanished from the jeweller's face, and he lowered his gaze as though embarrassed.

"Good heavens!" he exclaimed. "Don't tell me I was as bad as that, sir. I know I felt a bit merry before I left the club, and I can't remember how or when I got home, but— You don't mean to say that I was helplessly drunk, sir?"

Kilby, momentarily taken aback, managed to cover his confusion by saying:

"I am very sorry. But, believe me, I shouldn't have mentioned the affair if I'd had any idea it was you. Please forgive my seeming impertinence."

Mr. Smith courteously brushed the apology aside. Kilby happened to glance at a shelf high up near the ceiling where he saw a pair of bronze figures that seemed to be the exact counterpart of those he had seen on Sir Joshua Jordan's mantelpiece. Then his alert ears detected a slight sound behind the curtain, and he came to a sudden decision. He would immediately take the necessary steps to investigate the rooms at the back. Picking up his purchase, he took his leave of the jeweller, and strolled nonchalantly out of the shop.

The jeweller stepped to the front door and saw Kilby, who was apparently lighting a cigarette, walking slowly along the pavement. Then he went behind the counter, drew the red curtain aside, and opened the door it had concealed. Inside the doorway stood a man with a smile on his face and an automatic in his hand.

"Kilby, wasn't it?" asked this individual.

John Smith nodded.

"Yes, it was Kilby, sure enough. And I was almost tempted to let him come in here, as he wanted to. He's getting troublesome, and... the pistol would have been the easiest way out. You'd have used it, wouldn't you?"

The smile never left the other's face, but its nature seemed suddenly to change.

"Had you allowed Kilby to come in here," he said in steely tones, "I should certainly have used the pistol on you. Your duty, Mr.—er—John Smith, is to obey orders, and don't forget it. Fortunately, I was on the spot when you gave the warning, so I took immediate steps to pack off that prying cub, Davis, to a more permanent underground home. Kilby will come back, though. Let's be prepared."

Then, still smiling, 'Abie, the Mole,' hurried from the room by another door.

Chapter 27

The Prisoner

His teeth chattering, and his limbs stiff and sore, Jack Davis painfully rose from the cold flagged floor on which he had been lying. His gaze strove to pierce the darkness of his prison, but his hand held close to his face remained invisible, and the sound of his beating heart was magnified out of all proportion.

Before attempting to rise to his feet he made the agreeable discovery that he was no longer bound. Now upright, he stamped his feet and chafed his hands, and gradually the blood began to course normally through his veins.

As his brain slowly threw off the effects of the drug, he strove to estimate the predicament in which he stood. He did not attempt to disguise the fact that he was in considerable danger; but, at any rate, he was alive and uninjured. Reflecting on the merciless manner in which Mr. Hyde had been murdered, he wondered at the strange leniency that had been shown him. But he would have wondered still more had he been told the circumstances to which he owed his present comparative safety.

He searched for his matches to find that they were gone. Evidently his captors were taking no risks.

Feeling more helpless than a blind man, for the other senses of the blind are, as a rule, highly developed, he determined nevertheless to explore his prison. Hands outstretched in front, and feet shuffling along the floor, he cautiously moved forward until his hands encountered a wall that was cold and clammy to the touch.

Fifteen minutes later—although he himself had no idea of the time—Jack, having groped his way along the walls and encountered three different corners, had come to the conclusion that he was in a large underground cellar. As far as he could judge, the place contained not a single movable object of any kind.

When he came to the fourth corner he was certain that his conjecture had been the right one. Here he stumbled against the lowermost of a flight of stone steps that led upwards. He clambered up a dozen steps until his head came in contact with a closed door; and soon afterwards his bruised shoulders were testifying to the fact that the door was not only closed but securely fastened.

Realising the futility of continuing to dash himself against such a formidable barrier, he retraced his steps to the bottom, where, instead of giving way to despair, he fiercely clenched his hands and braced his shoulders. Had his abductor appeared just then, he would have met with an uncomfortable reception.

Not a sound came from anywhere, either inside or outside. Jack reasoned that he must be well away from the front of the house, for he knew that London's traffic never went wholly to sleep. Then he began to wonder whether he had been taken to London at all.

At last he heard a faint sound overhead, like a mouse scraping on woodwork. From his position near the steps he listened. The sound was not repeated, but after a moment's silence he heard something drop on the floor with a dull thud. Jack's imagination was particularly acute at the moment, and he pictured a man lowering himself through a trap-door in the ceiling and dropping on to the floor in stockinged feet.

Very soon, there followed the sound of another falling body. Had his enemies, thinking him asleep, or still in a state of drugged unconsciousness, come to finish him off? Well, he would do all in his power to make their task as difficult as possible. At that moment he would cheerfully have given all he possessed for a light of some kind.

And then, as if it were a direct answer to his unspoken appeal, a torch, with the light already switched on, dropped down from above—dropped on to the blankets which had already preceded it.

Rushing over, he picked up the torch and flashed it upwards. But already the trap-door had been closed, and only a faint crack, in the shape of an oblong, denoted its presence.

Then the reaction set in, and every nerve in Jack Davis's body began to tremble. The presence of two men ready to pounce on him out of the darkness with murderous intent had upset him more than he had realised at the moment. That the men were merely imaginary did not deprive his emotions of their reality. Metaphorically, he hastened to shake sense into himself.

"You dashed idiot!" he rebuked himself. "Pull yourself together and be a man!"

Again he flashed the light upwards, and saw an electric globe hanging from the ceiling. The switch would be somewhere near the steps. Why hadn't he thought of that before? He could easily have groped for it in the darkness.

However, when he found the switch and snapped it down, no light came from the globe.

Aided by the torch, he surveyed his prison, but discovered little that he had not already learnt by his sense of touch. High up on one of the mildewed walls was a little iron grille that provided the only ventilation of which the place boasted. Even if he could reach it, the ventilator was too small to offer a means of escape, and the trap-door, because of the impossibility of reaching it, was equally hopeless. When he had examined the door at the top of the steps, he resigned himself to the inevitable. His only chance was to wait until someone should enter the cellar, then, perhaps, he might be able to fight his way out.

But was that really the only chance? What of the unknown friend who had provided him with the blankets and the torch? There could be no doubt that the Unknown was his friend, otherwise the things, had he received them at all, would have been given to him openly. An enemy, in the house of the enemy, would have had no need to practise subterfuge.

"Thoughtful beggar, whoever he is," mused Jack. "Had he thrown down the torch without first switching it on, I should probably be dodging imaginary thugs at the present moment."

In the folds of the top blanket he presently discovered a packet of sandwiches and a flask of hot coffee. He lost no time in disposing of this very welcome fare, and when he had finished he felt new life coursing through his veins.

Again he blessed his unknown benefactor, and wished that a box of matches had accompanied the other gifts. Although his own matches had been taken away, he had been allowed to retain his well-stocked cigarette-case; and the presence of the cigarettes, without the wherewithal to light one of them, he found to be extremely tantalising.

At length he arranged the blankets as comfortably as he could, switched off the torch, and composed himself to sleep. Wisely, he had determined to conserve his strength for the encounter that must inevitably take place between himself and Doctor Peters.

Some hours later, he was roused to sudden wakefulness by the sound of stealthy footsteps descending the cellar steps. All his faculties were instantly on the alert, and his first action was to conceal the torch in the inner breast pocket of his jacket. He did not intend to be left at the mercy of the darkness again; and, moreover, the torch might prove a useful weapon in a sudden emergency.

He watched a pool of light, like a slowly-spreading lake, fall from step to step, spread over the floor, and flow in his direction. Behind that light—a torch like the one he had so mysteriously received—were two shadowy figures, which almost merged into the darkness that crawled behind the patch of brilliance.

Jack was now standing upright in a defensive attitude. A few paces in front of the bottom step, the intruders paused; the light was flashed full in Jack's face; one of the men stepped backward; there followed a sudden click, and the cellar became flooded with light from the globe that depended from the ceiling.

The torch was switched off, and the men boldly advanced. Jack Davis had no difficulty in recognising one of them as the individual who had been his guard on the way from Blackton. And he was quick to note that on this occasion also the burly man gripped a revolver in his hand.

"Pleased to meet you, Mr. Davis," said the smaller man, with unexpected geniality. Then his gaze dropped to the blankets, and a frown swept across his face, and was gone so quickly that Jack could not be sure that it was a frown. "Ah!" he went on, scratching his head, "I notice you've been making yourself comfortable." He kicked the blankets, thus exposing the flask. "Been feasting too, I see."

Jack Davis concluded that the speaker was not his unknown benefactor. His eyes were busy scrutinising the man, and he saw that, except for the eyes, the face was what is usually described as 'ordinary.' But the magnetic eyes made it a face impossible to ignore.

"Yes," said Jack at last. "I've been feasting... Doctor Peters."

Jack could not be sure whether the flash in the other's eyes was the result of amusement or anger.

"Is the name a wild guess, Mr. Davis? Or do you fancy you know?"

"I know!" was Jack's quick retort. "You cannot deny that you are the man who has called himself Doctor Peters—a thief and a cold-blooded murderer!"

Something in the other's eyes, and the manner in which his hand flew to his pocket, made Jack realise that those few words had very nearly been his last on earth. He had spoken them on a sudden wild impulse, for he had remembered that this was the man who had caused much sorrow to the girl he loved.

"Reckless words, young man," said the other, withdrawing his hand from his pocket, empty. "However, I can't see why I should take the trouble to deny them. I am Doctor Peters. But you are not likely to be in a position to spread the news abroad for some considerable time. What do you say, Silas?"

The broad-shouldered brute growled something unintelligible. But his scowling expression clearly expressed a desire to be permitted to use the revolver there and then.

"Mr. Davis," said Peters, with a return to his genial tone, "you saw fit to cross my path, and I saw fit to have you swept off it. So far, the balance is fairly even. But things cannot be allowed to remain like that. How much do you know?"

Jack's answer came like the cut of a whip-lash:

"Enough to hang you. When the proper time comes you will learn the full extent of my knowledge."

"The proper time, as you foresee it, Mr. Davis, will never come. But, as I see it, the time is now. Once more, how much do you know?"

The young man did some rapid thinking. What answer ought he to make? It would be folly to let Peters guess how little he really knew. But, on the other hand, it would be extremely dangerous to pretend to know too much. Only bluff, and the right amount of it, could carry him through successfully.

"Ask Inspector Kilby," he flashed back in obedience to a sudden inspiration. "His knowledge is at least equal to mine."

The shot told. But only for an instant did Peters's snarl betray his feelings. The next moment he was his old smiling self.

"As you will, Mr. Davis. I can see that you are determined not to speak, and I shan't attempt to force you... yet. It's a pity you're so obstinate, though. Had you been able to assure me that you had found out nothing really detrimental to my well-being, I was prepared to let you go without more ado. Well, you have made your choice. I must leave you now. And I fear I shall have to cut off the current again as soon as I get upstairs. You don't mind the darkness, I hope?"

Jack vouchsafed no answer, and the two men backed towards the steps. A short distance up; Peters stopped and gravely regarded Jack for several moments. Then he spoke in a voice that was apparently charged with genuine regret:

"It's a pity you've refused to speak, Mr. Davis; a very great pity. Your obstinacy now compels me to experiment on the tongue of Miss Connie Hyde."

As he walked away from the shop, Kilby, instead of lighting a cigarette, as the jeweller had supposed, was making the highly-polished surface of his case do duty for a mirror. Without having to look round, he saw John Smith come to the door, stare fixedly in his direction, and return to the shop. Then dropping his leisurely manner, Kilby made all possible speed to headquarters.

The Assistant Commissioner took immediate steps to obtain a warrant authorising Kilby to search the business premises of John Smith. So as not to reveal too much to the jeweller, the warrant vaguely stated that he was suspected of being a receiver of stolen goods.

While he was awaiting the fulfilment of certain necessary formalities, Kilby picked up a poker from the fireplace and smashed the vase he had purchased into many small fragments.

In less than an hour after he had left it, Kilby, accompanied by two plain-clothes officers, was back again at the jeweller's shop. It was now past closing time, and they knocked at the side door. John Smith, while professing both surprise and innocence, placed no obstacles in the way of the officers, and the search was expeditiously carried out.

His alert eyes noting every detail, Kilby, preceded by the jeweller and followed by the plain-clothes men, went from room to room. When they had descended to the cellar, he observed that the floor was littered with paper, straw, broken packing-cases, shavings, and various other odds and ends.

"Filthy, isn't it?" observed Mr. Smith. "But we do all our unpacking down here."

Kilby nodded and went back up the steps. Without seeming to bestow on it more than a cursory glance, he noted the unusual thickness of the door at the top. And, when the door had been closed, the whitish appearance of a certain part of the wall around it showed him that a cupboard, now standing near a corner of the room, had until quite recently blocked up the doorway.

They returned to the shop, where Kilby stood lost in thought for several moments. Then, remembering that the jeweller had glanced at the floor in a peculiar manner after taking the vase from the window, he stepped behind the counter. He discovered the projecting knob, and pressed it down. Again he went from room to room, and his expression steadily grew more grim as he observed that in every room a little red light was glowing. John Smith merely smiled, although he wished that there had been time to disconnect certain wires.

"Davis was undoubtedly a prisoner in the cellar," Kilby was saying to his Chief, some half-hour later. "I made a very big mistake in not going armed with the warrant in the first instance. While I was acting like a fool over the vase, the young man was removed almost under my very eyes. The jeweller signalled to someone at the back, and the job was done. Afterwards, the cupboard was moved away from the door opening on to the cellar steps, and the floor of the cellar was littered with all kinds of rubbish. Of course, sir, the idea of the rubbish was to hide all traces of the prisoner's having been there, and to make the cellar look as different as possible from Davis's description of it—should he ever get an opportunity to give a description. I may say that the cellar, with its blocked-up door, is ideal either as a prison or a hiding-place. The cupboard, I have no doubt, is furnished with a sliding back... But sir, there isn't a single thing for which we can arrest the jeweller, and the blighter knows it only too well. You should have seen the way he grinned when I found the red lights."

The Assistant Commissioner thoughtfully stroked his chin.

"Wonder where they've taken Davis to this time?" he said.

Before Kilby had time to answer, the telephone bell whirred, and General Norman picked up the receiver. A few moments later, he handed the instrument to Kilby.

"A police-station in Leicester is calling," he explained. "You are wanted, Kilby."

Kilby held the receiver to his ear and signified that he was ready to listen.

"There's a gentleman here who's very anxious to speak to you," said the voice at the other end. "Says his name is Davis. Know anything about him, sir?"

"Yes, yes!" cried Kilby with ill-suppressed excitement. "Put him on at once, please."

Kilby's excitement was as nothing compared with the agitation in the new voice.

"I'm Davis—Jack Davis. You have heard of me from Miss Hyde. I've just escaped from Doctor Peters. No time to explain, though... I'm setting out for Blackton in a minute or so... Miss Hyde is in deadly danger. Will you ring up the Blackton police and ask them to guard her until I get there? They'd hardly be likely to take instructions from me... You'll do it, Mr. Kilby, won't you?"

"Certainly, Mr. Davis. But—"

"Thanks. I must be off. Goodbye."

The receiver clicked, and Kilby put it down.

Chapter 28

A Stick of Grease Paint

Jack Davis had been allowed to retain his money; consequently he found no difficulty in hiring a taxi at Leicester. Moreover, he had the feeling that, even if he were penniless, the police would have helped him to obtain the conveyance he so urgently needed.

The car rushed through the night, and Blackton was reached in record time. Jack sat beside the driver to direct him, and the car pulled up with a jerk and a screech of brakes outside the house in which Connie Hyde lodged.

Jack sprang to the ground, to find that two police officers had materialised from, apparently, nowhere. A light was flashed in his face, and then switched off.

"All serene, Brent," said Inspector Parker. "This isn't the man we're waiting for."

Explanations quickly followed. Parker, having received Kilby's request to guard Miss Hyde, had decided to take charge of affairs himself. He and Brent had watched the front of the house, while a sergeant and another man were at the back.

"There hasn't been a sign of Peters or any other suspicious character," said Parker. "Of course, it's fairly early yet..."

Jack Davis warmly expressed his gratitude to the police, and then the landlady was called and despatched upstairs to Connie's room.

The motherly woman was delighted with the turn events were taking, for Connie had already confided in her.

The girl hastily dressed, rushed downstairs, and, despite the land-lady's presence—the police had remained outside—impulsively threw herself into Jack's eager arms.

"Oh, Jack!" she cried. "Thank God you're safe! What's happened?"

Jack endeavoured to persuade her to wait until morning, when he would tell her everything, but the girl refused to be put off.

"Tell me now, Jack," she insisted. "I can't possibly go to sleep till I know what's happened."

He saw that it was best to put an end to the girl's anxiety. The landlady had already discreetly withdrawn, and they sat down side by side while Jack related his adventures.

"Jack," cried the girl when he had finished, "I could act like a savage and cheerfully cut that horrid Peters into millions of tiny pieces! Yes, millions! No one will ever know what I have gone through since I learned at your lodgings that you hadn't returned from Hartby."

Jack patted the girl's hands reassuringly.

"Don't worry any more, darling," he said. "Your troubles are now over—apart from the loss of your father, of course."

"I wonder, Jack." The girl paused for several moments before con-tinuing: "I wonder. Now, I want you to tell me why you went to the Peak District on the day that—that Dad was killed."

Jack released her hands and rose to his feet.

"Because," he answered evasively, "I promised Fred Bates months ago that I would pay him a visit at the first opportunity."

Connie, too, rose to her feet and placed a hand on his shoulder.

"The real reason, Jack," she insisted. "I want to know the real rea-son."

Jack swallowed hard.

"Oh, hang it, Connie!" he suddenly blurted out. "If you must hear it, you must! Well, I decided to get away from you for a little while. I thought that out alone on the bleak hills I might be able to do the right thing, might be able to force myself to let you go for ever."

"Just as I suspected." There was a funny little catch in Connie's voice. "Jack, didn't it occur to you that I had the right to be consulted before you came to any such decision?"

"Knowing how unselfish you are, Connie, I felt that you would have made the right decision impossible. Somehow, before the trouble with your father, I ignored the fact that you would one day be very rich. I hardly ever thought of it. But your father led me to see how unfairly I was acting by you. I realised that the only decent thing for me to do—"

"Bosh!" interrupted the girl inelegantly. In a flash, she had seen that a complete change of tone was necessary. "Allow me to tell you, young man, that you can't shake me off so easily as that! When the proper time comes, I shall have you dragged to the altar, if you refuse to come willingly. And I wish you wouldn't be so frightfully old-fashioned about money matters. Money is very useful, I admit; but, after all, it's comparatively unimportant. Don't, however, ask me to give it to a Home for cats or dogs, for, although I am very fond of animals, I love my own comforts even more... Now, let's call my landlady and see whether she'll allow you to remain down here on the settee for the remainder of the night, whilst I go upstairs and make up for the sleep I have lost through worrying over an ungrateful wretch who's doing all he possibly can to repel my unmaidenly advances."

Connie found a refuge in Jack's arms for several minutes. Then the landlady was called.

There was no sign of Peters during the night; and in the early morning Jack took Connie to London and placed her in the care of her father's servants—now hers. Then he hurried off to Scotland Yard. Without loss of time, he was conducted to the presence of Inspector Kilby, and the long-delayed meeting at last took place.

But little time was wasted in introductions, and then Kilby put the abrupt question:

"By the way, Mr. Davis, what made you think that Miss Hyde was in danger?"

Recollection of the hours of soul-numbing fear he had suffered on the girl's account made Jack clench his hands until the knuckles showed white.

"Because that devil Peters threatened to make her speak when he saw that I wouldn't."

"I see. And what did he want you to speak about?"

"About what he thought I knew." Then Jack Davis went on to relate how he had pretended to Peters to have made important discoveries, whereas, in reality, he had merely succeeded in following a certain car to a certain house in Hartby, where he had been knocked unconscious.

"You say you tracked the car through several streets. That seems to have been no easy task, Mr. Davis. How did you manage it?"

Jack smiled. Remembering that Connie was now out of danger, his usual light-heartedness had returned.

"There was nothing clever about it," he confessed. "The roads were wet, and the off back tyre had a design that was easy to follow."

"The off back!" repeated Kilby. "You are sure it was the off back?"

"Yes. Had the design been on the front wheel, the back one would have obliterated it."

Kilby's fingertips met and formed a bridge.

"And the design was the swastika, Mr. Davis?"

Jack stared.

"Yes," he said. "But how the deuce did you guess it?"

"I happen to have seen the car—and the new tyre. In the circumstances one could hardly call it a guess, I suppose. But tell me, what happened after Peters had threatened to make Miss Hyde speak?"

"To begin with, I lost my head completely. With that devil's threat ringing in my ears, I rushed up the steps. But before I had got half-way up, I heard the door at the top slam to, and a mocking laugh came to me from the other side. With the strength of a madman—and I felt like a madman—I hurled myself against the door time after time. But I might as well have attempted to move a mountain. I believe that the door was barricaded on the other side."

"Merely a heavy cupboard," put in Kilby. "But please go on."

"After a time," continued the other, "I realised the futility of attempting to escape by that way. But I wished I had risked a bullet and made a dash for it while the men were in the cellar. At last I stumbled down the steps and attempted to switch on the electric light. But no light came. Peters had fulfilled his threat to cut off the current, and I would have to use the torch, although I wanted to save it as much as possible in case my imprisonment should be of long duration.

"Then began a period of inaction that seemed to be never-ending. After a time, I observed that the dawn was beginning to creep in through the little grille, and I switched off the torch. Apart from the approach of daylight, I had no idea of the time, for my watch and matches had been taken away. Peters's idea of refined torture, I dare say. He must have known how intense darkness and ignorance of the passage of time shatter a person's nerves."

"Perhaps he was afraid that the light would show outside through the ventilator," put in Kilby.

Jack Davis shook his head.

"I doubt it, Mr. Kilby. The watch couldn't be seen or heard from outside, yet he took that away. Well, the whole of yesterday—though it seems ages ago—I spent in pacing up and down the floor of the cellar or lying on the blankets. But my periods of rest were few and short, for I found it impossible to remain still for any length of time. Very little daylight entered my prison, for the cellar was large, and the ventilator small."

"They left you alone all the day, then?"

"No. Peters, attended by his bodyguard, came twice and repeated his demand to be told all I knew. I still thought it advisable to keep up the bluff, so I told him nothing. That my silence maddened him was evident, and he concluded each visit by repeating his threat to make Miss Hyde speak.

"Three times during the course of the day food and drink were thrown on to the blankets; but of the person who threw them down I saw no sign.

"Funny," was Kilby's comment.

"The cellar again began to grow darker," went on Davis as though he had not heard the other's remark. "Night was approaching, and there seemed no possible chance of escape. You will perhaps wonder why I didn't make a fight for it on either of the two occasions that Peters came down to renew his demand. Well, thinking the matter over as calmly as I could, I had come to the conclusion that such an attempt would be pure madness. I was unarmed, and the big brute carried a loaded gun. Had there been only myself to consider, I should certainly have risked it; but there was Miss Hyde..."

"Peters acted with deliberate fiendishness there," said Kilby. "He meant to madden you. I don't believe he ever had an intention of touching the girl."

"I think otherwise, Mr. Kilby. But he was prevented."

"Prevented?"

"Yes. He was stopped by a woman. We're coming to that, though. Well, when darkness had almost blotted out every square inch of the cellar, Peters and the other fellow came rushing down the steps. They switched on the light, and their faces showed me that something had happened to disturb them very much. But I held to my resolution not to act rashly. I would await developments.

"My period of waiting was, however, unexpectedly short. The men immediately threw themselves upon me, Peters gagging me, and the other tying my hands behind my back. I felt no desire to resist, for, at the back of my mind was the thought that I should find a more favourable opportunity to escape.

"'Attempt to make a sound, and I'll blow your brains out,' snarled Peters. 'Kilby is upstairs, and I'm pretty desperate.'"

Kilby smiled grimly.

"Just as I thought," he said. "The blighters carried you off under my very nose. Well?"

"Their warning was unnecessary, for to make a sound was impossible, except I started kicking out with my feet. And, as Peters had said, they were desperate. At the top of the steps I was blindfolded, pushed along in front of the two men, and bundled into a car that was somewhere outside the building—at the back, I presume. I began to feel hopeful. Anything was better than the horrible cellar. When the car had been travelling for some time, the bandage was I removed from my eyes, and I felt more hopeful still."

"Yes. Being able to see makes a vast difference."

"It does. But it wasn't that alone. As on the previous occasion, I found myself on the back seat of the car. But this time it was a rattish little individual who faced me with the revolver. Evidently the beefy chap couldn't be spared to ensure my safe delivery. Plans for escape at once began to germinate in my mind. There was a small light on in the car, but the blinds were down. If only my hands were free, I felt I could easily dispose of my mean-looking guard in less than half a minute. But my hands were tied—and my tongue as well.

"After a time, I observed that the drawn blinds were not fastened at the bottom. Now and then, I saw one or the other of them swing away from the window, owing to the motion of the car. And from that slight fact my hope steadily grew.

"From the looks of the fellow opposite, I concluded that bravery was not his strong point. It was plain that Peters was hard up for men just then or he wouldn't have trusted me to such a mean-looking wretch. Would the little rat have the courage to shoot me and risk the consequences? I wondered. I felt sure he wouldn't, particularly if there were many people about."

"Yes," assented Kilby. "Only a brave man—or a lunatic—will endanger his neck by shooting another in a crowd. But he could have used the weapon as a club, you know."

"I had thought of that. He was such an insignificant little blighter, though, he wouldn't have been able to put much force into the blow. Well, the blind on my side, the near side, swayed well away from the window, and I saw brilliant lights outside. I saw many people, too, and heard the sound of much traffic. Now or never was my chance. The car slowed down, probably because there was a slowly-moving vehicle in front. Bunching my shoulders as best I could, so as to save my face, I jumped. There was a crash of shattered glass, and I found myself sprawling on the kerb, dazed, bruised, but not seriously hurt. The blind must have saved me from being cut by the broken glass. If the revolver was fired, I never heard it. A crowd gathered round; a policeman came; I was picked up and helped to the police-station. The rest you know. But what afterwards happened to the car I cannot say."

"I can, Mr. Davis," said Kilby. "The moment you had jumped, it swerved from behind the bus that had been holding it up, dashed madly along the road, and was out of sight before anyone had time to realise what had happened. Later it was found abandoned a few miles beyond Leicester. And now, Mr. Davis, can you tell me—excuse my bluntness—have you any idea why Peters didn't kill you?"

"Yes, Mr. Kilby. I know. And I know why Miss Hyde wasn't molested, though I feared nothing would have restrained Peters once I had escaped... We were both saved by a woman."

"A woman!"

"Yes. I've been leaving this tit-bit till the last, you see. Well, a short time before I was dragged out of the cellar, someone partially raised the trapdoor in the ceiling, when Peters came on the scene. I recognised his voice, and he was rebuking the woman who was raising the trap-door.

"'You're a soft-hearted fool, after all,' I heard him say. 'If it hadn't been for you, I should have finished him off at Hartby.'

"Then the unknown woman spoke.

"'If you harm either him or the girl,' she said, and her voice sounded as though she meant it, 'I shall leave you for ever.'

"'What the devil has he got to do with you, anyhow?' snapped Peters.

"'The girl loves him,' came the answer, and her voice seemed to have a kind of a sob in it. 'I, too, love, and I know all that love means.' Then the trap-door dropped with a crash, and I heard no more."

Kilby, an inscrutable expression on his face, looked as though he were finding it difficult to digest this fresh piece of information. After a time, he asked:

"Do you think you could find that house in Hartby again?"

"I think so, Mr. Kilby. I have a very fair idea of the general direction I followed, and if I were to start at the point where I first saw the car I believe I could find the house again."

"Good. Feel like taking a run to Hartby now?"

The young man was willing, and four hours later found them outside the house where Davis had been knocked unconscious.

They repeatedly rang the bell and banged on the door, but received no answer. Kilby decided not to stand on ceremony.

"Scout around, Mr. Davis," he said, "and see if you can find a window easy to open. I don't like breaking one if it can be helped."

They entered by a suitable window, and searched the deserted house from top to bottom. Nothing, however, came to light until, as they were about to abandon the search in disgust, Kilby had a second look at the interior of an empty clothes cupboard.

At the bottom he found part of a stick of grease paint. It was about half an inch long, and of a greyish colour.

Chapter 29

The Dirt Track Meeting

Kilby attended the coroner's inquest on the body of Sir Joshua Jordan, and was instrumental in obtaining an adjournment. And it was he who induced the magistrates at the court which was subsequently held, to order that both of Sir Joshua's servants be remanded in custody.

Just as he was about to take his leave of the Chief Constable and return to London, word was brought to him that Sam insisted on making a confession. He lost no time in hearing what the man had to say; and then he decided that his obvious duty was to interrogate Ted. When he had warned the bandy-legged servant in accordance with the latest requirements of the latest Royal Commission he continued:

"Sam's confession seems to implicate you deeply. He's now of the opinion that you sent him into the study knowing that Sir Joshua was already dead. I'm not saying that I believe Sam. And I'm not asking you to speak. But if there is anything you would care to explain..." He stopped and watched the snarl on the other's face, and the savage manner in which the cruel-looking teeth bit into the quivering, animal-like lips.

"Damn Sam!" cried Ted at last, in a rasping, high-pitched voice. "So the treacherous beast's squealed, has he?"

"Cornered rats always squeal, eh, Ted?"

Ted's jaw dropped, and his bowed legs sagged farther apart at the knees. Then Kilby was treated to the spectacle of a fear-filled wretch possessed by the one all-absorbing idea of saving his own worthless skin. He, who had been delegated to prevent another from squealing, now acted himself, in deadly earnest, the part of the miserable rat.

"I didn't have anything to do with his death, sir," he whined in a voice that was not altogether free from venom. "As God's my Judge, I didn't!"

Kilby's face assumed a set expression. There must, he reflected, be a funny kink in the criminal mind with regard to the Deity. Over and over again he had heard even the most depraved wretches invoking God's name, in the belief, or the hope, that such an invocation lent weight to their wild protestations of innocence.

"If you're going to talk," he said, "cut out all the cant. And we'll leave Sir Joshua's death for the moment, and discuss the gang. Who's the leader? And where is he now?"

"I don't know, sir. Honest to God, I don't! As far as I know, I've never seen him. And I've never heard his name. Nobody seems to know who he is—except, perhaps, Sir Joshua. He knew him, I think. But I didn't—"

"Surely, man," broke in Kilby, "you got your orders from the leader?"

"Perhaps I did, sir. I don't know. At first I got my orders from Sir Joshua, and I thought that he was the boss of the gang. But now I know he wasn't. For the last few months, I'd been getting most of my orders from London. And several of the orders were to keep a sharp eye on Sir Joshua. The boss was getting to mistrust him on account of the drugs. And I was instructed that Sir Joshua was to be allowed the drug only at certain fixed times. My master fell in with the arrangement, too. Like me, like all of us, he dreaded to disobey the boss. But I don't know who sent the orders from London, sir. It may have been the boss. I don't know."

"I do," retorted Kilby. "Hasn't anyone ever seen the leader, then?"

Ted seemed to be regaining some of his lost confidence.

"That's more than I can say, sir. There used to be meetings held here, but I was never allowed to attend them. The boss may have been present then in one of his disguises. It was said that he'd got far more disguises than a cat's got lives. That's why we didn't talk about him among ourselves whenever any of us fellows happened to meet. We might be talking to the boss himseself, and not know it. But we did know that our numbers were up if he ever got to hear that we'd been letting our tongues wag."

"I see. Now tell me what happened to Mr. Hyde at Hopeview House. And don't forget anything. I already know a good deal about it."

Kilby's polite manner did not deceive Ted, and he omitted nothing. But he now spoke very warily, for he was referring to an episode in which he had played, or had been prepared to play, an active part. Ted's account of the affair placed many of Kilby's hypotheses on the plane of established facts.

As Kilby had deduced, Sam and Ted, acting on orders directly received from Sir Joshua, had stationed themselves behind the pine tree on the fateful Monday afternoon. They were to fall upon Mr. Hyde as he walked past, knock him unconscious, and take from him several banknotes which he would be carrying. That done, they were to return to the house. Mr. Hyde was to be left where he had fallen until he regained consciousness, or, which was more likely, until the taxi-driver had come to look for him. Sir Joshua and the two servants were prepared to swear that not one of them had been outside the doors of Hopeview House at any time that day. The servants did not fear being afterwards identified by Mr. Hyde, as they had taken the precaution to alter their appearance considerably.

All their painstaking preparations, however, had been rendered abortive by the simple fact that Mr. Hyde's taxi had driven up to the front door. Sam and Ted had then slipped into the house by a back door; and Ted, who had listened outside the door of the study, was now able to confirm Mr. Hyde's account of the purchase of the necklace.

When Mr. Hyde had gone, Sir Joshua had written, and Ted despatched, the telegram to 'Peter Jones' at Boxfield railway station. Before Ted's return from the post office, Sam had enacted the farce of binding, and releasing, his master. Another of Kilby's theories was thus verified, except that the sham attack had taken place after the diamond merchant's visit, instead of before it.

Ted and Sam were then ordered to go out through the town and let themselves be seen by as many people as possible so as to provide an alibi in case it should afterwards be needed. They were told the hour at which each was to come back. Upon Ted's return, he rang up the police, while Sir Joshua stood beside him at the telephone. Although Sir Joshua had given all the instructions to the servants, Ted was of the opinion that he had merely passed on certain definite orders which he, himself, had received.

Questioned about Sir Joshua's death, Ted vehemently protested that he had had no hand in the affair. But he was now of the opinion that the murder must have been planned long beforehand. Weeks before, he had received orders from London to break the trident off the bronze figure, conceal the damaged bronze, and pretend to Sir Joshua, if he should happen to miss it, that it had been sent away to be repaired.

Ted frankly admitted that the telegram which he had received through his wife was a warning to prevent Sir Joshua from making any dangerous disclosures. He did not consider, however, that he was expected to adopt drastic measures; and when he had realised, from his post outside the study door, that Kilby seemed likely to persuade Sir Joshua to confess, he had merely gone into the room and handed his master some dope before the proper time.

Prior to this, he had received orders, again from London, never to open a parcel addressed to his master, but to take it straight to Sir Joshua himself. This Ted had done as soon as the parcel containing the bronze had arrived. Later, he had returned to the study and found Sir Joshua dead. He had immediately cleared away all signs of the cause of death, even to the note which informed Sir Joshua that something of the utmost importance would be learned by pressing the false base of the bronze.

"But why," asked Kilby, "did you destroy the note? If you were able to produce it now, it would help me to believe in what you say."

Ted looked round him fearfully.

"If I were to show that note to anyone," he said in a voice that was hushed as though there were some dreaded Presence that might hear, I shouldn't have another twenty-four hours to live. The boss would get me and finish me off, even if I had a regiment of soldiers to guard me."

The rest of Ted's disclosures failed to reveal anything that Kilby had not already known or suspected. Ted did not know how the murder had been committed in Highpen Tunnel; and he had never heard of either Doctor Peters or 'Abie, the Mole.'

In company with a throng of eager enthusiasts, Inspector Kilby entered the 'popular' side of the White City enclosure, and turned to the left. If 'Abie, the Mole' were present, he was most likely to be found here, where a sharp curve in the track promised many delightful thrills—and spills. Disdaining the stands behind and above him, Kilby took up his position near the barrier which separated the spectators from two concentric tracks—the outer designed to test the mettle of dogs; and the inner, the stamina of men and machines.

Kilby was now attending his fourth Dirt-track meeting, but his first at the White City. The other three meetings had been barren of result. If Abie had attended any or all of them, he had managed to keep his presence a profound secret.

More than a week had passed since Ted's confession; and, excepting that Light-Fingered Freddie had been allowed to go his way, and the inquest on Sir Joshua Jordan had again been adjourned, matters in connection with the tunnel mystery had seemed to remain at a standstill.

Kilby, however, was hopeful tonight. Event No. 5 on the programme was a Challenge Match Race between riders representing England and the United States. If that event did not induce Abie to leave his hiding-place, Kilby felt that no thrill, short of the thrill of Abie's own attempted escape, would be able to do so.

A bellowing voice issuing from a loud speaker announced the first event, and soon afterwards thousands of pairs of eyes were watching the Grand Parade of Riders. Kilby's gaze, however, was not on the illuminated track or the roaring machines that tore round it, but on the cheering spectators, who, obviously determined to witness the thrilling events from close quarters, were massed alongside the barrier.

During the first four events, and the intervals between, Kilby strolled nonchalantly up and down—to discover that in a length of fifty yards there were at least a dozen persons, anyone of whom might conceivably be 'Abie, the Mole.'

The chief event was announced, and Kilby became doubly alert. After several moments of buzzing suspense, the two competitors raced round the track, ready for the flying start. They approached the starting-line all out, the eyes of the English rider alternately glancing from the track before him to the form of his American rival, who had drawn inside position.

Despite himself, Kilby was no longer able to curb his interest. He saw the flutter of the starter's white flag, saw the riders crouch farther forward as the roar of their engines increased in volume.

Three times the machines tore past, taking the curve with slightly diminished speed, and shortly afterwards a green flag was waved. The riders had entered on their last lap, and now the real thrill was at hand. The finish promised to be spectacular, for neither rider had yet shown any superiority over the other. Hats waved like the fluttering of demented rooks, and thousands of voices drowned the roar of the engines as the two riders raced down to the curve, abreast. The American, his left foot ploughing through the dirt, still retained the inside position. At such a sharp curve, however, the position was of doubtful advantage, for the Englishman, although describing a bigger arc, was able to maintain a higher rate of speed. Side by side, they negotiated the curve, and from there to the timekeeper's box one small tablecloth would have been sufficient to cover both riders.

A black-and-white flag fluttered—only once. The race was over, but no one near Kilby's corner seemed able to say which rider had won. Many loud-voiced comments could be heard, but the consensus of opinion favoured a dead heat.

Kilby suddenly remembered the object of his visit. Looking around him, he smiled to observe that several of the spectators, still under the spell of breathless excitement, had forgotten to replace their hats on their heads. But the smile set on his face as though it had been frozen there by some instantaneous process, for he had observed a man with uncovered head raise his left hand and scratch the centre of his crown with the first finger. The little finger was sticking up into the air.

"Doctor Peters!" Kilby almost cried aloud. "Abie, the Mole! The..."

As though he had received a message by mental telepathy, 'Abie, the Mole,' wheeled sharply round. But Kilby, apparently unconscious of the man's presence, was staring across at the illuminated indicator which now showed the result of the race. Kilby was hardly conscious that the Englishman had won, for he was finding it extremely difficult to keep his gaze away from Abie's face. While the winner was being announced by loud speaker, Abie turned away; and the inspector knew that he had been recognised. But he was equally certain that Abie had made the mistake of thinking that his own disguise had not been penetrated.

Kilby took little interest in the remaining events. All his attention was devoted to 'Abie, the Mole,' who seemed blissfully unconscious of the scrutiny that was being bestowed upon him. Kilby wondered what steps he ought to take. Would it be advisable to arrest Abie on the spot? Or ought he to allow him to retain his freedom a little longer? Free, Abie might unknowingly lead him to the rest of the gang.

Kilby was spared the trouble of arriving at a decision. The riders were forming up at the time-keeper's box for Event No. 10—the last event but two—when the White City enclosure was plunged into sudden darkness. Instead of turning on the lights that illuminated the track and then turning off those that lit up the stands, the man responsible for working the switches had, either through momentary absent-mindedness or because of some slight defect in the lighting arrangements, reversed the process. For a second or two, so sudden was the change from light to darkness, one could hardly see one's neighbour.

Matters were soon put right. But when Kilby looked towards the spot where Abie had been, the man was no longer there. He suffered a moment's keen consternation; but, glancing hastily around him, he soon caught sight of Abie strolling towards one of the exits. In this there was nothing remarkable. Several other people were also leaving the enclosure, obviously with the idea of avoiding the rush that would inevitably take place as soon as the final event had been run.

Keeping a respectable distance behind, Kilby followed Abie to Wood Lane Underground station. There he met with a slight surprise. Instead of catching a train that would take him back to the centre of the city, Abie took a seat in one going in the opposite direction. Kilby had no option but to do likewise, although he was careful not to enter Abie's compartment.

At each station he kept a sharp look out, lest his quarry should attempt to leave the train. Abie, however, rode all the way to the ter-minus at Ealing Broadway. Arrived there, he left the train and walked on to the platform of the Great Western railway, and Kilby began to wonder whether the leader of the gang was about to attempt to leave the country by way of Bristol or some other port served by the Great Western.

Abie, however, strolled along the platform, in company with dozens of others, towards the steps that led to the exit above. When he was about half a dozen yards from the staircase, he quickened his pace, thus putting several more people between himself and his pursuer. Kilby, too, hurried; but, by the time he had pushed his way to the bottom step, Abie was half-way up, a tightly-packed mass of humanity separating pursuer from pursued.

When Kilby reached the top, Abie was nowhere in sight. He glanced round the booking-hall, and then hurried to the exit. On the pavement outside he stopped and looked in both directions. But of Abie there was no sign. A short distance away, on the right, Kilby saw the entrance to the District Railway station. That was the explanation of Abie's quick disappearance. He was going back to London by another route. If Kilby lost no time he would probably be able to catch the same train.

No sooner had Kilby left the Great Western booking-hall than Abie stepped from behind the weighing-machine that had concealed him.

A peculiar smile was on his lips as he hastened down the steps, up which he had come less than a minute before. By good luck, a train had just come in from Slough, and Abie's journey to Paddington was undisturbed by any untoward incident.

Meanwhile, Kilby was also proceeding City-wards by the District Railway. But he had not passed many stations before the germ of doubt began to grow in his mind. Was Abie really on the train? With the doubt came the determination to make sure.

Making himself known to the inspector, Kilby received permission to pass along the train.

"Confound him!" were the only words that escaped his lips as he realised that Abie had eluded his vigilance. And he decided that it would be useless to return to Ealing Broadway. Abie was too wily to linger there longer than was absolutely necessary. Somehow he had learned that his disguise had been penetrated and that he was being followed.

As he considered the matter, Kilby's hopes rose considerably. Not knowing the means by which he had been recognised, Abie would no longer feel safe, and, consequently, he would be likely to hasten the crisis by attempting to leave the country. Kilby smiled quietly to himself, for he had the feeling that Abie was not the kind of man to vanish, leaving his hidden spoil behind him.

At Westminster Kilby left the train and hurried to Scotland Yard. Ten minutes later, he was in a fast car, ready to rush north.

"Barring accidents, we ought to be able to do the journey in less than three hours," said the driver, throwing in the clutch.

Kilby smiled as they flew along. The car was a powerful saloon, and the driver an expert. Barring accidents, as the driver had said, there was nothing further to fear. But, as he thought of a possible breakdown, Kilby regretted that he had not taken the precaution of sending a warning to Inspector Parker at Blackton.

Once they had to stop because of tyre trouble. And the driver twice lost his way because of his anxiety to avoid the larger towns; so that, instead of reaching Blackton at about half-past one in the morning, as they had hoped, it was nearly an hour later before Kilby was able to alight outside Blackton police-station.

The two inspectors held a hurried consultation, and then set out on foot together.

"Sergeant Hopkins ought to be somewhere about here," said Parker, when they had got a short distance beyond the North Eastern railway station.

A moment later, the sergeant's form loomed up out of the darkness, and, stepping over to him, Parker spoke in a rapid whisper.

"The damned mutton-headed idiot!" he cried in a vicious undertone, as he hurried back to Kilby's side. "They've been here already—been here and gone! And the fool actually looked on and said nothing!"

"What!"

"It's true, Kilby. They left nearly half an hour ago."

Chapter 30

A Wild Chase

Sergeant Hopkins literally trembled, for he expected to be soundly berated by the Scotland Yard officer; but Kilby merely said:

"Which way did they go?"

"They drove into the town, sir. I'm very sorry, sir, that I misunderstood my instructions. But Inspector Parker mentioned no names, and when I saw that they—"

Kilby, however, waited to hear no more. As though their lives depended on the haste they made, he and Inspector Parker hurried back to the police-station.

Parker set about making enquiries in the town, whilst Kilby got busy on the telephone calling up various police-stations and describing the fugitives and the car in which they were escaping. Before he had finished, word was brought in that the wanted car had been seen leaving Blackton in an easterly direction.

"It's only a matter of time now," said Parker, as Kilby put down the telephone. "Let's follow in my little Falcon, for your driver must be pretty well played out after his dash from London. If the Falcon doesn't overtake Abie within the first forty miles, I'll—I'll send her to the Midtown museum."

Kilby looked thoughtful.

"Don't be too confident, Parker," he warned. "Abie's car must be a flier, or he couldn't have got here so quickly from London."

Parker's answer was a tolerant smile. He fancied he knew the capabilities of Abie's car.

They quickly disposed themselves in the Falcon. Kilby and Constable Brent rode inside. Parker took the wheel, and the chauffeur who had driven from London sat on the driver's seat beside him.

The station-sergeant came out to see them off.

"Keep the wires busy," Kilby instructed him, and then the little car darted forward.

The light from the headlamps tore a gaping rent in the darkness as the car rushed along. Now and then, as a village or town was reached, Parker stopped to make inquiries; and, thanks to the use Kilby had made, and the station-sergeant at Blackton was still making, of the telephone, a police officer was always at hand to direct them. Several attempts had been made to stop Abie, but he had ignored all signals. Though the pursuers knew beyond the shadow of a doubt that Abie was in front, they gradually became aware of the disquieting fact that the Falcon, instead of gaining on the fugitives, was slowly but steadily losing ground.

At a village beyond Newark they were informed that the police had placed a row of red lights across the road. But Abie had not been deceived by the ruse. He had dashed past at a speed that would have meant instant death had the road really been up.

"Flew past as silent as a greyhound, and twice as fast," said the sergeant who gave the information.

"What did I tell you, Parker?" called Kilby. "It never pays to be over-confident."

Just then the storm broke.

Parker and the London driver changed seats, and once more the Falcon flew forward. As though in mocking defiance, thunder crashed and rumbled across the sky.

"A very fitting ending," observed Kilby to Brent. "The elements were angry when Mr. Hyde's murder took place, and it's quite appropriate that they should herald the crack of doom for the murderer."

"You think you'll catch him, sir?"

"Of course. He can't keep on flying before us forever. Somewhere, sooner or later, he'll have to stop, and then 'Abie, the Mole's,' number is up."

During the past few days Brent had had an uneasy suspicion that Parker was being unduly secretive about the progress that was being made in the investigation of the tunnel mystery. The thought had rankled considerably, consequently he had refrained from mentioning that he had received a letter from Freda Lowe three days before. It is doubtful whether he would have mentioned it in any case, for he did not consider it was anyone's business but his own; nevertheless, Parker's reserve provided justification for his own lack of frankness. This letter had stated that Freda hoped to be returning to Blackton in a few days, as her aunt's health was steadily improving. She did not enclose any address, because it was quite likely that she would be on her way back to the cottage before George's reply could reach her. Quite casually, Freda had mentioned that she was going for a run in the Tin Lizzie, and would post the letter in whatever town she happened to stop for lunch. The town, according to the blurred postmark on the envelope, seemed to be Warwick, but, of course, as George had told himself many times, that gave no clear idea of the town or village in which the letter had been written.

"Abie, the Mole!" George Brent now repeated. "Who's 'Abie, the Mole,' sir?"

"The leader of the gang we've so often talked about. Until about three years ago he was famous, or, rather, notorious, in America. Neither property nor life was sacred to him, and in his time he has used the knife, the bullet, and poison. A female relative is said to have been responsible for some of the deaths by poisoning. Personally, however, I doubt that statement. Whatever his other failings, Abie is really very fond of this relative of his, and I fancy things would have to be in a bad way with him before he'd allow her to stain her hands—or her soul—with the guilt of murder. In the present case, she very nearly did, but—well, the tunnel murder was an exception. There are some who say that the relationship between the two is assumed, but I have proof that it is genuine."

He paused while the thunder rattled and crashed, and then continued:

"Eventually the States got too hot to hold Abie, and he came over here, bringing some members of his gang with him. But he recruited some others in England. Among the latter was Sir Joshua Jordan, a swindling Company promoter. Sir Joshua was very useful. His house provided a rendezvous for the gang; and I have no doubt he often played the game which he played with Mr. Hyde. But, thanks mainly to drugs, Sir Joshua's nerves gave way in the end, and Abie put him out of harm's reach."

Once more the car stopped while Parker made enquiries. Abie was still in front, heading towards the coast.

"He's probably making for Hull or some other port on the east coast, sir," said Brent. "I suppose his idea is to cross over to the Continent?"

"Yes. I have no doubt that he's going to try to cross over. But I don't believe he'll make the attempt from any of the ports. More likely he has a boat waiting for him along some lonely part of the coast."

For a few minutes neither spoke. At last the young constable said:

"Abie, of course, is Doctor Peters?"

"Yes, Brent," said Kilby after a long pause. "Abie is Doctor Peters. Or perhaps it would be more correct to say that Doctor Peters is, or was, 'Abie, the Mole.'"

"And he had another headquarters at Hartby, sir?"

"Hardly a headquarters, I should think, Brent. It was merely the place in which he effected his various disguises. Mr. Davis was the first to discover it, and his discovery nearly cost him his life. He would have paid the penalty had it not been for"—Kilby paused—"for Abie's female relative."

They were now nearing the coast, and conversation ceased. The storm had increased in fury, and the rain lashed against the window-panes as though giant hosepipes were trained upon them. When the thunder of the sea had drowned all sounds, save the thunder from above, Parker, who was again at the wheel, swerved the car sharply to the left. The road now ran parallel to the coast, and so mountainous were the storm-driven waves that a flying spindrift added to the volume of water that descended from the clouds.

The four men were now in the grip of spell-binding excitement. At any moment they might come upon Abie and his fellow fugitive attempting to make their escape by boat. But to attempt to board a boat while the sea lashed in such insensate fury seemed nothing short of suicide.

The Falcon tore through the storm in the wake of the fugitives. Darkened towns and villages became bright for a moment or two, but quickly retreated backwards into the darkness again. At last Parker applied the brakes with such suddenness that the car skidded, and, had he been a less experienced driver, there is little doubt that the Falcon and her occupants would have come to an untimely end over the cliffs.

Three police officers stood on the road, looking like three wet, shiny seals. The car came to a throbbing standstill, and one of the officers—a superintendent—hurried over to the driver.

"Chase over!" he yelled with dramatic terseness. His words could hardly be heard, although he shouted at the top of his voice.

Kilby sprang out, followed by Brent.

"The chase over!" he repeated, also shouting. "What do you mean?"

"The car you were pursuing has gone over the cliffs. Learning that it was coming in this direction, we decided to use a spiked mat. About a quarter of a mile farther back, and just outside the town you passed through a minute or two ago, we put the mat across the road... The car came on and rushed over it. The mat was effective, for the car at once began to wobble and zigzag. But the driver never lost control, and he continued his flight in this direction, though at a greatly-reduced speed. Knowing that he would soon be compelled to abandon the car altogether, we hurried along after it... We heard a crash and a wild cry—a woman's cry, I think—and when we got here we found— But see for yourselves what's happened."

The beam from his electric torch flashed on the puddles and footprints and dancing raindrops. But the tyre-marks, particularly those of the new tyre with its swastika design, were not yet quite obliterated, and the officers had little difficulty in reconstructing the terrifying catastrophe that had happened. As though the scene were being re-enacted before their eyes, they saw Abie lose control of the car because of its punctured tyres; saw the car swerve sharply to the right and crash through a frail wooden paling; heard the fearful cry of agony as the vehicle plunged over the cliffs and down into the raging inferno below.

"Poor devils!" shouted Kilby. "What an end! How long is it since it happened?"

"Well over half an hour."

"And you did nothing?"

"What could I do?" was the yelling protest of the superintendent.

"Nothing, I'm afraid. But I should like to make sure whether there's any hope. Will you send one of your men back to the town for lamps and ropes? The driver will take him there and back."

While they waited, they walked up and down the bleak, wind-swept road, none attempting to speak. Presently, the lamps and ropes arrived, and Kilby announced his intention of going over the cliff.

"It's madness!" cried Inspector Parker, hardly able to make himself heard above the howling of the storm. "You'll be dashed to pieces!"

"I must risk that. They may have landed somewhere on a ledge."

"But, even if they did, the waves will have washed them away."

Kilby's mind was made up, and he refrained from answering. The ropes were long and stout. Selecting one, he fastened it securely round his waist, and, as an additional precaution, he fastened the other end to the car, which had been drawn up close to the side of the road. Brent did likewise with another rope, and no one offered any remark, except that Kilby nodded his approval.

Lamps were attached to the ropes round their waists, and then, on Kilby's instructions, they were carefully lowered over the edge of the cliff, three men to Brent's rope, and two to Kilby's.

The wind caught hold of them, tossed them about, and screamed like ten thousand raging demons. The sea took a hand and endeavoured to drench them in showers of stinging spray, but already their clothing had reached the saturation point.

Dangling perilously above the churning foam, they made their slow descent, their eyes eagerly scanning the cliff side for traces of the hapless fugitives. But when they had reached a point beyond which it would be madness to attempt to proceed, they had to acknowledge that their search seemed fruitless. Managing to find a foothold, Kilby gave one tap on his rope, and those above checked the descent of the two men.

Neither Kilby nor Brent had attempted to speak since they had begun their perilous venture, and now they hung there in silence, swinging their lamps about as best they could in all directions. It seemed as though nothing were likely to reward their scrutiny, when a mountainous wave thundered towards them, bearing on its crest something black and shapeless. The wave broke its fury against the face of the cliff and then retreated. But it had left its burden behind it, perched drunkenly on the jagged point of a massive rock. They directed the light from the two lamps on to this object, and then Brent would have plunged headlong into the raging inferno beneath, had not the rope been fastened securely round his waist.

"Kilby!" he screamed, forgetting difference of status. "Kilby! It's Dick the potter's car!"

"Yes, Brent. Dick the potter's car," agreed Kilby. "One of the fastest cars in the country very cleverly disguised."

Another giant wave charged forward, and in its retreat it carried away with it the twisted heap of metal that had so often carried Freda Lowe and old Dick, her uncle.

There came a sudden lull in the storm.

"Poor devils!" said Kilby again. "But their death must have been almost instantaneous. I daresay they would have preferred it so, had they been given a choice."

He tapped twice on the rope, and a minute or so later they had regained the road, Constable Brent speechless with agonised amazement.

Day was breaking, and the local superintendent invited them to hurry to the police-station for hot drinks and a change of clothing.

"There are numerous details," said Kilby, "which leave no doubt in mind that Abie, or Peters, or the old potter—call him what you will—committed both murders. Taken singly, each detail may seem somewhat trifling, but their total provides an overwhelming mass of circumstantial evidence."

Once again it was night, and the three officers who had played such a prominent part in the tunnel mystery were seated in Inspector Parker's office. On the principle that a poisoned wound needs painful cauterisation, Kilby had insisted on the presence of Constable Brent:

"Let me put the whole affair as clearly as I can," went on Kilby. "As we know, Abie came over to England determined to carry on the work that had become too dangerous in the States. He organised his gang with a thoroughness that was almost perfect. He had agents and meeting-places in London, Hartby, Donmoor, and Heaven knows how many places besides. He himself, struck by the strategic importance of Blackton, leased the little cottage and went to reside there with his niece. At the cottage he was always Dick, the potter, and the house at Hartby was a place to which he could easily and quickly retire to change into one of his various disguises. It was only as the potter that he drove the car, which was deliberately made to look ramshackle in keeping with his appearance. His apparently clay-smeared face, I should say, was the result of the clever use of make-up."

"But," objected Parker, "I myself read a telegram which informed you that Richard Lowe and his niece were genuine."

Inspector Kilby smiled.

"Quite true, Parker. But that was only another example of Abie's thoroughness. Abie and his niece borrowed the names and the history of two perfectly respectable persons. And I may here admit that that telegram very nearly threw me off the trail. Abie, of course, had to steal the name of a potter, since he meant to pose as one. I've already told you, Parker, that he used to conceal the precious stones in vases and other articles he made and send them quite openly to the Euston Road jeweller, who disposed of them in some manner I haven't yet discovered. Every piece of pottery that contained a jewel was indicated by the intertwined serpents with the projecting fangs, and each box or packing-case by concentric circles. Of course, many of the articles were perfectly innocent.

Despite the doubts and hopes that were tormenting him, Constable Brent had been carefully following the narrative, and he now felt it his duty to register a protest.

"But, sir," he said, "nothing that you have yet told us shows that the man had anything to do with the murder of Mr. Hyde."

"I'm coming to that, Brent. You already know the parts which Sir Joshua and his servants played. I shan't repeat all that, but shall go on to the part taken by the chief actor. Murder was provided for, and, anticipating subsequent enquiries, he sent his niece to Little Faston to purchase a ticket. Probably she went there in the car.

"That afternoon, each travelling by a different route, the pair went to Boxfield, where Abie received the telegram that had been sent in care of the station-master. We know how the various passengers afterwards bestowed themselves in a particular compartment of the train. And we know that Abie, from the compartment behind, shot Mr. Hyde while the train was in Highpen Tunnel. Perhaps we couldn't prove it to the satisfaction of a jury, but... we know it."

"That's a point," threw in Parker, "which seems to have depended too much on chance. What would have happened had there been other passengers in Abie's compartment?"

"I don't know, Parker. Perhaps he would have covered the pistol and fired, trusting that the darkness and the storm would conceal his actions. Or perhaps he might have dogged Mr. Hyde all the way to London, if necessary, and finished him off there at the first favourable opportunity. But I don't really think it was ever his intention to let the man go farther than the tunnel. He wasn't depending on a pistol-shot alone. Mr. Hyde was very nearly poisoned."

"Poisoned!" exclaimed two voices in chorus.

"Exactly. Miss Lowe—we'll still call her that—very nearly poisoned him with a prepared chocolate. Starting with the children, she could have passed the chocolates round the compartment, reserving the poisoned one for her intended victim, and he could hardly have been so boorish as to refuse it. You may remember, Brent, that when the girl was entertaining us a week or two ago she told us quite emphatically that she detested chocolates. Yet she had a box that day... Anyhow, she didn't poison Mr. Hyde. Instead she gave her uncle the necessary signal by throwing the paper through the window. The attaché case gave her an excuse for keeping out of the line of fire, as well as preventing anyone else from taking the corner seat."

Kilby took a sip from his glass before continuing:

"Abie fired the shot, and you know what followed. After leaving Blackton that afternoon he went to Hartby, taking with him the pistol and the pouch containing the necklace. There, he became old Dick again. Returning to the cottage, he burned the tobacco pouch in the furnace—that's where I found the stud—and that night or early next morning before you, Parker, had thought of placing a guard, he threw the pistol into the tunnel. He used the car either for returning from Hartby or to convey him to the tunnel. You may remember, Brent, that you found the girl washing it next morning.

"Of course, luck also favoured Abie. It was fortunate for him that Light-Fingered Freddie and John Lofthouse were present to divert your suspicions. And it was doubly fortunate that the precocious schoolboy, having found the expelled shell, kept it for such a length of time.

"Without these advantages, however, Abie would have been quite safe, or, at any rate, he would have had a much longer run had he simply kept quiet and let well alone. But he was too anxious to make his the perfect crime. That was why Freda made friends with Miss

Hyde, and why he himself pretended to be a keen student of crime: he wanted to be able to know, and combat, whatever steps were being taken to unravel the mystery. And I need hardly say that old Dick's sick sister was invented to provide an excuse for their leaving Blackton when they began to find things getting too hot.

"I very soon began to suspect old Dick. But I knew that my real difficulty would be to connect him with Doctor Peters, or with the crime in any way whatever. My only chance was to make him give himself away. That was why I let him know a good deal of what I had discovered. When I learned that potter's clay, and no putty, had been used on the carriage window, I determined to obtain a specimen of the clay he used. But he stood over me while I washed my hands, and I was unable to obtain any in that manner. Afterwards he thought it safer to slip out, force the staple, and pretend that some unknown person had stolen some of his clay. I knew it was he who had forced the staple, because only a few minutes before I had examined the door with the intention of committing a burglary myself that night. Then, when he had offered me a piece of clay, and thus in a sense, taken the wind out of my sails, I determined to take a bolder step. And that was the step which induced old Dick to send a warning to Sir Joshua Jordan through the Euston Road jeweller. That message established the necessary connection, and I felt that everything else was only a matter of time. The photograph, of course, showed me that old Dick was really 'Abie, the Mole.'

"One other thing I must mention before I stop. You may remember that I took a walk by myself before I returned to London a week or so ago. Well, my walk took me to the cottage, and there I discovered in an underground hiding-place—a worked-out coal seam, by the way—several vases bearing the familiar design of red serpents with protruding fangs. I broke the vases and found a diamond in each. Last night I felt that Abie would not be likely to flee without first attempting to regain possession of this treasure. As it happened, I was right. And I believe this underground chamber was to be used as Jack Davis's second prison. Davis tells me, by the way, that he's going to be married as soon as a decent interval has elapsed…"

Kilby paused. Then, turning to Brent, he said:

"I'm sorry for the girl called Freda. She had the makings of a good woman in her. And if she was ever responsible for any person's death—which I very much doubt—she has balanced the affair by saving the life of Davis. At one time I believe it was her intention to cast suspicion on him and Miss Hyde, but... she changed her mind. I'm sure she would have helped him to escape from the cellar had she had the chance. Love had redeemed her. Or it would have redeemed her. And... she had found love. Brent, I am sorry. From my heart, I wish that she had met with a different end—the end you would have wished."

Brent, with downbent head, walked quietly out of the room. Again he was torn by torturing doubts. From his pocket he pulled an envelope, which he had received by the seven o'clock post that evening, and withdrew its enclosure—a sheet of cheap notepaper containing the briefest of messages:

"Goodbye.—FREDA."

George turned to the envelope, addressed to him in Freda's firm handwriting. For once in a way, the postmark was not an undecipherable smudge.

"Hull, 8.30 a.m.," read Police Constable Brent.

He remembered that the car had gone over the cliff before daylight. And he remembered, also, that the letter could not have been posted before the accident.

Hugging his secret to himself, he stepped out into the clear, starlit night.

THE END